OLLIE'S DILEMMA

BY

OTIS L. SCARBARY

12-1-14
For Bobbie —
Thanks for your
support & for reading my
second work. Hope you
enjoy it.

Otis

ACKNOWLEDGMENTS

I want to thank all the readers and fans of my first book, Leo's Redemption, for encouraging me to undertake the writing of my second book, Ollie's Dilemma. All of your kind words and support were taken to heart, and I hope you enjoy this effort.

Fortunately for me, I had a select group of beta readers who offered their assistance to this project. They included Cindy Adams, Darryl Bollinger, Misty Peterson, Donna Scarbary, Mandy Scarbary and Shirley Scarbary. Each of them provided me with corrections, suggestions, and much needed constructive criticism as I created this work of fiction.

Once again, I depended on two professionals to work on the book's appearance. Carl Graves of Extended Imagery created a wonderful front cover, and Cheryl Perez completed the spine, back cover, and final formatting.

Finally, I would also like to thank a friend of many years, Greg Guest of Hairball Productions, for helping me with his technical expertise. Whether it involves fixing my computer, shooting a photo of me for marketing purposes, or creating a book trailer, he is always willing to lend a hand.

Any remaining mistakes are mine.

DEDICATION

*For the best three mentors from whom this lawyer learned,
personal thanks to the following:*

*Mr. Virgil Shepard, for all the practical advice on running a law
office and for referrals that kept me afloat.*

*Honorable Clarence H. Clay, Jr., for giving me a job as a
prosecutor and letting me develop as a trial attorney.*

*Honorable J. Taylor Phillips, for critiquing my efforts in the
courtroom and teaching me for over thirty-five years.*

*All of you helped save the world as members of The Greatest
Generation. You are my heroes, and I miss you all.*

CHAPTER 1

Present

The cocktail glass contained the usual amber-colored liquid covering a few ice cubes. There were two dark plastic stirrers set at an angle in the yet untouched beverage, providing the purchaser not only the means to better blend the content, but also a substitute for chewing other than the desired Cuban cigar concealed inside his Brooks Brothers jacket.

The man shifted slightly on his barstool and gave the drink a swirl with the straws. He picked them up and placed both in his mouth savoring the taste of the single malt. His eyes closed as the familiar smoothness lingered on his tongue. Biting and then chewing the straws ended the ritual.

He looked into the mirror behind the bar and wondered about the man looking back at him. The blue eyes were clearer than might be expected from someone his age and having gone through all they had over his sixty-seven years. The face was creased in places, but it held a ruggedness others had found handsome in his youth and which had not been completely lost in the later years.

His salt-and-pepper hair was much shorter than it had been back in the late sixties and seventies when he wore thick brown locks over his ears and down to his shoulders. He still had a headful though, unlike most of his contemporaries. Male pattern baldness was not a part of his genetic pool.

A slight smile crossed his face as it occurred to him how much he favored one of his deceased uncles. The family had always said Ollie looked enough like Uncle Joey to be his own. That would've been okay with Ollie because his father had been way too hard on him when he was young, and his uncle had always seemed to understand what was going on in his life better than his dad had. Everybody thought Joey was a handsome guy as well, so having some of those looks couldn't be a bad thing.

"Hey, counselor. You admiring your mug in the mirror or thinking about the fresh meat over there?"

The memory lost in the greeting, Ollie Tucker glanced in the mirror to his immediate left and saw another regular had joined him at his favorite downtown bar. Tom West was a realtor and a former client with a warped sense of humor and a penchant for the ladies. *Too bad for Tom women didn't necessarily feel the same way towards him*, thought Ollie.

"Neither," replied Ollie as he shifted the straws from the center of his mouth to the right side.

Tom plopped down on the stool beside Ollie, and a young bartender appeared. He had a tall beer in hand and placed it in front of the real estate agent without speaking. As the kid turned, he gave Ollie a glance with one raised eyebrow and then shook his head without comment. Such silent conversation with the wait staff was the rule unless the customer chose otherwise. They all knew the regulars well and would more often than not appear magically with the preferred drink of choice when needed.

Tom leered into the mirror at a thirty-something brunette sitting in a booth across from the bar. Ollie followed the other man's stare, and the woman looked into the mirror at the same time. She smiled at the old lawyer, and he was stunned at the gesture. He would have smiled back, but thought it would've looked stupid with the straws he still sucked and chomped.

The agent looked over at Ollie and said, "She just smiled at me, did you see?

"I saw her smile," answered Ollie.

"You're so vain I bet you thought she was looking at you, ancient one," said Tom.

"Even if I am, and even if she was, the girl is young enough to be my daughter, at the very least. Maybe even my granddaughter, Tom. You're not that much younger than me either, you dirty old fool," said Ollie.

"I bet she's into older more experienced men. Maybe she's looking for a sugar daddy with a successful business. Somebody with the means to buy her nice things, and with the know how to give her the attention she deserves, if you know what I mean. The kind of guy I am," Tom said as he licked his chops like a hungry dog.

"Have I ever told you what a sick dick you are?" asked Ollie.

"Indeed. Just about once a night, counselor," said Tom with a laugh. "Why are you breaking my balls anyway? You've had your flings with younger women. All the guys are jealous of your reputation with the opposite sex."

"Never that kind of age difference, Tom. I've learned my limitations, if I've learned nothing else. Lately those limitations have become more pronounced," replied Ollie.

"Sounds like a personal problem. Don't worry about how disgusting I am. My ex-wives will be glad to tell you all about that. Anyways Ollie, I'm younger than you by almost ten years. That's equal to seventy in dog years. You should acknowledge my youth," said Tom.

"Whatever," said Ollie as he looked back into the mirror toward the woman.

She demurely sipped her drink, which looked green and salty. Ollie noted she held her glass with her left hand and no ring was present. The woman continued to look at him in a way that made him feel uneasy yet excited for some reason.

Ollie was thinking the woman looked familiar in that way you couldn't put your finger on. Maybe she had been on a jury of his one time. There had certainly been enough of them over the years. For the first time since the drink had been set in front of him, he picked it up and took a swallow. He let the chilled warmness slide down his throat into his stomach and settle. *Hello, old friend,* he thought.

He took another sip and Ollie felt relaxation take over his mind and body. When he looked back into the mirror, the younger woman was even more unnerving with her gaze. For whatever reason, he felt she wanted to talk to him. He couldn't imagine why.

As he pondered the situation, the woman got out of her seat and headed toward the bar with drink in hand. Ollie felt somehow trapped as she walked to the empty seat beside him on the other side from Tom.

She sat down on the stool and set her lime concoction on the bar. The fragrance she wore was light floral and pleasant in his nostrils. She leaned in close to the lawyer and spoke in private hushed tones so no one could hear but him. Tom strained to make out what she said as he craned his neck in that direction.

"Good evening, Mr. Tucker," she said in a breathy voice.

Her voice didn't have the usual southern accent of so many people in the middle Georgia area. Ollie could usually tell where people lived from hearing them speak, and she didn't sound like she was from around here.

Ollie turned in his seat to face the woman as Tom got up and moved to another section of the bar. His exit did not seem to be missed by the two remaining.

"Forgive me, Miss. You obviously know me, but I don't believe I've had the pleasure," replied Ollie as he searched her striking face.

"I don't guess so, Mr. Tucker, but I've heard a lot about you. You might remember my mother, though. Her name was Nancy Lee. She told me she loved you with a passion nobody else could ever understand. I know I never understood and was hoping you could enlighten me."

Ollie swallowed hard and went back in time to his early thirties. He was invincible and afraid of nothing. He was a young lawyer who would not back down from anything or anybody. There was a difficult case he handled involving bank fraud where a beautiful witness was necessary to prove his case in court. Nancy Lee was her name, and Ollie was smitten from the start. For a while, they both had been, and a white-hot affair followed.

When the case was over, so was the relationship. Ollie had been too consumed with his career in those days to get seriously involved with any woman no matter how smart or attractive she was. Come to think of it, he had never found the time to stay with anyone for any extended period of time. He had not thought about Nancy in ages, but then again self-analysis had long ago diagnosed Ollie as emotionally crippled. There was no time to think about all that baggage now.

"You're Nancy's daughter?" stammered Ollie.

"Yep, one and only. I wanted a brother or sister, but never got one. Mom never got married no matter how much I tried to find her the perfect mate."

"So, how is your mother?"

There was a cloud that passed over the woman and sadness filled her otherwise pretty face. "She died December of last year. Breast cancer. It wasn't easy, but I was there until the end, and we talked about a lot of things including you. "

Ollie felt a twinge of undisclosed grief and wanted to retreat somewhere else. There was nowhere to run and nowhere to hide at the moment, however.

"I guess I should tell you what Mom told me about you." She paused and looked into his eyes. "She said she loved you with every fiber of her soul, but she couldn't or wouldn't tell you. I don't understand why, but Mom was a free spirit and felt if she let you know about me, it would change things for the worse somehow. She also said you are my father."

The lawyer's jaw dropped and then he downed the rest of the cocktail. "Holy shit," said Ollie.

CHAPTER 2

July, 1958

Ollie and his friends ran through the tall grass without worrying about anything that might be lurking underneath. There were no fears when he was twelve years old.

Life was simple. The neighborhood was tightknit and they would play from sunup until sundown when their parents finally made them come inside. Made-up games were the best. Capture the flag, dodge ball, pinecone wars, and whatever sport was in season provided fun for all the kids in the vicinity.

Ollie was the leader of the pack and his word was the law. It didn't hurt that he was the oldest. It also didn't hurt that he was the smartest. He would tell the group of kids what they needed to do, and they did it. No questions asked.

Today, they were pirates, and they were looking to plunder. If they could find anything of value, they would take it as booty.

They all carried their pretend swords fashioned from broom handles, fallen branches or discarded boards that were swung with reckless abandon at anything resembling a threat to the horde of buccaneers.

The wooded area across from Ollie's house provided a maze of trails and paths worn by the kids trampling. Since it was the heart of summer, it was lush and overgrown with all sorts of greenery. It was the perfect place to spend time away from the heat of the Georgia sun and still enjoy youthful activities.

"Whoa, mateys. Argh, methinks I spy yond fort," cried Ollie as he pointed to several pines with mounds of pine straw placed in between. Sometimes their beloved fort provided safe haven from attacking Indians, today they would be the attacking party.

"Methinks thar is much gold and silver for us if we can breach it," continued Ollie in his best Captain Blackheart's snarl.

The other boys stopped in their tracks and watched Ollie as he held his weapon of a short piece of picket fence sharpened on one end. The leader then slid the cutlass into his belt and turned to his crew.

"Everybody get the canons ready. We'll blast 'em first and then scale the walls. Take no prisoners," he rallied.

The kids started grabbing pinecones. They held them at ready while waiting on their leader to give the order to attack.

"Fire in the hole! Let 'em have it, mateys," yelled Ollie.

The boys began hurling the cone missiles toward the fort with only a few actually falling inside. Ollie's were on target while most of the others lacked the necessary arc or strength to make it.

"Owww. Quit it, you idiots," a young female voice rang out from inside the fortress.

Ollie was surprised to hear someone inside. He was even more surprised not to recognize the voice. He held up his right hand signaling the crew to stop the attack and waited. He couldn't imagine who might have discovered their secret hiding place. After a few moments of silence, he began to approach with the rest following behind at a safe distance.

When he got to the waist-high straw, Ollie looked over and saw a girl. He recognized her as somebody from his sixth grade class and who lived farther up the road. Her name was Elizabeth, but everybody called her Libby. She always seemed quiet, but not unpleasant like most girls he knew. Most of the ones he knew from school seemed silly. Always talking about stuff he didn't care about. Libby didn't associate with them, and that was a plus as far as he was concerned.

"Hey, Libby. I, uh, didn't mean to throw pinecones at you. What 'cha doing in here?" asked Ollie.

She looked at Ollie with defiance. Her print dress ended just above her knees revealing slim legs and white ankle socks above her black patent Mary Jane shoes.

"I didn't know you owned this property, Ollie. I was looking for a private place for a little peace and quiet," said the girl.

Ollie didn't know what to say. Nobody had ever challenged that the place belonged to his bunch.

"Uh, me and the guys just play back here. I'm really sorry if we hit you with any pinecones."

She smiled at Ollie. She had one dimple on the left side of her mouth that he had never noticed before. For the first time in his life, Ollie saw something in a girl that made him forget playing with his guy friends.

"It's okay, Ollie. I was just getting away from everything for a while. You couldn't have known I was in here."

Ollie had forgotten his crew, and he now wished he could talk to Libby without others being near. Poochie began snickering behind a hand. He was a younger kid who could be annoying if you let him.

"Hey, Captain. You found a wench?" asked Poochie.

Ollie felt his face turn crimson as he turned to the other kids. Most, if any of them, couldn't have known what he was feeling at the moment.

"Listen up, pirates. There's been a change in plans. I've decided we need to check out the swamp for buried treasure," said Ollie.

The swamp was another area they frequented while playing. It was nothing more than a shallow creek running with murky water, but it often provided much to contemplate in their fertile imaginations.

"Yeah, hidden gold in the swamp. We'll be rich," said one of the other kids wearing a patch over one eye.

Ollie looked over the straw wall at Libby and tried to smile. Their eyes met and for a moment his heart fluttered. He didn't understand the feeling, but he knew he wanted to talk to her again without the rest of the guys being around. It would have to wait for now.

"See 'ya around, Libby."

"I expect so, Ollie," she replied with a wink.

CHAPTER 3

Present

At a high-top table across the bar sat four regulars. There was Jimbo Barbour, a Macon/Bibb County captain in charge of the major crimes division; Jacques Montand, a car salesman; Bobby Henry, an architect; and Tom West who had left the bar when Ollie started talking to the pretty brunette. They were in an animated conversation that had been played out many times before, but always resurfaced when they got together at the bar.

"Hey, Bobby. You gonna pay the tab tonight, right?" asked Jacques in his New Jersey flavored foreign accent.

"Yeah, right after you blow me, frog," replied Bobby.

"There ain't going to be any sexual propositions in my presence, or I'm running both you guys in for solicitation," deadpanned Jimbo.

Tom laughed at the dialogue and chugged a third of his beer. He interjected, "Speaking of propositions, what do y'all think of the girl old Ollie is hitting on at the bar? Is she a hot babe or what? She's too young for that old fart, but I'd say she's perfect for me. You know what I'm saying?"

All of the men turned their attention to the bar where it appeared Ollie and the younger woman were having an intimate conversation. She was doing most of the talking, and he was chewing on a cocktail straw.

"You wish, Tommy Boy. She's got his attention, all right. Based on my superb interpersonal skills and many years training as an officer, I would say his body language is screaming major discomfort," said Jimbo.

"You can tell he's taking in what she's sayin' by the way he's gnawin' on that damned stwah," chimed in Jacques.

"Indeed, she could gnaw on me, and I wouldn't mind," said Tom.

"You so fwiggin' cwude, Tom. That's why you never score with the gulls. Why don't you learn some class? That and get yourself a new wardrobe. You look like a John McEnwoe exile from the eighties," said Jacques.

"There goes that jealousy thing again. Just because I've got nice legs and I'm not afraid to show them in public; and you've got those big-assed hams of yours covered up, as they should be, you let your pettiness shine through every time," responded Tom.

"Gentlemen, and I use the term loosely, haven't we worn out that subject many times before?" asked Bobby.

"Yeah, stick something in your pie holes, or just do what we do when in an establishment such as this. In case you've forgotten, it's a bar. Bottoms up," said Jimbo.

The four men drank in silence for a few moments. All stole glances at Ollie and the woman with more than a little jealousy. The couple at the bar, on the other hand, paid no attention to the group.

***

Ollie was in a state of disbelief. He hadn't thought about Nancy Lee in years. The intense affair they had over thirty-five years ago seemed nothing more than a dream now.

No way. I'm not anybody's father, he thought.

He studied the pretty girl's face and even with many years past could see the resemblance to her mother. They had the same jawline and perky nose. The almond shaped eyes were the same, too. The color was a little different and could best be described as bluish-green. Ollie bet they would change colors depending on the light or the color of her outfit. Her hair was lush and thick, parted slightly to one side of her head and curled around her slim shoulders. It was the same pigment his had been at her age.

Same hair color doesn't make me her daddy.

"Excuse my language, Miss. I've never even come close to that kind of introduction before. I still don't believe I got your name," said Ollie.

The woman laughed and shook her head. "I've heard a lot worse language. I'm sure being introduced to someone claiming to be a thirty-five year old daughter you never knew existed requires at least such an utterance. No apologies necessary. You can call me Holly, rhymes with yours," answered the woman.

The old lawyer's instincts took over and questions poured out of him. "Did your mother do that by design?" he asked.

"She might have, I guess. I asked her once when I was a teenager how she came up with my name, and Mom told me it came from an old friend," she replied.

"How did you find me?" asked Ollie.

"You mean generally speaking or here this evening?" Holly said with a smile and a question of her own.

"Yeah," Ollie said.

Holly had a throaty laugh and a devilish smile, thought Ollie, and she showed off both. Her teeth were white and straight, probably assisted with braces in junior high school.

"Sorry, asking questions is part of my job, too, counselor," she said. "I'm an investigator. Or, I guess I should say I was until a couple of weeks ago.

Ollie studied Holly as she took a dainty sip of her cocktail. She became even more attractive in her appearance than he had first noticed. It occurred to him he had become much too complacent about women in general, and it was a flaw in need of professional help.

"Investigators typically poke around what they're hired to look into. Can you say what were you working on and for whom? Public or private?" asked Ollie.

Holly looked at the man she had earlier dropped a bombshell on and lobbed another grenade. "Among others, an old client of yours. I'm sure you remember Tyler Crenshaw. He was a person of interest in a case I was working on for the Fulton County DA's Office. Unfortunately for me, budget cuts by the state and local governments just cost me my job. Since I was snooping around close to your home, I decided I'd check out this area and finally look you up."

Ollie tried to maintain his best poker face as her answers to his questions exploded in his brain. Crenshaw starred in many memories best left alone. For sure, Ollie didn't want to talk about him with her.

CHAPTER 4

August, 1958

The kid was hidden in a weathered pine twenty feet off the ground. Hiding had become a specialty of his. He had a knack for concealment and could find places no one else thought about. He would do it at home in a corner of a closet spying on his brother or under a bed listening to his parents' private conversations. In the woods, he especially enjoyed scaling trees that other kids wouldn't attempt. There he could listen to their child's play in silence and pretend he was invisible. That was a fantasy he savored more than anything.

Today the thin kid was scouting new trees to climb down the street from where he lived. He recognized the boy and girl as they walked underneath the tree where he crouched on skinny haunches. They all lived in the neighborhood and attended the same school. They weren't really friends since the kid usually kept a distance from everybody. As the pair sat down on straw padded ground, the kid had to strain and use his super powers in order to hear the conversation.

"So Ollie, where are all your mateys today?" asked Libby.

Ollie's face blushed at the reference to his brothers, friends and other adolescents who made up the pack he most often hung out with. Of course, he remembered when they had clunked her with pinecones while acting like pirates. He hoped she wasn't making fun of him in some fashion. Ollie had decided he liked this girl enough to ask her if she wanted to be his girlfriend. He wasn't sure what that entailed, but his best friend, Mike, had one and he wanted to be like him. Mike was the neatest guy he knew and a trendsetter.

"Uh, my brothers went to town with my parents to buy school clothes. I'm not sure where the rest of the guys are today," said Ollie.

Libby smiled and teased, "So, how about new school clothes for Captain Oliver Tucker? It looks like he could stand some new jeans at least."

Ollie looked at the right knee of his faded jeans and self-consciously placed his hand over a patch his mother had ironed on. The color of the denim square was darker blue and stood out like a sore thumb. He knew Mom used every chance to save money for the family living on a tight budget. Since he and his brothers were rough on their play clothes, patched blue jeans were seen often.

"Uh, well, I picked out my new clothes last month when we all went to Sears, but my brothers wanted to look in Penney's. We didn't have time then 'cause Daddy spent too much time looking at tools, so they were going back downtown to look today. I got two new pairs of blue jeans, one pair of black ones and some new Sunday school slacks. I can't start wearing the new ones 'til school starts," said Ollie trying not to sound as self-conscious as he felt.

"That's nice, Ollie. I'm supposed to go next week and get some clothes, too. I can't wait for school to start back and get to wear something new again. Do you like school?"

Ollie felt more relaxed the longer he was near Libby. He had never been around very many girls and talking to them didn't come naturally. There was something different about her, though. He experienced an attraction that was fresh and new. A tingling sensation in the pit of his stomach was not unpleasant, but it still made him more than a little nervous.

"Yeah I do, a lot. I like learning different stuff and seeing some of the guys I don't get to see during the summer. I also like being able to check out books from the school library and playing sports for the school team. To a lot of the guys it's probably weird, but I'd rather be in school than out. I think it'll even be more fun when we get to junior high next year," said Ollie.

Libby's single dimple disappeared as she frowned. "I'm not so sure about next year. It's hard to believe this will be our last year at Union. I don't know if I want to be with so many others in high school. We'll be like little fish in a big pond. And, we won't get to see each other as much since we'll be in separate schools."

Ollie thought she looked worried, and he wanted to help. He had forgotten about the gender separation of the local high schools, or maybe he had never really thought about it before now. It would be different not to have girls in his class. He reached over and took her hand in his. They looked into each other's eyes for a moment before he spoke.

"It'll be okay, Libby. We'll still get to ride the same bus, and we can talk before and after school."

She smiled and the single dimple reappeared. Then Libby squeezed his hand and leaned forward kissing him on the cheek before Ollie could react. He felt his face warm, and the palm of the hand holding Libby's turn sweaty. He was more scared than he could ever remember.

"You're the sweetest boy, Ollie. I really like you. Do you like me?"

"I-I-I do like you, too." He hesitated and then continued. "Do you want to be my girlfriend?"

She giggled and said, "I've never had a boyfriend before. I can't think of anything I'd like more, except maybe a new pair of shoes."

It was Ollie's turn to grin and his flushed face began to regain its normal color. He had never felt happier. It was just like the first time he hit a baseball over the fence.

"You kid me just like one of the guys. I think that's one of the reasons I like you so much. You're funny for a girl," said Ollie.

"I'm not kidding, Ollie. I like you, but shoes are special to me."

Ollie looked at the girl and her smile was mocking. He was just about to make a witty reply when there was a cracking from above followed by pine bark debris falling on his and Libby's heads. They both shielded their heads with their arms and Ollie glared upward.

Ollie didn't see the kid at first. He blended in with the foliage and he was small. However, the gentle swaying of the lower of two close branches disclosed white rubber on the bottom of a tennis shoe as Ollie focused.

"Hey, who's up there?" shouted Ollie.

Libby and Ollie got off the ground and back-pedaled from directly underneath the branches where the kid remained in a crouched position. Although not clearly visible, the two of them could make out the small figure clad in a green shirt and jeans clinging to a branch with both hands while balanced on another with both feet. Neither of the limbs looked strong enough to support much weight.

"We can see you," called Libby. "You might as well tell us who you are."

Several silent moments passed with no movement from the tree. Ollie couldn't tell if the kid was going to answer or not. Just as he was contemplating whether to try climbing and confronting the mystery kid, another more ominous breaking sound occurred and both limbs began to swing again.

"You better get down from there, now," hollered Ollie. "You're gonna break your stupid neck."

Now a faint voice answered, "I'm afraid. I don't want to fall."

Ollie and Libby moved a few steps closer and peered through the pine. Finally, there was a sharper picture of the kid and the situation he faced. The limb supporting most of his weight was visibly cracked a few feet between him and the trunk.

"Hey, I know you. You're one of the Crenshaw boys," said Libby.

"Yeah," was all he said.

Ollie was studying the branch and knew it would fall with too much pressure. He had fallen from such a tree last year at a much lower distance and it had hurt his ankle when he fell. Daddy had whipped him after he found out and warned him about the dangers of climbing pine trees, especially those infested and weakened with beetles.

"Listen. You need to hold on with your hands more than stand with your feet," said Ollie. "Do you understand?"

"I'm tryin' but I think there's a crack in this top branch, too," said the Crenshaw boy.

Ollie looked at the other branch and saw there was indeed another danger. At least that break didn't appear as pronounced even though that branch was not as big in diameter. However, it was going to be a tricky proposition to get back to the trunk and climb back down before one or both limbs crashed down. No doubt, the kid would be hurt badly if that happened.

"Alright, be still as you can for a minute," Ollie said.

He looked at Libby who had turned pale as a ghost. Help was too far away, but something had to be done quickly.

Dropping his voice and holding Libby's shoulders in both hands, Ollie spoke to her. "Let's get as much straw as we can and put it under here. I'm afraid he's going to fall and we need some padding if he does. Let's pack it in here before he tries to move again."

There was no shortage of pines in the area, and the pair grabbed double arms full of the golden brown straw before dropping them underneath the boy's spot. They worked as fast as they could while constantly looking up afraid the branches might fall on them. In a matter of minutes there was a mound nearly as tall as they were.

"Okay, we've got you some protection down here if you fall," said Ollie. "Now, you need to take it slowly and move closer to the trunk. Baby steps and keep the pressure off the bottom limb. If you think you're going down, try to flatten out."

Ollie saw that Libby was biting her bottom lip while he talked to Crenshaw. She was worried, no doubt. Tears were welling in her eyes and her lips were quivering. She almost seemed to be praying. Ollie was even more scared than when he saw and heard his daddy snapping off his belt before dispatching punishment. A whipping would be better than watching this.

The Crenshaw boy had few choices left. He'd never been in such a mess. He swallowed hard as he looked toward the trunk and then down at the two below him. This was about as bad as he could imagine.

All three of them could only hope for the best. At that moment in time, they were joined.

CHAPTER 5

Present, three months earlier

In the suburbs there was a certain complacency not readily available in other parts of the community. There was crime everywhere in the city and nowhere was considered completely safe, but the burbs were generally considered havens. That's what they said anyway.

This night was not unusual. This part of the suburbs was not anything special either. It was just another night away from the lights of town. Nothing was supposed to happen in the cul-de-sacs hidden away from the ills of society. Cookie cutter homes insured conformity first and safety a close second.

There were houses up and down the three streets with stories of their own contained within. There was the one with an accountant worrying about his unfaithful wife and the unethical practices at work complicating his life. There was another holding a sales manager with a drug problem, and he wondered if anyone suspected. Yet another contained a young female pharmacist laboring with her lesbian lover's propensity for gambling. Life was complicated for them all, but they remained private.

There was also a single woman with fetching looks others found beautiful. However, Holly Lee was not worried about her appearance or what other people thought. She rented the house where she resided and was not concerned about what the future might hold. That's what she told herself often. Everything in her life seemed temporary anyway. She knew one day she needed to discover her life's plan, but for some reason Holly kept putting it off to another time.

She studied the screen on her laptop. The text was starting to blur, and she pinched the bridge of her nose hoping it would help her focus. This job was getting to her. Being an investigator had its rewards, but there had to be something more to life than snooping. Yeah, she was pretty good at her job, but wasn't there something else she could do that was more fun and a better use of her talents? She hadn't been on a date since her mother's death, so maybe she should stop turning down the offers she received on a regular basis.

Maybe it was time to think about a career change, too. Maybe she should look up her father and see if he had any words of wisdom. Mom wouldn't have thought so, but perhaps he could reveal a few things she didn't know or hadn't thought about. That is, if he really was her father.

Yeah, Mom wouldn't lie about anything like having a successful lawyer as my father. There's always DNA to prove one way or another. I'm good with that, she thought.

I wonder if he would object to a blood test. It's not like I want any money or anything. Besides, it's the only way to find out the truth.

Holly got up from her chair and stretched. She glanced at the clock sitting on the bookshelf and saw it was 10:30. It was getting late and she was still working. Sex crimes had been her life for the last five years since she left Atlanta PD and joined the Fulton District Attorney's Office. So many sickos, so little time to get them off the streets. But, the state had cut funding for jobs and since she was lowest on the totem pole, she had to stand out or she might just get let go real soon. She had to keep working hard, at least until she figured out what she wanted to do forever.

Yeah, I think I need to make a trip to Macon soon.

***

Amongst the quiet solitude of the suburbs sat The Viewer. That's the name he gave himself because that's what he did. He had learned long ago tricks of the trade and loved the game involved. He blended better than the most skilled hunter in a dense forest. He could change colors better than a chameleon. He smiled to himself as he sat concealed in some bushes near the woman's house.

He had learned she was interested in him. It tickled his inner core that he was observing her as she was investigating him. She would never know him like he knew her. Nobody ever had except maybe a friend or two from childhood.

She was pretty. She was smart. She took her job seriously. He knew all that from watching her and other more intimate things from invading her living space.

Yeah, she was smart. But, he was way smarter, though.

CHAPTER 6

Present

The Law Offices of Oliver Tucker, P.C. were contained on the first floor of a historic house in downtown Macon. It had been purchased after Ollie settled a personal injury case twenty-five years before which resulted in a nice six-figure fee. His realtor friend, Tom, found the house only blocks from the courthouse. The previous owner had been reluctant to spend the necessary funds to improve the property, and it had fallen into a sad state of disrepair.

Because the old home looked like it was about to collapse, Ollie was able to buy it for a song. He then parlayed connections with a couple of his clients in the construction trade and took advantage of swapping legal work for services rendered in the restoration process. He also took advantage of available grant money from the Historical Society and used the expertise of other friends to plan what he wanted. His architect buddy, Bobby Henry, drew the plans and his best friend Ty was his de facto supervisor. When the project was completed, the once dilapidated structure had been transformed into a first-class law office on the main floor. The home office had even been featured in some regional publications.

All of the older homes on the street were well maintained, but Ollie's stood out. It appeared stately on a slightly elevated lot with its white columns and black shutters contrasted against the red brick exterior. The designed landscape caused visitors to stop and snap photographs every spring during the Cherry Blossom Festival since the grounds contained several of the beautiful trees.

Inside, the office space was spacious and inviting. There was a comfortable reception area filled with leather chairs for clients located next to a grand staircase near the front door. An antique grandfather clock stole the attention of visitors as they entered and announced the hour faithfully for those in attendance. Additionally, there were two over-sized offices where Ollie and his associate, when he had one, conducted their business. The other space consisted of a separate office area for two secretaries and a small eat-in kitchen located in the rear.

The second floor could only be accessed by climbing up the winding stairs of the house and was Ollie's residence. Only a select few had been granted a view. It had been remodeled by a former female interest that had long since departed for greener pastures.

In a word, it was comfortable. It's where he found refuge. It was homey and had all of his favorite things. He spent most of his down time in the central living area relaxing in a soft, well-worn, leather lounge chair, but he had a huge master bedroom with an equally impressive master bathroom that he enjoyed as well. There was a state-of-the-art sound system in the living room and speakers located throughout the space allowing Ollie to hear classic rock-n-roll no matter what room he was in.

All the rooms were impeccably furnished and most kept clean by a Hispanic housekeeper named Rosa who came at least twice a week. The kitchen was open and modern although not used very often. Ollie had once enjoyed cooking, but he had become lazy as he aged. Now he preferred eating out and most often sat at a bar for his meals.

There was another bedroom and a smaller bath on the opposite side of the floor for guests, but no one had stayed there in years. For the most part, the extra bedroom's main purpose in recent times was storage. A cursory inspection would reveal at least two pieces of unused exercise equipment and various boxes of discarded files. A more thorough inspection would find all sorts of boxes underneath the bed, many covered with spider webs. Rosa never ventured there which was as fine with her as it was with her boss.

As Ollie entered home following the memorable evening, the security system sounded its familiar monotone whistle letting him know he had thirty seconds to disarm it before the alarm would wake up half of downtown. He closed the heavy wooden front door and walked to the partially concealed keypad. He punched in the required code with seconds to spare as his brain continued to process the night.

He was not convinced Holly was his daughter even though she had been persuasive by requesting a DNA test. Ollie thought that was an idea worth exploring, because he had used such tests for cases in the past. He knew the science had been perfected and would ensure the results, whatever they showed.

It made no sense to him that Nancy would have accepted the burden of raising a child without ever contacting him and asking for his help. He had handled several hundred domestic cases involving child support issues. They were often nasty matters that dragged on to the point of making him want to pull out his hair.

Bottom line, however, children deserved to be supported and if there was a parent not pulling his or her weight, they should be made to. Ollie knew for all of his faults he would've done what was necessary to help with such expenses had Nancy ever asked. He simply couldn't imagine why she would have chosen to take on such a heavy load by herself.

Ollie racked his brain as he trudged up the stairs trying to remember if Nancy had ever indicated she was pregnant before their breakup. It had been so long ago and too many women before and after for him to recall the scene. Surely he would remember such an important event.

The first thing he did upon entering the living area was find some Jackson Browne and turn on the stereo. He hoped the soothing sounds would help him think.

Leaving the great room, Ollie slipped off his jacket and began loosening his tie before arriving inside the bedroom. He crossed the floor to the walk-in closet and finished undressing down to his tee shirt and boxer shorts. The expensive suit was hung on a cedar hanger and placed on one end of the rack alongside several others. Because he was somewhat OCD, the suit wouldn't be worn again until all of those on the other end were worn and then placed behind that one.

He walked back into the bedroom, pausing for a moment in front of the freestanding mirror located in a corner away from the bed. He turned from side to side and saw that his once athletic body was telling its age. There was a paunch instead of the flattened stomach long admired by women and men until just a few years ago. His arm and leg muscles were sagging too, but were not as noticeable. The daily four-mile walks and lightweight workouts at least kept them toned to a degree. Altogether he was still in pretty good shape for his age, even if his personal critical view told him otherwise.

Downstairs the clock chimed nine times as Ollie slipped on soft cotton pajamas and his old bedroom shoes. Though the sound could be heard clearly throughout both floors of the house, he rarely paid attention as his senses had long since become dulled to the regular noise.

After getting into what his mother would have called "wallowing clothes," Ollie walked back into the kitchen and retrieved a bottle of The Glenlivet 15 year-old single malt scotch from where he had left it last night. He got his favorite glass, added a few ice cubes from the dispenser on the refrigerator door and poured himself a generous amount. He took a quick Ollie taste test and then headed to the inner sanctum where the lounge chair awaited.

He settled in the chair and placed the drink on the table to his right. For the next several minutes he listened as JB crooned about lost love. Intermittently, he sipped on the drink as his mind drifted. Soon enough Ollie was a kid again.

CHAPTER 7

August, 1958

O llie was scared like no other time ever experienced. The Crenshaw boy had edged toward the trunk of the pine an inch at the time. As he shuffled his feet sideways, loose bark fell near Ollie and Libby. There had been cracking sounds along the way reinforcing the belief that the kid was going to fall any minute.

Libby was standing beside Ollie but slightly behind him. He glanced back at her and saw she was holding both hands at her mouth with eyes wide open. When the bottom branch where the kid's feet balanced groaned and finally broke, the boy and girl on the ground audibly gasped in unison.

They watched in horror as the limb fractured a couple of feet from the tree and crashed to the ground leaving the Crenshaw boy holding on with both hands to the limb above him. It dipped dangerously and looked as if it might break as well any minute.

"Hold on," screamed Ollie.

He ran directly underneath where the boy swung and began pulling at the fallen branch. Part of it was buried in the mound of pine straw Ollie and Libby had heaped making it difficult to budge even though it didn't seem all that heavy. With Libby joining in to help him, they were able to get most of it out of the pile and then began to replenish the displaced straw.

All while the process took place below, the kid hung to the limb like a rung on the playground monkey bar. He was about four feet from the trunk where there were available footholds that would allow his descent. The bark was rough on his hands, but he began moving in that direction.

Ollie and Libby could only watch as the skinny boy made slow and steady progress. Ollie wondered if he could somehow catch him if he did fall, but knew they probably both would be hurt if that happened. Maybe the straw would keep him from breaking all his bones.

After several agonizing minutes that seemed much longer, the Crenshaw boy was able to position himself with his feet on a sturdier part of the tree. He rested a moment before climbing down.

Libby was the first to reach him. She was taller than him by a head, but was only slightly meatier. She hugged him with ferocity and without reservation. He stiffened at first and then gave in to the gesture without hugging in return. Ollie watched the scene with interest as his heart still worked to get back to a normal rate.

"What were you doing up there?" she asked while separating her grasp.

The kid's eyes held her gaze for only a moment and then dropped staring at the ground as his chin rested on the shallow chest he possessed. When he answered the voice was soft and measured.

"I was looking," he said.

"For what?" asked Libby.

"I don't know."

"That makes no sense."

He shrugged and replied, "It does to me."

Ollie joined the two of them and said, "I've seen you around the neighborhood and know you ride the same bus. Your last name is Crenshaw and you've got at least one older brother. I think you're a year or two behind us in school, right?"

The kid's head nodded up and down as he maintained his stare at the ground. Ollie thought he appeared as a scolded child or a mistreated animal. Maybe he was just shy.

"Name's Tyler. Live up the road. Be in the sixth grade this year."

"Let me tell you something, Tyler. You scared the dookie out of us. We thought you were going to break your neck," said Ollie.

"Didn't mean to scare you. Climb these trees all the time. Most of the time nobody pays me any mind," replied Tyler.

"I see you a lot," interjected Libby. "You're only a few houses down from where I live."

"I know," was all he said.

Ollie and Libby exchanged glances. The girl then frowned.

"Please don't tell anybody I almost fell," Tyler said as he looked up.

Ollie studied the face of the younger boy for the first time. His dirty blonde hair stood in a butch waxed flattop, and his blue eyes drooped at the corners giving the appearance of perpetual sadness. He was fair-skinned with a hint of freckles across his nose. He was not an ugly kid, but he wasn't exactly cute either.

"I can't speak for Libby, but I'm no tattletale. You need to watch climbing some of these trees, Tyler. I fell out of one last year not nearly as high as you were, and I was lucky I didn't get hurt bad. Daddy told me about some bugs that can make them die," said Ollie.

"I don't see any need to tell anybody, Tyler. One thing I want to know is were you spying on me and Ollie," Libby said.

Tyler dropped his eyes again and started shuffling his feet. After a pause, he replied, "I saw y'all coming when I was already in the tree."

"Why didn't you say anything when we got here?" she asked.

"I heard some of what you said, but I didn't know what to say."

"It's not nice to listen to other people's private conversations," responded Libby through a frown.

"I didn't mean to do anything wrong. I just don't have any friends, so I play by myself most of the time. I like to practice hiding and lots of times I climb trees because people hardly ever look up when I'm in one. I didn't mean to make you mad," said Tyler still talking to the ground.

"Okay, Tyler. We're not mad at you. How about if Ollie and me become friends with you? You think that might help you from climbing so high in dangerous trees?"

For the first time, Tyler Crenshaw raised his head, looked both of them eye-to-eye and smiled. "Really? I'd like that."

CHAPTER 8

Present

Ollie woke with a start and was disoriented. He was still in his chair and holding a mostly empty glass except for watery ice cubes. It was at an angle in his hand that was precariously tipped toward his groin, but he did not feel wet, yet. His aging bladder warned of impending disaster if he didn't make a bathroom run in the very near future, however.

A large decorative clock on the living room wall indicated it was a few minutes after 1:00 a.m., but he had not heard the chime downstairs signaling such. Music still played on the sound system telling about another sad tale of love. *How appropriate is that?* he thought.

He placed the glass on the table next to the chair and wondered if another scotch might be necessary before going to bed. His back groaned as he leaned forward and attempted to get out of the chair that no longer felt like an oasis.

"Watermelon," he mumbled. It was a reference to his long deceased grandmother who had often told a tale of toddler Ollie referring to his overflowing diaper as "what a mess" but sounding like the southern delicacy that was red, juicy, and delicious. She had thought he was asking for something tasty rather than warning of something nasty. He now used the term anytime things weren't going exactly like he would like.

This night had been one honking, fat watermelon, all right. Here he was well into his sixties and he'd never thought about being a father. Hell, he'd never seriously thought about marrying. Yeah, he'd come close enough a couple of times, but then old memories came back and he would know he'd only make a mess of building a life with a woman, much less bringing another life into this shithole of a world. He couldn't do that to another person after what he'd seen. It was all too complicated, he told himself.

Could he handle being somebody's father? It was bound to be the biggest challenge he could imagine, especially at his age. If tests showed he was, he could only try.

***

Noise humming from downstairs indicated his office was getting ready for the day's work. As always when employees arrived before him, Ollie knew he had overdone the activities from the night before. His head felt more than the usual pressure caused by hypertension that had bugged him the last few years, and he hated to admit he had drunk too much again. That last one before stumbling to bed had been the proverbial one too many.

He had no one to blame but himself. As in the past when he succumbed to the desire to have one more drink, he resolved to work through the pain and do what must be done in his professional life. Otherwise, booze would be the winner. At least it was Friday and he had no court appearances, so he could dress casually and hopefully enjoy a less stressful day. Part of him wanted to stay snug on his Tempur-Pedic mattress wrapped away from the realities of the world.

The LED display on the nearby clock indicated it was 8:38 a.m. He pulled the covers from his body, sat up on the side of the bed and picked up the phone from the nightstand. Before getting ready for work, Ollie wanted to make sure his memory about the daily schedule was as he remembered. Lately his mind had played tricks on him, and he didn't want to look foolish to the staff if he had indeed forgotten something.

"Hey, Boss," answered Suzie the auburn-haired receptionist otherwise known as Red.

"Good morning, Red. I'm a little slow waking up. Anything going on in the sweat shop, yet?" asked Ollie.

She snickered before answering, "Just the usual, Boss. Did you have a rough night?"

"I plead the fifth. How about looking at the schedule and making sure I don't have anything needing my attention before ten?"

There was a moment of silence before she answered. He could hear her tapping on the computer keyboard and flipping a paper page as well.

"It looks like you have an appointment at 10:00 and another at 2:00. Other than that, nothing is listed on my calendar. Hey, maybe I could leave after your last appointment and get an early start on the weekend, okay?"

Ollie was relieved he had remembered the first appointment. Maybe his slipping memory wasn't as bad as he thought. He didn't recall knowing anything about the afternoon meeting, so that could be one made by somebody else in the office. No matter, it would be an easy enough day in the state he currently felt.

"I'll think about it. I'm going to jump in the shower and I'll be down in about an hour. How about going down to Jeneane's in a little while and getting me a sausage and egg biscuit? If the rest of you want anything, you can take the money out of petty cash. See y'all in a little while," he said before hanging up the phone.

After making a quick bathroom run, Ollie went into the kitchen and started the Keurig. He found it quicker, easier and less wasteful to make a single cup of coffee at a time as wanted or needed. In a couple of minutes, he was sipping his first "cup of ambition" as one of his friends liked to call it.

Some mornings Ollie would fix his own breakfast before getting ready for work, but since he had slept later, he got busy preparing his mind and body for the day ahead. He took the coffee to the chair where he had awakened earlier in the morning and set the cup on the table to his right. His MacBook was located there as well, and he picked it up before sitting down.

Clicking on the Macon.com bookmark, he began reading the local paper online. There were all the usual types of stories Ollie had been reading about as long as he could remember. Too often it seemed as if everything could be under what he titled, More Bad News. He scanned a number of headlines and read the first couple of paragraphs of a few pieces. There was nothing really of interest until he noticed a short article under the local news section. He read as he sipped the full-bodied roasted coffee.

Sheriff says there is a serial burglar in the area

After a rash of recent break-ins, Sheriff Derek Davidson said yesterday there is a serial burglar in the middle Georgia area stealing personal items of little value. Although the thefts have resulted in no injuries to persons or property, the victims all reported the stolen items have sentimental worth.

"It's really unnerving to the folks who've had their homes violated by this perpetrator," said Sheriff Davidson. "The Sheriff's Office is taking this threat very seriously, and we'll be taking measures to patrol all parts of the county and apprehend

this felon. It's only a matter of time before the person or persons responsible will be arrested and brought to justice."

According to sources within the department, there have been at least eight reported incidents in the last three months. Chief Investigator, Michael Singletary, said there might have been more unreported events because of the nature of the burglaries. In each investigated case there have been no signs of forced entry, and there was a "calling card" left by the thief. He refused further comment when asked for additional information.

Ollie shook his head and thought it was weird behavior. He had seen a lot stranger in his time, however.

He finished his cup of coffee and noticed the clock was marching double-time. Putting the computer back in its place, Ollie got up and went to get ready for the easy day he had planned.

CHAPTER 9

Red was talking on the phone when Ollie came down the stairs. She smiled at him as he walked by her desk and motioned for him to wait. Her animated southernese speech patterns always cracked him up, but the clients seemed to identify with the sunny disposition and the always-present smile.

"Okee-dokee, I'll tell him what you said, and I'll call you back if there's a problem. If you don't hear from me, just plan to be here around 3:30 this afternoon...Yes, ma'am, nice talking to you, too," Red said as she hung up the phone.

"So, you just made me another appointment, Miss Red? I was looking forward to a quiet day," said Ollie.

The young receptionist had not stopped smiling since he had come down from the living area. It somehow made her appear sneaky or that she had some untold secret.

"Mornin', Boss. How ya' feelin'?"

"Tolerable, Red. Don't change the subject. You did hear me ask whether you had made me another appointment, right?"

"Yes, sir. I heard you, and yes, sir, I made another appointment. She seemed really nice and said she talked with you last night. She said y'all had things in common, and she was sure you would be okay with meeting her this afternoon. Holly Lee is her name. Hope I didn't mess up. Hot date?" said Red raising an eyebrow.

Ollie couldn't help the frown that appeared on his face, but tried to maintain his composure. He remembered from the night before the discussion about getting together soon to further discuss what would happen next in the relationship. It seemed she wanted to push it faster than he thought prudent. He felt agitated and wanted to cuss a little. He didn't, though and forced a smile.

"So, you want to get off early today? You need to learn how to make me happy every chance you can in order to earn those kind of benefits. Number one way to do that is to make sure I don't have any late appointments on Friday afternoons. I think you just failed that exam," said Ollie straight-faced.

"Come on, Boss. I've been working hard all week. Chan and I've been planning a romantic weekend for two months. I've got a babysitter, and this is the first weekend he's not planned to hunt in a while. We need some adult time. Plus, I got the impression she's important in your life, or I would've never put her on the schedule in the first place," said Red.

Ollie thought about when he was forty years younger longing for a weekend, and knew he couldn't resist. Where did the time go?

"Alright, Red. You can leave when the last appointment arrives. However, you owe me big time," he said.

The girl squealed like she was at her favorite boy band concert and broke out a huge grin. Bouncing up and down made her pleasure evident if nothing else did.

"Thanks, Mr. Tucker. I'll do whatever you say. By the way, I left your biscuit in the kitchen. Mine was real delicious."

Ollie nodded and walked past Red's desk heading toward his office. He glanced at his secretary, Joyce, but she was busy typing at her computer and didn't seem to notice as he walked by. Upon entering his space, he took a quick inspection before going to his sizeable walnut desk and taking a seat in the high-backed leather chair. The large window behind him provided natural light that was especially bright illuminating the expansive area.

The desktop was polished and bare except for a couple of files on the left-hand corner and a phone on the right. Everyone in the office knew of his penchant for neatness and made sure the office was in order before he appeared ready for work each day. He had once fired an associate simply because the young lawyer kept stuff piled everywhere. Ollie surveyed the space and found it to his standards.

He felt clear-headed after taking a steamy shower and drinking another cup of coffee. He was not hungry, but had learned skipping meals often got the system off kilter and made him grumpy. Even a smaller meal helped him to stay regulated, so he only sat a moment at the desk before going back to the small kitchen.

There was a tiny table with two functional chairs that allowed the staff room to eat their lunch inside rather than having to go out if they chose not to. Ollie opened the brown bag showing signs of grease and pulled out the biscuit. It was dense and not as warm as he preferred, but he ate about half before folding the rest in its original wax paper and replacing it in the sack. He wiped his mouth with a napkin and threw it in a plastic wastebasket underneath the sink.

Joyce stopped him as he walked by her desk again. Her professional style was always evident. Well-dressed and soft-spoken, she took pride in doing her job with very little supervision. She had worked for Ollie about ten years and seemed to always be at least one step ahead of him.

"Good morning, Mr. Tucker," she said showing off her gleaming white teeth.

"And to you, Ms. English. Any problems I need to know about?" asked Ollie.

"No sir, everything's under control. I've finished all the correspondence you dictated yesterday, and it's ready for your signature. There's nothing major, so I left all in one file on your desk. I've also drafted the Smith complaint for your review. It's in the other file left in your office. The only other thing I need to do right now is the payroll, but that will take just a minute."

"I don't know what I'd do without you, Joyce. Barring any catastrophe, why don't you take the afternoon off? You've certainly earned it, and my day should be easy enough. I've already told Red she can leave around 3:30 since she made an appointment for that time, but you can leave after the 2:00 arrives. Speaking of that, I didn't remember who was coming in then. Can you remind me?"

"Thank you, Mr. Tucker. If you really don't mind me leaving early, I could spend some time getting my house ready for a weekend visit with my granddaughter. I need to do some child-proofing," Joyce said as she clicked open the calendar on her desktop.

She continued, "The 2:00 appointment is with Mr. Tyler Crenshaw. He told me he was an old client. I didn't remember his name and I couldn't find any file, but he said you would recall him. I hope it's okay."

Ollie fought against showing any signs of discomfort. With his best poker face he replied, "Yeah, don't worry about it."

CHAPTER 10

April, 1959

Both sixth and seventh grade classes were outside for mandatory physical education. At least once a month a male and female coach hired by the county made sure all the students learned the basics of exercise and fitness. The boys had gathered on a hardened clay area that served as a football field in the fall and the baseball/softball field in the spring. The girls were on the asphalt basketball court that also doubled as a place to play volleyball.

Ollie had his baseball glove, as did several of his friends who played on the school league team. They were all on the squad that would be practicing after school, but all knew the P.E. instructor would let them use their own equipment in the planned softball game during the day's scheduled period. The rest of the boys in the class either didn't own a glove or didn't care to play the game for a variety of reasons. The boys owning one would share with those without which worked out for most of the kids when they were on defense.

Coach Tom, as all the boys called the teacher, most resembled a barrel. He was a genial sort with a waddle walk and a booming voice. Everybody liked him, even the kids who didn't like playing sports, because he had a knack for not making anyone feel inadequate. His sometimes bark was much worse than his threatening bite.

"Alright, then. Everybody stop the milling around and let's have some fun and maybe even get a little exercise in the process. Oliver Tucker and Wayne Wheeler, front and center," he said as he dropped a green canvas bag containing well-worn gear.

Ollie and Wayne were friends and the best two players on the baseball team. Wayne was the taller of the two and usually played first base since he was left-handed. Ollie could field most positions, but usually pitched because he had a good breaking pitch to go along with his fastball. Both were good hitters and consistently hit the ball farther than anyone else they played with.

When the two boys joined Coach Tom, he got in between them and put a meaty paw on each of their shoulders. Although he was not much taller than Ollie, and Wayne even had a couple of inches on him, the coach outweighed both boys together.

"These two baseball stars are going to be captains for our softball game today. That means they are going to take turns choosing their teams, and they'll be responsible for setting the positions and the lineups. I don't want any fussing and lip from anybody unless you want to run laps or even worse, get a whack from my paddle, got it? So, I'm going to flip a coin and Ollie can call it. Heads or tails?" said Coach Tom as he looked at Ollie.

Ollie called heads and a quarter was snapped into the air. Wayne grinned as he saw the tail side of the coin bounce upward on the packed grassless ground of red clay that was hard as concrete and about as forgiving. Ollie shrugged and began studying the faces of the kids to be chosen. Between the classes of kids there were over twenty to choose from and Ollie's competitive streak was sizing them up.

As he looked over the small crowd, Ollie noticed Tyler Crenshaw inconspicuously located in the rear. Over the course of the last few months Ollie had taken steps to include Tyler in some of the activities enjoyed by the neighborhood boys with only mixed success at best. Most of his other friends found him strange and difficult to talk to, and a couple of them called him weirdo behind his back. Ollie felt somehow responsible and felt he could only keep trying.

The selection of the teams was quick through the first six rounds as the baseball team regulars were fairly divided. The pace slowed as the remaining boys either were not athletic or appeared uninterested. It was during this part of the process that Ollie chose Tyler to be on his team. There were a couple of groans as the thin boy walked over to the group.

For the next fifty minutes the game seesawed back and forth as the two teams traded runs in each of the first three innings. The highlights included homeruns from each of the captains the first time at bat in their respective innings. Wayne hit a towering drive over the right fielder's head, and Ollie hit a gapper between the left and center fielders that rolled forever. Since the baseball teammates were used to playing with smaller balls thrown much faster, hitting the bigger softball lobbed into the strike zone seemed too easy. For the kids who never or rarely played the game, it was difficult to even hit the ball, much less with any power or authority.

As the top of the fourth inning was to begin and with the score knotted at five, Coach Tom boomed that it would be the last one of the game. Good-natured kidding followed as the teams changed places on the field, and some of the boys loaned gloves to those on defense. Ollie took his place at shortstop and shouted out instructions to a couple teammates who seemed lost. He looked over at Tyler playing second and told him to come in closer.

The first batter was an overweight boy named Russell who was more interested in academics than sports. He wore pants that were not jeans and shoes that were not sneakers. In his first at bat he had missed on each of three swings, so Coach Tom had taken him aside to give pointers and offer encouragement before he stepped to the plate.

He made contact on the second pitch and the ball dribbled weakly to the right side of the pitcher. Tyler showed quickness as he rushed to pick up the ball and tossed it under-handed to the first baseman before the batter was halfway down the line. Tyler looked sheepish as Ollie slapped the pocket of his glove and yelled, "Good play."

The next boy in the lineup was Danny Channing, a loudmouth bully, who was repeating the seventh grade. He was bigger than the rest of the class, and most kids stayed out of his way. He mumbled something derogatory as Russell walked past, making the other kid appear despondent and ready to cry. That only made Danny's wicked grin bigger as he picked up the bat. He began his practice swings while shooting menacing looks at the pitcher.

Ollie watched the hitter's practice and shifted slightly deeper in the hole before the first pitch. Crouching with his glove resting on his left knee and his right hand on the other, he watched the arc of the ball and the tension uncoiled as the bat was swung. Contact was flush and the ball screamed on a line between Ollie and the third baseman. He didn't think he had a chance to get to the ball, but dove to his right at the last second with the glove arm stretched across his body.

Somehow the ball stuck in his glove but squirted away as Ollie hit the unforgiving ground. He lay stunned and noticed his left elbow had been scraped red with a mixture of blood and clay.

Danny had been running since striking the ball and was already at first base by the time Ollie got off the ground. He located the ball a few feet behind him and cocked his arm as soon as he picked it up. He hesitated a moment before throwing because he knew Tyler was still learning how to catch and a hard throw could be missed giving the runner at least one more base.

Tyler stood at the base and held a borrowed glove in front of him. Ollie didn't think any more about it and threw as hard as he could. The ball flew straight as Danny bore down on the flattened square straddled by the skinny guy.

Danny had a demonic expression as he barreled toward the base. Tyler didn't even look in the runner's direction. Ollie watched his throw intently as it flew toward the climatic destination.

The scene was one to remember. Ollie's throw was true and went into Tyler's glove the instant before Danny exploded into him. Tyler was thrown backward several feet and looked like a rag doll slung akimbo. When all was said and done, the ball was held tightly in Tyler's glove, as he lay crumpled on the ground.

Ollie ran to the kid and fell down beside him. Tyler had his eyes closed at first, but opened them after his friend knelt to check on him. There was a smile exchanged before Danny stood over them.

"You little punk. I ought to stomp you in the dirt," said the boy.

Ollie stood up and dropped the glove off his hand. He had never felt such rage.

"You want some of my friend, you'll need to start with me first," screamed Ollie.

Ollie was breathing through his nose and feeling strangely calm. He hadn't been in many fights, but he was ready for this one. Danny had balled up his fists and had hate in his eyes.

"Fine with me, hotshot," said the bully.

Before anything else could happen, Coach Tom appeared. He grabbed Danny underneath his arm and told him to come with him. Ollie felt his heart beating like a drum, but reached down to pull Tyler off the ground.

Coach Tom stopped walking as he throttled Danny. He made an announcement over his shoulder, "Okay, guys. I guess we have a tie today. Gather up the gear and get ready to go to your classroom."

Tyler stood up and both boys exchanged looks of admiration. Tyler used his hands to shake off the red dust that covered him. Ollie dabbed at his bloody scrape with his glove. Unspoken words cemented their friendship.

CHAPTER 11

Present

Ollie sat at his desk killing time. He absent-mindedly surfed different websites while pondering his life. At one time, he had thought he could make a difference in the world. Today, he wasn't sure if his life had ever been worthwhile or had any real meaning. He had pretty much screwed up everything important except for work. His relationships with women had all been disasters if he was completely honest, and there was no one to blame but himself. What did it matter anymore? Now all he wanted was a little peace of mind, and he wasn't sure how best to accomplish the goal.

Sure, professionally he was a success. He owned a picturesque home office that was the envy of lawyers around town, if not the entire state. He was debt-free and had accumulated personal wealth that he was sure some would be willing to kill for. He knew other people thought he was crazy to still be working at his age when he didn't need to. It was sad on some level that work was all he had, but it was all he had ever known. He didn't think this old leopard could ever change his spots.

Many of the attorneys he knew were struggling to make a decent living and had told him they would work until they died because they had saved nothing toward retirement. It was no wonder suicide was considered a problem for the profession. The pressure was enormous, and the general public would never believe a lawyer's life was not the glamorous existence portrayed on television or in the movies.

Maybe he should retire. He didn't even like the practice of law that much anymore, did he? He was good at what he did, but why should that matter? He didn't get satisfaction from helping unfortunate clients like he once did, and he really didn't know what was the attraction that caused him to keep doing the job. He just needed to do something, and this was all he knew. It was all inertia, at this point.

Ollie realized he was tired. Not so much physically, but mentally. His age was catching up with him. He could take some time off, but what would he do then? Until recently he had not really thought about it, but now he believed there had to be something more. What it was he didn't know.

The website he now surfed was of a Caribbean island. There was a pristine beach and a cloudless blue sky. A sailboat was in the distance, and an attractive couple was closer in the shot with masks and snorkels evident. Everyone was happy in the picture. To one side in the shot was a tiki bar with cold beverages. You could almost taste the banana and pineapple. Ollie wanted to be there right now.

He was losing himself in the scene when Joyce buzzed him. The moment was lost as she said, "Your two o'clock appointment is here, Mr. Tucker."

Ollie closed the site from his computer and answered, "Okay, send him in."

A few seconds later, Tyler Crenshaw came walking into Ollie's office. Ollie had not seen him in a couple of years, but he was surprised to see his old friend had not changed a bit. Still slim and fit, with a youthful haircut and form-fitting clothes, he looked at least ten years younger than his age. His sandy hair was plastered down with some product. The red bow tie he wore seemed out of place and made him look like a poster child for the Republican Party. Ollie thought it was the first time he had ever seen his friend wearing anything around his neck.

"Hey, old buddy," said Tyler as he walked in the room with his right hand extended.

Ollie couldn't help but wonder what had happened to Tyler over the years. This man did not resemble the insecure boy he first met fifty-plus years ago at all.

"How ya' doing, Ty? Still climbing trees?" asked Ollie.

Tyler laughed as they pumped hands. "That was a long time ago," he said.

"Well, you look like you could still scale one if you wanted to. You're in great shape, man. How do you do it?"

Tyler laughed and replied, "I run a little, but I love hiking. Been all over the southeast the last few years. Probably been on every trail at least once. Nothing like getting back to nature, Ollie. Sleeping under the stars, catching a fish in a cool stream, cooking and eating it after walking all day...It'll make you fit and feel energized like nothing else. You should come with me. Be glad to take you sometime."

"That sounds like fun if I were thirty years younger, Ty. I'll take a pass on that one and leave it to you kids," said Ollie.

"Okay, but you're only a year older than me, remember?" said Tyler.

"Yeah, don't remind me. Come and sit down. Can I get you anything? Coffee, coke, water?"

"No, thanks. I don't do caffeine anymore, and I'm fine anyway," said Tyler as he sat down in one of the chairs across from Ollie's desk.

Ollie walked around the desk and took his place in the high-back leather chair. He resisted the urge to rock back and prop a foot.

"So, are you still in business for yourself? As I recall you had your hand in several pies," said Ollie.

"Yeah, I've slowed down a good bit and have become more selective, but I'm still taking on a few construction projects. Mainly renovations. Nothing as nice as you've done, though. We did a good job in here, and I'm glad I had a little bit to do with your showplace. I sold the burglar alarm business a couple of years ago, and I quit doing landscape designs about the same time. How about you counselor? Are you still going at it as strong?" asked Tyler.

"My practice areas have changed a bit over the years. I'm pretty fortunate that I can pick and choose what I want to do now. It's not like when I first got started and had to take whatever came through the door. I try not to do any domestic stuff anymore and very little criminal work at all now unless one of my old clients needs something. I still handle some probate cases and a little real estate now and then, but mainly I like representing plaintiffs in personal injury litigation," said Ollie before pausing.

He continued, "The only problem is everybody and their brother chase after the available cases. There are several lawyers who spend crazy amounts of money advertising and often do a disservice to their clients by settling for less than they should. They depend on quantity, not quality. Some of these guys have never tried a case and may never see the client at all. It drives me crazy and denigrates the profession, in my opinion. Sorry, didn't mean to get on my soap box."

"I don't watch much television, but when I do, I have to agree, old friend. I find those ads pretty disgusting. Probably would never consider hiring an attorney like that. I pretty much prefer word-of-mouth recommendations, and everybody I've ever heard talk about you says you're the ultimate professional.

That's good enough for me. I'm damned glad I know a first-class one like you," said Tyler.

Ollie's face turned a shade deeper. He was always embarrassed by any praise and often wondered if the person giving it was truthful. Having known Tyler as long as he had didn't change that aspect of his personality.

"I appreciate that, Ty. So, is that why you wanted to see me today? You need a lawyer?" asked Ollie.

Tyler was poker-faced at first, and then an enigmatic smile crept into view. Some people might even think it a little unnerving, but Ollie didn't find it so.

His old friend shrugged. The smile disappeared, and he got out of his chair. Tyler walked around the office and stopped when he saw a photograph of Trunk Bay hanging on the wall. It was a picture Ollie had taken twenty years before when on a vacation. He had enlarged the picture and had it mounted in a custom frame. Over time it had faded somewhat, but it still was one of the most beautiful places to the lawyer. It had inspired others he knew to make a trip to St. John to see the sight for themselves.

"Now, that's where we ought to be, Ollie. A cold one or a rum drink would make the perfect partner," said Tyler.

"I was just thinking something similar before you got here, Ty. There's nothing like the waters of the Caribbean," replied Ollie, not moving from his seat.

As Tyler kept staring at the photo, Ollie couldn't help but wonder what this meeting was about. His old friend had always been a private person, probably the most secretive he had ever known. With the knowledge he had acquired over the passage of time, Ollie felt certain there was something important on Tyler's mind, but years as a lawyer had taught him to be patient with clients.

"Ollie, you probably know me better than anyone ever has," said Tyler as he turned away from the picture and looked at him. "I'm curious. What do you really think about me?"

Ollie's puzzled look was genuine. He fumbled for the right words and answered, "I don't know what you mean, Ty. You're a friend, in fact, the best one I've ever had, and I accept you as you are."

Tyler walked back to his chair and sat down again. He rested his elbows on the arms of the seat and brought his fingers together to form a temple. "What does that mean exactly? You accept me as I am implies that there are some aspects of my personality you find distasteful. Could it be you've never forgiven me for what happened?"

Ollie felt his blood pressure start to rise causing his face to flush. He had no idea where the conversation was going, but it was not what he had imagined when it started. Some things were better left in the past. Nothing could change history.

"I'm not trying to imply anything of the sort, Ty, although I must admit I resent the implication you seem to be making. All I meant was that whatever differences there may be between us on a whole range of subjects, you are my friend no matter what."

Tyler's expression changed as he said, "Sorry, Ollie. You're the only friend I ever had. Stuck up for me when nobody else did. I know that had to be hard sometimes."

"All that is ancient history, Ty. We all deal with life in our own way, and just because you've handled yours differently than me or anybody else doesn't make it wrong. I've never judged you and never will," said Ollie.

"Maybe so, Ollie. But, I've never forgotten Libby, and I don't think you ever have either, if you're honest with yourself. The fact of the matter is she's still affecting our lives.

CHAPTER *12*

April, 1964

It was an exciting time in all of their lives. Ollie and Libby were soon to graduate high school, and both had been accepted at Mercer University to begin classes in the fall. Neither had even thought about going to school anywhere else and felt certain their educations would be as good as any of their friends who had decided to leave Macon for Athens, Atlanta or other places. Tyler was thinking about Georgia Tech, but he still had to finish his senior year, and it was only because he wanted to become an engineer. Ollie's dream of becoming a lawyer and Libby's of becoming a teacher were perfectly suited for their desire to stay in town and remain close together.

Junior high and high school now seemed to be a blur. There had been times during the last five years when the days dragged by. For Ollie those included sitting through all the advanced math and science classes his advisor insisted were necessary if he was going to college. He simply refused to believe he would ever need to know how to solve some problem in geometry, trig, calculus, or chemistry. It made no sense to him, anyway. That side of his brain lagged behind the other.

Ollie had loved all the other courses, though. He especially liked history, civics and literature. He devoured the textbooks and whatever extra reading the teachers recommended.

He had continued playing baseball and was one of the better players on the team, but had given up football and basketball because they took up more time than he was willing to give. There was some speculation he might be offered a scholarship, but he didn't count on that. In the meantime, he continued to work part-time with his Uncle Joey and earned enough money to buy an old Ford from the good-natured relative. It was a source of pride he could wrap his arms around.

The car was a '57 and had been babied for the seven years Uncle Joey had owned it, so it looked good and ran like a top even though it was pushing 100,000 miles. Ollie felt fortunate to have his personal vehicle, and it was big enough to accommodate the occasional double date with Ty and a girl to the drive-in. More often it was used to transport him, Libby and Ty back and forth to school with the happy-go-lucky girl always present in the middle between the two guys.

Now, he was driving home after a Saturday helping his uncle repair a bathroom that had multiple plumbing leaks. A widow, who had insisted on feeding the two of them lunch when the job took longer than expected, owned the old home. At least she hadn't balked when Joey told her it was going to cost more than he had initially figured. It had been a good day, and now Ollie had a few bucks in his pocket he could spend on his girl that night. He felt like he was on top of the world and sang along with the A.M. radio as he drove.

Ollie was a few miles from his house when he saw a lone figure walking down the stretch of road. Since he was going under the speed limit, it was not difficult to recognize the guy as Ty's older brother, Mathis. He looked to be plodding along without paying attention to traffic, but had his left thumb stuck in the air. Ollie didn't give rides to hitchhikers often, but he would on occasion when he knew the person seeking the ride. Although he really didn't know Mathis very well, this was his best friend's brother, and he was going the same way, so Ollie figured it was the neighborly thing to do.

Pulling the vehicle partially off the road ahead of the walking man, Ollie waited for him to open the passenger side door. Ollie was a little surprised when he got in abruptly and slammed the door much harder than necessary.

Mathis Crenshaw looked disheveled and had a sour odor associated with a mixture of sweat, lack of bathing and stale cigarette smoke. Ollie realized only at that moment he hadn't seen the guy in a while. They had never been friends because he was older than Ollie and ran with a much wilder and rougher crowd. Ty rarely talked about him, and the last conversation about his older brother resulted in Ty telling Ollie that Mathis had moved out of the family home.

"Matt, how ya' doing?" said Ollie.

The man looked at the driver and scratched his head. "I'm a little bit out of sorts right now, but I appreciate the ride."

Ollie glanced at his passenger. Mathis didn't seem right. He wasn't sure what he should do, but Ollie thought the best he could hope for was to get him to a safe place as soon as possible. That would be his home, if they would take him.

"What's wrong, Matt?" asked Ollie.

His passenger looked at Ollie, and there was no doubt things were happening behind his bloodshot eyes. He was haunted and helpless, not a combination that brought comfort.

"My girlfriend's pregnant, and I ain't got no money. Don't know what to do."

Ollie wasn't sure what to say. All the grown-ups he knew would frown at such a situation. He hadn't expected such a conversation.

"Can't you get married?" was all he could think to say.

The smelly man beside him started laughing. It sounded maniacal and spooky like in a horror movie.

"Her parents think I ain't no good. They're probably right. They ain't the first to tell me that. My own daddy said the same thing."

Ollie felt uncomfortable. *Why did I ever stop and pick up this guy,* he thought.

Mathis raked his right hand through his greasy hair. He had a faraway gaze and a sneer on his lip that made Ollie think about Elvis for some reason.

"Hey Matt, you've got a lot more problems than I can imagine. Can I help?" asked Ollie.

Mathis had a gaze that showed a moment of clarity. As fast as it showed, it disappeared. "Need a job, know where I can get one?" asked Crenshaw.

"Sorry, I'm not sure about that. Most of my friends only work part-time in grocery stores and stuff like that. I can ask around," replied Ollie.

Mathis shrugged as if it didn't matter. He turned his head and stared out the passenger window without further response.

Ollie drove and approached the neighborhood where they lived. He was ready to dispense his passenger and get ready for Saturday night. He could almost taste Libby's lips. Mathis had become a distraction he was ready to dispose of as quickly as possible.

No need to worry about this loser, thought Ollie.

"Let me off up here," said Mathis.

Ollie slowed the car and coasted to a stop at an old path leading to the playground where the neighborhood kids had spent so much time throughout the years. The well-worn trail could be distinguished from a flattened area containing a makeshift field. It was a place all the kids knew and where they could escape from home if need be.

"Thanks for the ride," mumbled Mathis as he exited the car.

"Hey, I'll ask my dad if he knows of any jobs," called out Ollie as Mathis shuffled down the path. He made no acknowledgement of whether or not he heard Ollie. It didn't matter to the teen because he was in love, and that was the most important thing in his life.

***

Ollie had shaved, showered and splashed on a dab of Old Spice. His hair was parted on the left and slicked back. His jeans were pressed and his starched cotton shirt was neatly tucked in. His penny loafers were polished and colored socks matching the shirt peeked between the shoes and pants. He scanned his image in the mirror one last time before heading through the house toward the back door.

It was nearing dusk, and Ollie wanted to pick up Libby before it got dark. Saturday night dates were the best, and this one promised to be even better. He couldn't wait to see his girlfriend and give her the ring he had in his pants pocket. It wasn't an engagement ring, but what the jeweler called a pre-engagement one. He had been saving for a while to buy it, and he was ready to give it to her to show how much he cared for her. The way he saw it, this would suffice until he got her the real deal in another couple of years and then the wedding ring would happen about the time they graduated from college. He had it all planned out perfectly.

"Ollie, wait a minute and let me get a look at you," called out his mother.

The teenager stopped dutifully at the kitchen door leading to the back yard. Annie, his mom, entered the room and walked to her son. She looked into his face and then appraised his clothes before smiling.

"You're a handsome boy," she said.

"Thanks, but you're prejudiced, Mom."

"Where are you and Libby going tonight?" she asked with a slight smile.

"Shoney's and maybe a movie. Not exactly sure, whatever Libby wants to do," he answered.

"As long as you let your girl choose what she wants to do, you'll live a long and happy life," she said with a laugh.

Ollie grinned and reached down to hug his mother. She hugged him back harder than normal.

"Y'all be careful and be back by eleven o'clock," she said before he left.

Ollie crossed the yard and got into his car. The keys were in the ignition where he had left them, and the engine came to life as he twisted the set. The Beatles were singing as they had for the last couple of months since the Ed Sullivan show debut. He smiled about that night when he and Libby were mesmerized in front of the television set instead of going to church services. They had both bought records since and loved the music. Ollie turned the radio down as he placed the gearshift into drive.

The half-mile to Libby's house was familiar enough that Ollie felt he could drive it blindfolded. He was a careful driver and never took chances while driving, no matter what. He pulled into the driveway behind her parents' Chevrolet and glanced into the rearview mirror before getting out.

Almost as soon as Ollie knocked on the front door, Libby's mother wearing her work uniform and a worried expression opened it. Ollie was astute enough to know something was wrong, but he asked anyway, "Hey, Mrs. Chancellor. Is everything okay?"

"I'm not sure, Ollie," she replied and chewed on the corner of her bottom lip. "I was hoping Libby was with you. I sent her looking for Timmy almost an hour ago, and she hasn't come back."

Timmy was Libby's younger brother known for roaming the neighborhood and playing with every dog around since he didn't have one of his own. As his name was mentioned, the boy appeared from behind his mother.

"Timmy just got back a few minutes ago and said he hadn't seen Libby. That's when I figured she had run into you and y'all were together. I know she'll be upset that she's late for your date," said Mrs. Chancellor.

"Don't worry, Mrs. Chancellor. I'll find her. She's more than likely up the road. I'll be right back," said Ollie.

"Oh, thank you, Ollie. You know how we mamas get about our babies. I was just about to wake up the husband since he's working the nightshift, and now I won't have to disturb him just as he's getting up. Libby has already dressed for the evening, but please stop back by the house before y'all go out, okay?"

"Sure thing," he replied.

***

Ollie was scanning both sides of the roadway as he travelled slowly away from Libby's home. The spring weather allowed him to roll down the driver's window and not get chilled. Darkness was falling, and he switched on the headlights of his car so he could better see the surroundings. The shadows all around him played tricks with his eyes.

Within a minute of driving, Ollie spied Tyler walking in the same direction at a fast pace. Ollie slowed down and called out, "Hey, Ty. Where ya' headed?"

"I'm looking for my brother. He had a big argument with our parents and left in a huff. It's not good, Ollie. I'm worried about him," said Tyler.

"Jump in, buddy. I'm looking for Libby. We'll make it a joint operation," said Ollie.

Tyler got in the car and looked at Ollie. "Hey, man. You got a hot date tonight?"

Ollie grinned and glanced at his friend. "Libby told me she's got a secret to tell me, and I've got one for her, too. That girl drives me crazy, man. I'll let you in on a secret. I've got a present for her. I got her a special ring because I love her."

"Y'all are really perfect, Ollie. I must admit, I'm jealous," said Tyler.

"I'm a pretty lucky guy, Ty. Life is so good. I wish everybody could feel as happy as me," replied Ollie.

"Yeah, I hear you," said Tyler.

"Hey, I gave Matt a ride earlier. He didn't seem like he was quite with it," said Ollie.

"Yeah, he's out there alright. I'm worried about him. I don't know what's wrong with him, but he's acting nuts."

Ollie pulled the car near the area where he had earlier left Mathis. He parked and looked over at his friend. "Let's start here. This was the last place I saw him."

Both teens got out of the car. The darkness started to creep around them as they looked about. "I'm not crazy about this, Ty. Look in the pocket and get the flashlight."

Tyler opened the passenger door and fumbled around before pulling out an aluminum cylinder. He clicked a button and then bumped it on his leg before a beacon came up. "A light in the night," he said.

They both started down the path bordered by trees. It caused a gloomy effect that was the opposite from how the site appeared in daylight. Just before getting to the end of the path as Ty swung the light in a back and forth arc, a scene from hell flashed in front of the boys.

A few feet off the path was the splayed body of Libby Chancellor. Blood had splattered on her ripped blouse. Her beautiful face was frozen in a terror-filled façade that burned immediately into both boys' brains. Neither could move for what seemed an eternity until sudden activity near the scene caused Ty to shift the light.

There stood Mathis holding a switchblade that gleamed in the light. He had a demented expression fueled by the displayed violence. Without warning, he charged at his brother and screamed, "You little spy. I'm going to kill you."

What happened next was never fully clear to anyone. A monumental struggle between the two brothers and Ollie occurred primarily in the dark because the flashlight went out when it crashed into Mathis Crenshaw's head. At the end of the fight, the older Crenshaw was dead, and the two boys were injured.

Everything changed after that. Nothing was ever the same.

CHAPTER 13

Present

Ollie and Tyler were in their own worlds as the thoughts of Libby alive and dead flooded their heads. The lawyer absent-mindedly rubbed his left arm where a long faded scar was hidden by an expensive custom shirt. He had long since stopped giving explanations about how he got it on a spring night fifty years ago. There were scars on his friend, too, and Ollie watched him to see if he had the same habit of touching the areas when thinking about that evening. Tyler made no such move and sat still awaiting Ollie's response.

"It doesn't serve any purpose to think about Libby now, Ty," said Ollie with a trace of sadness.

"Doesn't serve any purpose to think about Libby? Come on, Ollie. You know damn well we both have, countless times. Look at us. We're both screwed up as Hogan's Goat. Neither one of us has ever gotten married. Hell, I'm not sure about you, but I've never even been able to have a long-term relationship with a woman," said Tyler.

"Look, I don't want to talk about any of that. If I ever do, I'll let you know, okay? Is that why you wanted to see me today?" asked Ollie.

Tyler nodded slightly and said, "Ollie, we've been friends a long time. I've always known I could count on you even when we went through periods of not talking or seeing one another. I've been thinking a lot lately, and I believe we might be able to help each other finally resolve our long-standing problems with women. So yeah, that was one of the reasons I wanted to see you. But I'll respect your decision not to, if that's what you want."

"Sorry, Ty. I can't. Now if there's something else, you want to talk about, that's fine. Otherwise, I've got another appointment in a few minutes."

"Alright, Ollie. There is one other thing I wanted to discuss. Don't know if it's anything I'll need your professional services for, but I thought I'd run it by you just in case you think I should be concerned," said Tyler.

"What is it?" asked Ollie.

"I'm not sure exactly. I've been out a good bit lately and haven't been at home as much. One of my neighbors told me an investigator has been asking questions about me. Wanted to know everything she knew about my business and even asked some personal questions about me. The neighbor said the woman was friendly enough and quite professional.

"I don't think I would've even known about it, but the neighbor, Ms. Bobbitt is her name, asked me if I was still thinking about taking out a new mortgage. You would have to know her to understand she gets things mixed up sometime. I didn't think much about it until she told me that the nice investigator was getting some background information, and she knew I would qualify."

"Any idea who she's working for," asked Ollie.

"No, none at all."

"Hmm, I'm not saying you shouldn't be concerned, but I wouldn't worry too much about it. Maybe some potential customer is doing some preliminary background check before hiring you. If somebody officially contacts you, or should you hear from anyone else like Ms. Bobbitt, let me know and we'll check it out further," said Ollie.

"I guess it could be something like that, but it seems to me there are easier ways to find out my experience. You'll be the first to know if I hear anything else," said Tyler.

Red interrupted the conversation. She knocked on the office door and then poked her bright tangled curls into the space.

"Boss, I hate to interrupt, but your last appointment is here, and I was hoping I might be able to leave soon."

Tyler stood up abruptly, and Ollie followed suit. They gave each other a knowing glance before Tyler stuck out his hand to Ollie. Each clasped and shook with firm grips.

Ollie looked past Tyler and told Red to be patient for just a few minutes more. He really liked the girl, but she sometimes lacked as much polish, as he would prefer. She nodded, grinned and headed back to her desk.

"It's always good to see you, Ollie. Let's stay in touch. And think about going on a hiking trip with me," said Tyler with a smile.

"Yeah, it's good to see you, too. I really mean that, Ty," Ollie said pausing. "Let's get together soon, and maybe I'll reconsider our conversation about Libby. I don't know about the hiking thing, but we'll see."

Ollie led Tyler out of the office toward the front door. Standing nearby in the waiting area was Holly Lee thumbing through the latest edition of Macon Magazine. She was stylish in form-fitting slacks and heels. Her long tresses were pinned up in back giving a dressier appearance than the night before. Her stunning looks caused both men to stop in their tracks.

"Hello again, Mr. Tucker. I hope I'm not too early," she said.

"Um, we were just finishing our business. You're fine," said Ollie.

Tyler cleared his throat and took a step closer to the woman. She broke eye contact with Ollie and looked squarely at the other man. Her smile didn't waver as he spoke to her.

"Forgive my manners, Miss. I'm Tyler Crenshaw. I don't believe I've had the pleasure of making your acquaintance."

"I'm sure the pleasure is all mine, Mr. Crenshaw. I'm Holly Lee, a new friend of Mr. Tucker, and took a chance that he might be available to see me late on a Friday afternoon. Please forgive me if I interfered with your time together," she said.

Tyler moved another step closer to the woman. Ollie watched as Tyler studied her face as if he were an artist getting ready to create a masterpiece.

"The chance to meet you even makes my reunion with my old friend that much sweeter, Ms. Lee. I see Ollie has been holding out on me," he said with an enigmatic smile.

She laughed and glanced at Ollie. "He's full of mystery as I'm sure any old friend would know," she said.

"Holly is the daughter of another old friend, Tyler. We just met recently," Ollie said.

"Well, let me say what you've probably heard many times before, you are a beautiful woman. I wish I could stick around and maybe have a drink with y'all after you finish your business. Unfortunately, I have other plans that prevent it. I would love to get together again sometime more convenient," said Tyler.

"Sounds good to me," said Holly.

Ollie looked uncomfortable as Tyler finally left, and he stood shifting weight on alternate feet near Holly. Red grabbed her pocketbook and took the opportunity to get out before the boss changed his mind. She offered a timid wave as she departed. Ollie watched her departure in bemused silence.

Holly's single dimple that made him think of Libby again only seemed to mock the rapidly aging lawyer. He saw things changing and wondered if it was for the better or for worse.

CHAPTER 14

The Viewer liked his self-named title because it was descriptive of what he did the best. He referred to himself that way or sometimes as another nickname he had come up with, Ispy. He had even come up with a clever business card that contained an image of an eye that he sometimes left behind when conducting his craft.

He sat in a nondescript van parked down the street from the law office watching the comings and goings into and out of the building. The tint on his windows was legal, but it was impossible to see through with any clarity if you were trying to look into the vehicle from the outside. It really didn't matter, however, because he had hidden peepholes drilled in various locations throughout the sides and back of the van, which allowed him to observe without being discovered. He would simply close off the front and wander around the back until he found the best location to study his subject. A collection of telescopes and other equipment were stored in the area that helped with his tasks.

He was not a particularly big man, but he was in good shape for his age and could be mistaken for someone several years younger. That was a plus when he was viewing. A stint in the military had taught him discipline that he had not forgotten and also assisted him while on his quests to observe without discovery. His knowledge of technology likewise helped in the pursuits of his hobbies. His skillsets were perfect and made him into the ultimate Viewer. It never failed to give him pleasure better than sex, power, or money when he was on such a hunt.

Now he moved to the inside rear of the van with eyes trained on the combination home office of a guy who seemed pretty messed up to him. No matter, the older man had a primo arrangement and a location that challenged and excited The Viewer. Old Man, as he had privately dubbed Oliver Tucker, seemed almost like a hermit and only roamed in short circles. No doubt, he was fairly predictable where he went during the day and in the evening after work.

The Viewer wanted to get inside and check out the digs, especially the living areas. The waiting was always the most nerve-wracking part of the process before going in. Patience would persevere, however. He only needed to wait until everybody had left the premises and nightfall before making entry. Then the fun would really begin again.

***

Ollie led Holly around the main floor of his office giving the tour she had requested. She showed genuine interest in the furnishings, art and the layout of the work areas. Her keen eye for details that helped in her chosen profession now catalogued the substantial personal possessions her father had accumulated.

Her father. That's what she was already thinking of Ollie Tucker even though this was only the second time she had ever been around him.

She listened as he described various items and thought he had the perfect voice for a lawyer. His speech was measured, and the timbre of his voice was on the deep side of the scale.

Holly watched her father's movements, too. He had a certain grace in the way he carried himself that was rare in most men she had known over the course of her lifetime. It projected confidence and not nervousness as he gestured and articulated whatever he was describing at the moment. She was sure his presence in the courtroom could sway a jury more than most. Having been around trial attorneys many times during her career as an investigator, Holly could tell he had special talents that many litigators lacked. He had a healthy dose of what she would describe as magnetism.

She couldn't help but wonder again why her mother had never wanted her to meet him. Her vague assertions that he was a flawed man when it came to relationships with women belied the charm he now showed. It was a mystery that she intended to clear up on her own, and Holly wanted to do just that without any baggage her dearly departed mother might have had.

I need to know for sure. He does, too, she thought.

As he was talking about an antique bookcase that adorned a wall of his office, Holly interrupted, "I'm not sure what to call you. I know you haven't had enough time to process what was said last night, but I want to make up for lost time and get to know you better. It would help if I knew how to address you."

Ollie stopped mid-sentence and his eyes seemed to bore into Holly's. She held his stare as she quivered internally. She hoped he didn't think her to be too forward.

"How about Ollie for now?" he asked.

"If that's comfortable for you, it works for me." she replied.

At different times in her life, Holly had wanted a dad even if he was part-time like so many of her friends with divorced parents. She had learned to cope without one because her mother had been so attentive to her needs during the bad intervals that cropped up occasionally. Now that she was gone, Holly found herself hoping her newly found father might embrace the idea of becoming the other parent. She knew her inner strength would help her get through if he didn't want to accept the role, but the yearning for acceptance from this man was quickly becoming a burning desire.

"I'm sorry, but I haven't put my arms around the possibility of being your father, yet," said Ollie.

"Totally understandable, Ollie," she paused before finishing. "When you decide to find out the truth, I'm ready to submit blood samples to whatever lab you choose."

"It's not that I don't believe you. I hope you understand. After thinking about it, I agree DNA testing is a good way to find out. I'll set up something soon.

"How about I take you upstairs and show you around the inner sanctum that I call home? I could fix you something to drink and we could talk awhile. We can go to dinner later, if you want," said Ollie.

She smiled a million dollar one and responded, "All of that sounds nice to me."

"For me, too," he said, as he began up the stairs.

CHAPTER 15

August, 1969

It was so fucking hot and sticky. Lush jungle greenery was all around him as he lay perfectly still. Being the point man required him to blend in and be watchful of his surroundings. Vietnam sucked out loud as everybody knew, and if he could make another two months, he was going home to Maconga, USA. He was getting the hell outta here the first chance he got. That represented a pretty big "if" at this moment in his young life. He'd seen too many others maimed or killed already.

He had always been good at blending into the surroundings. It was probably the reason he ended up in the situation he now found himself in.

Just grown up childhood games. Don't do anything stupid, he kept telling himself.

PFC Tyler Crenshaw was by himself, and it was all right. The rest of the squad was behind him off the trail. He lay on his stomach and had his locked and loaded rifle in front of him in case danger presented itself. His mind raced as his eyes darted all around his location.

As he remained still, Tyler reflected on how he ended up here at this moment in his life. He was not so different than others finding themselves serving a hitch in this hellhole. All that was required was an attitude to not avoid the draft and the desire to serve the country he had grown up to believe in.

The main thing now was all the crap disillusioned him. Tyler was pretty sure this war was not worth the loss of life and destruction he'd seen. No wonder so many of the guys he knew got drunk or high whenever they got a chance. Whoever said war was hell was right on.

If Matt hadn't gone off the deep-end and killed Libby, it would be so different. I really lost my two best friends that night, thought Tyler from seemingly out of the blue. Thoughts of the nightmare they had endured that night came to him way too often whether asleep or awake.

The young Marine remembered how close he had been with Ollie and Libby, and it saddened him to his very core. They had made him feel a sense of normalcy that he had not known before they came into his life, or since. More than five years had elapsed since Libby's death, and a hole had formed in his heart. It was nowhere near the destruction his best friend had suffered, though.

He wondered how Ollie was doing. After recovering from their physical injuries, he and Ollie had stayed friends, but the dynamics had been drastically altered. Ollie was no longer the eternal optimist, and the once outgoing personality had become much more reserved. Ollie had retreated to a shelter inside himself where Tyler was not allowed entry.

It hadn't helped their friendship either that Tyler and Ollie had chosen different career paths. Ollie had maintained his desire to stay in Macon and attend Mercer for undergrad. He now was a student in the law school as he had always said was his dream. Tyler wasn't totally sure, but he thought somehow Libby was the main motivation for Ollie's seeming determination to finish the drill.

Tyler had gone into trade school after finishing his high school education and had earned his certification as an electrician. He enjoyed working with his hands and had begun earning good money right away. He had moved around some chasing work, but stayed in middle Georgia.

Then it looked like the draft was going to get him because of a low draft number, and he opted to join the Marines. They were the elite according to the recruiter. He longed to be the best he could be. It was not difficult to join once his doctor wrote a letter clearing him from past injuries.

Ollie was safe at home with a college deferment, and Tyler probably would've been as well if he had stuck with his old dream of going to Georgia Tech and becoming an engineer. *No matter now,* he thought.

It all led to a renewed sense of the isolation that he had felt as a young boy, but had disappeared until recently. What he had been through had toughened him; however, he longed for the times he had known with Ollie and Libby.

God, I'm far from perfect, but if you're up there, please watch over me and get me home safely. I'll try to make it up to you one day. Also, can you tell Libby hello from me? I loved her and I miss her so much. One last thing, please help my friend Ollie. I think he needs you the most. Amen.

He wasn't sure about the power of prayer. It couldn't hurt, though.

CHAPTER 16

Present

Ollie awakened with a start. He struggled but couldn't remember what day it was. He was still in the bed and hoped his old brain would start working better soon. He knew he was drinking too much, and it was affecting the way he processed life.

Damn it! What the hell is wrong with me? I'm smarter than this. You've got to get a hold on yourself, Ollie.

He couldn't remember when he had started talking to himself, even if it was only in his head. It was becoming more constant, and not for the first time he wondered about his sanity. He hoped no one else could see through the façade of confidence he tried to maintain publicly.

Through the fog he remembered last night. He had taken Holly out to dinner after she looked around his residence. They had gone to the Tic Toc Room and the meal was delicious as always. He had insisted on martinis that were off the chart good and had way too many of them. Now his head felt like he was in another time zone.

But, he had learned stuff he hadn't known. He hadn't had enough time to process it all because of the vodka consumed. He tried breaking through the haze to recall. It cut him to the core as parts of the conversation played back.

"I don't think I could ever be a father. I can hardly take care of myself," said Ollie while he sipped his third dirty martini.

"Mom said you had been traumatized when you were younger and that was your main problem. She never gave any details. What happened?" asked Holly.

He paused as the memories crept inside and chewed on his psyche while popping an over-sized bleu cheese stuffed olive in his mouth. He wondered if he could just order a plateful of the delicacies rather than dinner. That was the last one on the toothpick from his drink and he wanted more.

"I lost my innocence, I guess," he said as he munched.

"You don't like talking about it, whatever it is, do you?"

"It's funny, not ha-ha so either, but you're the second person to ask me essentially the same thing today," said Ollie with a frown.

"Really? What a coincidence," she said.

"Maybe, but he knows plenty, and still he wanted to talk about ancient history. I'll tell you what I told him, I don't want to talk about it."

"Alright, I'll drop it, Ollie. But, I'm still hoping that maybe you can try to be my dad, assuming the tests verify you are," she said.

"I'm afraid I'll mess it up. You deserve better than me."

"I need you, but I don't want to cause you pain. Believe me, Ollie. I've wanted a father all my life. Now that I've finally met you, I don't want to lose you again."

"Look, Holly. I'm not sure what you're searching for. I'm far from being a prize. I'm trying to think what it means to be a dad. I really don't have a clue. What do you want from me?"

"Let's just get to know one another," she said.

"I'd really like that," he said.

"Do you know I used to wish you would come and rescue me?'" asked Holly.

"From what?"

"A boring life," said Holly.

Those were the memories he had from the alcohol-hazed night before. Back in the present now, he wanted to get moving and enjoy the weekend ahead.

Holly had seemed genuine, but could he be sure? His addled brain was no help.

Ollie climbed out of his Tempur-Pedic bed, and tried not to stumble. There was a sway to his stance as he attempted stability.

He headed to the bathroom in a lurch and sat down rather than try to aim. Maybe he was turning into an old woman. Whatever, he didn't want to clean up piss later in the morning.

When he finished, Ollie trudged toward the kitchen. He looked for his favorite Tervis tumbler mug to fix his coffee. He had bought it while in Key West a few years ago. Typically, he added a little half-in-half first before pouring the coffee on top. It was nowhere to be found, and it bugged him to no end.

"I wish I had a woman who loved to decorate," he said to himself as he looked around.

His living space was the oasis he longed for whenever life closed in. Everything had its place and order was king. For some reason, this morning it didn't seem that way. Just as he was trying to come to grips with the feeling, a voice startled him.

"Good morning, Ollie," said a feminine voice behind him.

Ollie, still more than a little confused, turned to see Holly clad in an extra-large tee shirt belonging to him that went almost to her knees. Disoriented even more than he had found himself when he first got up, Ollie pulled out a barstool located in the eat-in kitchen and sat down heavily.

"You'll have to excuse me. I guess I must've really tied one on last night. I didn't remember you were staying," he said.

She laughed and replied, "I think we both had a good time getting to know each other a little better. That's the most I've had to drink since I was in college at Georgia."

Ollie's head was swimming a backstroke trying to recall the rest of last night. *Yeah, it's coming back now. I invited her up to the top floor after dinner, and then we started drinking tequila while we talked.*

"Oh yeah, I seem to remember a little better now. One tequila, two tequila, three tequila, floor," he said.

Her laugh brought a hint of a smile to his lips. His head only brought a piercing pain that caused the illusion to disappear as quickly as it happened.

"Hey, I really slept pretty well, considering," she said.

He rubbed his temples as he realized his drinking had elevated to the point he couldn't remember stuff. *Not good,* he thought.

"Holly, I'm sorry if I said anything or did anything inappropriate last night. I don't know what's wrong with me lately."

She looked at him and her smile turned upside down. Her look was something he couldn't figure out.

"Ollie, you didn't do anything wrong. You were a complete gentleman. We had a wonderful dinner at a nice restaurant I'd never been to before. I learned things about you, and maybe you learned things about me, too. We came back to your beautiful house, and you showed me around. Yeah, you and I probably drank too much in celebration of finding one another. But, it was one of the best nights of my life, Ollie," she said.

"Quite honestly, I don't know how good it was for me since I don't remember some of it. I have to admit something else, all of this is blowing my old mind," said Ollie.

"You need coffee, and I could use a cup, too," said Holly.

She walked over to the coffee maker and added water to the reservoir. After retrieving a couple of cups from the nearby cabinet, she loaded a small plastic container of Southern Pecan flavored coffee and set it to make the associated whirring sound. After the two beverages were done, she sat next to Ollie.

"You want to know what I think? You're too hard on yourself," she said.

He sipped the coffee before responding, "If I am, believe me, I deserve it."

Holly's hair was still mussed from sleep and her eyes were puffy. Without fresh makeup, Ollie thought how she must have looked as a young girl waking up. He continued drinking the coffee as he studied her face.

"Did you really mean what you said last night?" she finally asked and broke his stare by changing the subject.

The coffee was helping, but he wasn't sure what she was talking about at first. He had vague memories about discussing her future and what his role would be.

"I'm thinking I'll take you up on your offer, if I can start calling you Dad."

Ollie was still searching his brain when he remembered the lost moment. How he could've ever forgotten was only further evidence his alcohol consumption should be cut immediately.

He set the cup down on the countertop and placed his hand over hers. He hoped the bloodshot appearance of his eyes appropriately conveyed the honesty of conviction as he told her words that would bring her tears of joy.

"I was pretty drunk last night. Sometimes, I drink too much and I know I need to stop. But, I always try to tell the truth. When I told you I would pay your way so you could go to law school, I meant it. I'll help with your other expenses, too. You can work with me when your schedule allows. It's the least I can do for my daughter. I don't need any blood work to prove it."

CHAPTER 17

A few months had passed at a whirlwind pace since Ollie and Holly first met. Early spring had become mid-September. Summertime could be miserable in middle Georgia, but neither had noticed because of the happiness found in each other.

She was content with her new relationship with her dad. No way she could've ever predicted where her life was headed after that initial get-together. Even though he had said it wasn't necessary, she had insisted they should submit blood samples for DNA testing. The lab report had proven beyond any doubt they were father and daughter, and it led to positive results.

Ollie had drastically cut back on the booze. The lawyer seemed to be rejuvenated in everything he undertook, and thought he felt and appeared years younger. With his newly reinstituted workouts, life was more wholesome for him. He told

Holly that he had rediscovered that law practice was fun, and that he loved having a younger person to teach and follow in his footsteps.

The relationship between father and daughter was becoming closer by the day. It had been tentative at first since neither had ever experienced such a connection before. Now, every occasion to be together was refreshing. Each of them felt more love and respect with every passing day.

"Dad, is there anything you need me to do?" asked Holly as she stood in the doorway of his office.

"I can't think of anything else at the moment. By the way, this work you've done on the Davis case is top shelf. I think we can settle this without a problem. Not only will we get justice and restitution for our client, we'll get a good payday, too. Really, this is stellar. You're a natural, Holly," he replied while looking up from an open file on his desk.

Lindsey Davis had been a client for a number of years. He was somewhat of a screw-up, and Ollie had dealt with the problems Davis seemed to encounter on a regular basis. There had been a couple of minor criminal cases filed against him when he was younger. Then he had gone through three divorces, at least two contempt citations and a bankruptcy. That he kept coming to see Ollie with every new difficulty was a testament to the trust felt for the lawyer.

The latest legal problem had not been through any fault of his own. Davis had been on his way home from his job as a plumber when another car had struck him in the rear causing his truck to run off the road and crashing into a tree. He had not seen the other vehicle, and the person driving had left the scene. He had sustained injuries that included a broken ankle making him unable to work for three months.

The major problem with the personal injury claim Ollie had encountered was due to a poor job by law enforcement investigating the accident. Holly had found a witness that led her to the operator of the other vehicle. Together with the assistance of the Sheriff's office, she was able to discover the driver was only sixteen and had been operating the car inattentively while talking on her cell phone. There was now another insurance company with more coverage to tap into for the client. What had been a small case had just become a bigger one because of Holly's work.

Holly beamed. "I think very few of the kids in my class have a clue what the real practice of law is all about. I think my age and experience in investigations will get me through. Not to mention I've got a really cool mentor."

"You're way ahead of the game, alright. You make an old man proud," Ollie replied.

Holly had begun to love the seasoned lawyer and the way he praised her constantly. She could tell he wanted her to succeed, and it only served to drive her more to please him.

"All of the pain and suffering Mr. Davis has endured could've been avoided if the girl had been paying attention to driving rather than talking on her phone," she said.

Ollie picked up his cell and said, "These damned things are a blessing and a curse. When I was a kid, such a device was only a fantasy we could dream about. Now, everybody and their brothers have one including all their kids. I've seen preschoolers using them as play toys many times as I'm sure you have. They can do amazing things with them, too. More than I can for sure. But, this technology comes with a downside or two. Try to take one away from a kid who has never had to live without it, and see how they do in the world. I bet they can't even do simple math. I'm going to get off this soap box before I rant on how dangerous they are when somebody with a two ton missile in one hand has one of these in the other hand."

"It's generational to a certain extent. I know people younger than you, Dad, who refuse to own a computer or a cell phone. But, I agree with you. At least the part about people trying to use one while driving. That's just plain stupid," said Holly.

Ollie closed the file and considered his daughter as she observed him. There was no doubt mutual respect was in the room. Feeling the love was nice for both.

Just as he was about to say something else about how she had changed his life for the better, his phone rang. It was Red on the front desk according to the phone identification screen.

"Yes."

"Boss, I have the sheriff on the line wanting to talk to you."

"By all means, put him through."

"Hey, Derek. What have I done to have the honor of the High Sheriff giving me a call?"

There was a pause before Ollie recognized Sheriff Davidson's voice. He seemed way too serious to suit the lawyer.

"Ollie, we've known each other for a long time, and I hate to call you about this. I'm cutting right to it without any sugarcoating. I've just arrested your old friend, Tyler Crenshaw. He's requested your presence before he'll talk to us. Can you come down to the LEC?"

Ollie's eyes darted to Holly's. "I'll be right there."

CHAPTER 18

O llie made the drive to the LEC by himself. Holly wanted
to go with him, but this was a situation that he wanted to
handle alone. Tyler was only going to be honest with his old
friend if he were by himself. He couldn't imagine what was
behind Tyler's arrest. The sheriff had been cryptic when Ollie
asked what the problem was.

All Sheriff Davidson had said was, "It'll be a headline in
tomorrow's paper. I won't say more over the phone. Come
directly to my office when you get here, and we'll get you in to
see him."

As he pulled into the parking lot, Ollie scanned for an open
spot to slide his Lexus ES350 into. He didn't get to the law
enforcement center as often as he did twenty years ago, and it
seemed business was booming. It had been a lot easier to find a
parking place when he was younger. If he were a betting man,

he would've wagered the crime rate was booming just based on the lack of available spaces.

The only slot he could find was next to an ancient Cadillac with rust spots and holes that could've been due to gunfire. On the other side was a four-wheeler that would require a ladder to climb into. Both vehicles were encroaching on the lines making the place even smaller to try to negotiate.

Geez, what some people drive, he thought.

He couldn't bear the thought that his beloved car would be nestled between the two vehicles, so Ollie drove out of the lot and spied All-State Bonding Company across the street. He had done business with them many times over the years, and he knew the owner wouldn't mind if he left the car for a little while. Ollie found a place near the functional structure and got out of the automobile. A sign at the front of the property advertised they were open 24/7. Just as he locked the vehicle and started walking toward Oglethorpe Street, Kyle Stillman came out of the office and waved to the lawyer.

"Hey, counselor. Haven't seen you in a while. You lookin' good," the bondsman said in his husky voice.

Ollie smiled at the affable employee. The big man had always been accommodating to his clients, as had all the other professionals associated with the long time Macon business. The lawyer wouldn't even consider using another bail bonding company. He knew he might need to arrange their services in short order.

"Good morning, Kyle. Yeah, I try to stay out of criminal practice these days. Thanks for the compliment because I feel better than I have in years. You're looking pretty good yourself. Looks like you could play line for the Falcons. They sure could've used you last season," replied Ollie.

"I probably wouldn't have been much worse," he laughed.

"I've got to see a client right now, and I may need your services in a little while. Are you going to be around?" asked Ollie.

"Must be an important one for you to come over here. Yeah, I'm here all day. You know I'll be glad to help," said Kyle.

"I like to think all of my clients are important, big guy. I'll check with y'all when I'm done over there," said Ollie while pointing across the street. "I need to meet with the sheriff before I see the client, so I've got to run," he continued.

"We'll be here if you need us," said Kyle.

Ollie waited for traffic to clear and then walked in a fast pace across the busy street. His mind raced, as he couldn't imagine the turn of events. He hadn't talked to Tyler much since he and Holly had established their relationship, but their friendship had always been like that. Months and even years could go by in between times they saw one another, but they always seemed to pick up where they left off as if they had just seen each other the day before.

Upon entering the Law Enforcement Center, Ollie recognized several people he knew. There were civilian employees as well as deputies and other ranking officers milling around the front entrance. Some waved and others spoke to him as he passed them on his way to the Sheriff's personal office.

Derek Davidson had risen through the ranks to become the top law enforcement officer for Macon-Bibb County. Although he was not quite sixty, he was approaching forty years experience in the office. His competence and easy-going personality had made him a natural for the first sheriff of the combined administration upon the recent merger of the municipal and county governments.

He sat behind his desk talking on the phone when Ollie was led into the inner sanctum. The old lawyer couldn't help but remember the fresh-faced jailer he had met years ago when he was a young attorney visiting incarcerated clients. The jail had then been located on the fifth floor of the courthouse. Now it was a stand-alone facility that held probably four times the amount of inmates as it did back then. Ollie thought if the truth were known, it could stand to be at least half again as big and still be full of offenders.

The youthful faced sheriff motioned for Ollie to have a seat while he continued his conversation. The only thing that gave away his age was the balding head that was often covered with a Texas styled hat when he was outside.

"Look, I can't confirm anything other than an arrest has been made. I expect to make an announcement in the next few hours. As soon as I'm ready, I'll let you know," Davidson said into the phone.

As the call ended, both men got up from their seats and shook hands. They smiled genuinely at each other and considered themselves friends.

"Good to see you again, lawyer. I don't think I've seen you since election night and that's been a minute," said the sheriff.

Ollie had supported Davidson's campaign when he ran for the office almost two years before and had gone to the election night party afterwards. Ollie had felt Derek was much better than the other candidates and had been happy to be an active supporter in the effort.

"I guess it has been a while, Sheriff. I'm hearing good reports about all the positive work you're doing. I know you've got your hands full."

"Keeps me busy, alright. Sorry it's got to be under such circumstances in order to see you again. Thought the least I could do would be call you first before all the publicity hits about the arrest of your client. I guess he's your client. That's what he said at least," said Davidson.

"Tyler Crenshaw is more than a client, Derek. He's the best friend I've ever had. I've known him since childhood. I can't imagine why he's under arrest."

The Sheriff had an inscrutable look. He shook his head slightly as he responded, "We have proof that he's the serial burglar we've been looking for the last several months. I'm sorry he's your friend, Ollie, because he's probably going away for a long time."

***

Ollie sat across from Tyler separated by thick clear glass. They shared concerned looks before either spoke. His friend looked skinnier and older dressed in the county issued orange jump suit. They picked up the phones simultaneously.

"Tyler, what the hell?" Ollie said with brow furrowed like two caterpillars.

"It's good to see you, too, Ollie," responded Tyler.

The lawyer took a couple of deep breaths. He had come across harsher than he normally did, but he couldn't seem to help himself.

"I've been told you're being charged with at least five counts of burglary here, and there may be some other counts coming in this circuit as well as from additional counties. I don't know what evidence they may have, but I can't believe they would charge you unless they feel pretty strongly about it," said Ollie.

"Sounds like you've already made up your mind about my guilt, too. Not that's supposed to matter, right?"

Ollie paused. He was right. *I shouldn't sound accusatory.* As he had told most, if not all, of the criminal defendants he had represented over the years, it was not his job to decide his client's guilt. He was there to protect his client's rights and put the state to its burden of proving the case.

"I'm sorry, Ty. I didn't mean for it to sound that way. For a second I was treating you differently than I would anybody else in your shoes. I guess that comes from your being my friend first and client second. Let's start over, okay?"

Tyler nodded, "Believe me, this is the most stress I've felt
since Nam. It's surreal to be behind bars. I don't understand how
it all happened. It's weird, Ollie. Can you get me out of here?"

"I should be able to get that done fairly soon since this is
your first arrest. Burglary doesn't normally cause much of a
problem in getting a bond set unless you have a record for that
offense. The main concern I have at this point is the possibility
there may be other jurisdictions involved. If other charges arise
outside of this jurisdiction, we'll have to make bail in every
other one, too. There is no telling what problems we could run
into in some other county. Sheriff Davidson promised me he is
having that question checked out as quickly as possible. I'll tell
you this; if there are other counties, we need to think carefully
how to proceed. I'd rather you stay here until we find out for
sure," said Ollie.

"You're making me nervous, Ollie. I don't even want to
spend one night here. It sounds like you're telling me I could be
locked up for much more than that."

"I'm going to do everything possible so that doesn't
happen, Ty. First, I need to find out everything you know about
the charges and how you came to be in custody."

Tyler pursed his lips and his eyes shifted. Ollie had
witnessed reluctance on the part of clients to share what they
knew countless times. Sometimes it was due to the natural
inclination to minimize the situation. Other times, clients lied to
their lawyer for reasons that were hard to understand. Many
times a client thought the attorney wouldn't take the case if he

knew the client was guilty as sin. Whatever the reason might be, Ollie had to give the speech routinely made when first taking a criminal case.

"Ty, I'm going to tell you something that I've had to say to most of my clients in your position. That is, I can't help you if you're not honest with me. I don't like being surprised by some prosecutor springing something that you should've let me know in advance. It may not be easy for you to be completely forthcoming, and you might think it's easier to hide certain information. Believe me, nothing pisses me off faster with a client than that. It shouldn't be an issue between us anyway."

There was a flash of an emotion behind Tyler's eyes that Ollie couldn't read. *Anger, maybe disbelief,* thought Ollie.

"Maybe so, Ollie. I'll tell you all I know about this situation, and then do what you need to do and get me out of here."

Tyler dropped his head for a minute, laid down the handset and rubbed his eyes with the heels of his hands. When he looked back at the lawyer, Ollie had a flashback to the school kid that he remembered from a lifetime ago. It was a time when the young Ty worshipped Ollie, the neighborhood leader and idol to many.

Before Ollie could say anything else, Tyler picked up his phone and continued, "I got a call early this morning to meet somebody at a neighborhood near Lake Tobesofkee concerning a potential job. The guy on the phone said Lindsey Stevens who lived down the street had referred me. I had done some remodeling for her a few years ago and knew where to go without having to look up the address."

He looked around his surroundings as if checking to see if anyone else was there. Ollie waited patiently before Tyler started again.

"Anyway, I drove over to the street and was going slowly so I could find the number on the mailbox. Just as I was about to the place, a sheriff's car appeared behind me and bumped his siren. I don't know how long he was back there before I heard it, and I wasn't aware if I'd done something wrong. I pulled the van over and waited until the deputy came to my window. I watched him approach in the side view mirror and noticed he had his hand on the grip of his weapon. I got pretty nervous, but I kept my cool as best I could.

"It all kind of went to shit when I reached for the glove box so I could get my registration. He yanked out his gun and screamed at me to place both hands on the steering wheel. I yelled back at him that I was only going to get my registration. He pulled open my door and asked me if I had any weapons in the vehicle. I told him I had a pistol under the seat. He then told me to get out of the van, and he patted me down.

"I was getting pretty mad by this time, and I'm sure I cussed some at the guy. I kept asking him why he was doing all that to me, but he wouldn't answer at first. He finally said there had been a tip about a burglary suspect and I matched the description. I told him I'd never done anything like that, and I was in the neighborhood to meet with somebody about a job.

"It was like he wasn't listening to me. He had made up his mind already. He kept asking me questions about being there, and then he asked me if he could search the van. I was pissed about that, but I thought maybe that would get him off my back so I said okay.

"He handcuffed me for his safety and mine, so he said. Then he put me in the backseat of his cruiser and started looking through the van. In a little while, he brought some stuff out. He had a wicked smile as he put all of it on the front seat of his car. He asked me if I recognized any of the items, but I didn't. It looked like a bunch of trinkets to me. I don't know where they were in the van because I'd never seen them before. It was crazy and seemed like a set up to me."

Tyler stopped talking and resumed rubbing his eyes. Ollie thought his friend was looking older by the minute.

"It seems to me your van was a part of a profile they were looking for. Is there anything about it that's unique?" said Ollie.

"Not really. It's functional. It's white. I can store lots of shit in it. There's nothing special about it, Ollie."

"What can you tell me about the items taken out of the van?" Ollie asked.

"I'd never seen any of them before. It looked like a bunch of crap to me."

"So, is that all you said to the deputy? You gave him permission to look inside?" asked Ollie.

"Yeah."

"Okay. That's enough for now. I need to find out what they've got. I take it you didn't talk after you got arrested and were brought downtown, right?"

"They wanted me to give a statement, but I didn't. I thought I needed to talk to you first. After that, they locked me down. I've been going crazy since."

"I know it's not pleasant in here, Ty, and I'm going to work getting you out asap. In the meantime, don't say anything to anybody about why you're arrested, not to the deputies or any of the inmates. From now on, I speak for you until I say otherwise. Are we clear?"

"Just get me out quick, please," said Tyler with a note of desperation in his voice.

"Let me see what I can do and I'll let you know. Hang in there, buddy. We've been through a lot worse than this," said Ollie as he hung up the phone.

CHAPTER 19

Ollie walked out into the bright sunlight behind the LEC and looked around. He really hated coming to this place anyway, but having to see his old friend behind bars only served to sour this visit to a new low on the scale. This was not how he had expected the day to turn out.

That's the way it was being an attorney. There was nothing better than the high experienced when winning a trial or seeing a client's face break into a huge grin at the sight of a big check you secured in a settlement. But, the depression that followed when the jury went the other way or the look on a client's face when you told him there was nothing that could be done to help the situation could be devastating to the spirit. Maintaining equilibrium in a lawyer's life could be impossible if one couldn't keep personal feelings out of the equation, and there was just no way to do that when representing someone like your best friend.

He had represented friends and other people he knew many times in his career. Sometimes it had been rewarding, but other times it was far from it. He had discovered it was not unusual for people he knew to often expect Ollie to represent them at a greatly reduced rate or even for free. And God forbid if a friend didn't get the result they expected. Maybe he should take the approach of other colleagues and not represent people he knew so well. Ollie had never represented anyone so close to him in such a predicament, and it presented a daunting challenge.

Ollie pulled his cell phone from an inside jacket pocket and dialed the office. Red answered on the second ring. He asked her if Holly was there and then to connect her when she answered affirmatively.

"Is everything okay, Dad?"

"Not for Tyler, I'm afraid. I need you to find out as much as you can about the deputy who arrested him. His last name is Chaney according to Tyler. I know you've got some contacts in the department, but I don't want you compromising any of them if you can help it. Right now I'm more interested in general perceptions about the guy. Also, whatever you can find out about the investigation of a serial burglar in the area would be helpful, too. I expect I can get all of that information during discovery, but I want to get a head start if possible. I'm counting on your expertise," replied Ollie.

"I'll get started right away. Are you going to be able to get him out of jail today?"

"The sheriff is checking on possible charges elsewhere, and that's key about a quick release. I'm going to get with the magistrate's office and maybe the DA's office for anything they might be able to tell me."

"Dad, this is not the right time, but I need to tell you something about your friend. I probably should've told you more about it before now. I mentioned it when we first met. When I was with Fulton County, we looked at him as a possible burglar with a sexual fetish."

Ollie remembered the first night he met Holly. For some reason, he had not thought about her mentioning Tyler as a person of interest in an investigation. He had put it out of his mind, and since then the subject had not been revisited. He guessed the excitement of the last few months had caused the memory lapse, or could it have been due to not seeing his old friend since their last meeting in the office? Come to think of it, Tyler had mentioned something about somebody investigating him. He didn't know if there was a connection, but Ollie knew he needed to get further information from his daughter.

"Dad, are you still there?"

"Yeah, sorry. I was having a flashback. You mentioned Tyler the first time we met, and I had forgotten that. What can you tell me about that investigation?"

"I still have my notes somewhere. I put them all away after I lost my job. Really, I haven't thought about any of that since I changed my life, thanks to you. I recall there was a string of break-ins where relatively minor things were stolen. I was specifically looking at suspects with connections to burglar alarm businesses. It was suspected an employee or former employee of such a company was responsible. Tyler Crenshaw was on a list with those credentials, and that's why I was investigating him. In all fairness, there were others on the list. I never finished my work on the case, so I was never able to clear him as a suspect," said Holly.

"Were the burglaries around Atlanta?"

"We had reports all around the area. Fulton, Clayton and down south to Henry. The thinking was somebody had to have an inside angle. We noticed most people victimized had burglar alarm systems. That went against the grain and against the norm. You wouldn't think that people who had such protection should be broken into with a greater rate, right? Well, every victim we investigated had systems. It didn't make sense."

"So, you started looking at the companies that installed systems?" asked Ollie.

"Yeah, there were several and we had to look specifically at ones with connections to the victims. Tyler Crenshaw fit that profile. I was assigned to look at him and a few others. He was somebody who was on the radar because of his background. There were others in the office theorizing the perpetrator was a contractor of some sort, and he also fit that profile."

"Okay, Holly. This is stuff I need to know. It's making me a little nervous, though. Did you ever have a moment that you thought Tyler was guilty?" asked Ollie.

"Hmmm, I can't say that, Dad. I can only say he wasn't eliminated as a suspect."

Ollie sat down on the concrete wall outside the jail. He held the phone close to his cheek as his mind went to another place. This experience made him want to go somewhere else away from here. His conflict with all that was happening would be better in another time zone.

"Damn, this is crazy, Holly. I can't believe Tyler is guilty of this. This puts me in a position I don't like. It's a dilemma I don't want to face. I need your help to find the truth. Don't leave me on my own with this," said Ollie.

"I won't, Dad. We'll get to the bottom of this mess."

"I hope so. Otherwise, I don't know if what I'm doing is the right thing."

CHAPTER 20

Ollie was up early for the first time in weeks, and he blamed Tyler for it. Since the life changes made over the last few months, he had begun sleeping much better. The stress level had also become more manageable than he could ever remember. He felt the still growing relationship with his daughter was the main reason behind the good feelings. Now he had to worry about a life-long friend, and a good night's sleep might be harder to accomplish until he could solve the problems.

He thought about yesterday and the frustrations he had felt. Ollie had always been effective in getting clients out of jail even when it looked as if they might be there a while. He had failed yesterday, and it didn't sit well with him. It was magnified because it had been his friend who suffered.

The chief magistrate had been worthless, and Ollie hated he wasted his time and effort even going by to see him. Any time a case had any sort of publicity, it seemed he would not take any chances in doing anything that could result in being held in a negative light. Therefore, when Ollie had requested a bond be set immediately, the magistrate had deferred until the District Attorney could weigh in.

The attempt to get the DA's office to agree to bail had been equally frustrating. Ollie had major difficulty finding out who might be assigned the task of handling the case. The usual assistant charged with prosecuting such cases had been warned not to make any recommendations. Ollie knew the DA himself, as the person in charge, would want to take the lead because of potential undesirable publicity. It was a job that required a certain amount of press, and this district attorney seemed more attuned to promotional efforts than others in recent memory.

Ollie had contacted the Chief Assistant, Jessica Mooney, and her usual confidence about what was to be expected had been wishy-washy. He was sure she was getting her marching orders from the boss. She had not even made her usual wise cracks, and Ollie was sure she had been stripped of any authority she might normally have. What it meant in the short term was that Ollie was unable to get Tyler out on bond until there was a hearing. That would happen today, and he was confident he could make a good case that Tyler should be released on a reasonable bond.

He prepared a cup of flavored coffee, and took it into his lair to read the paper on line. It still pissed him off that he couldn't find his favorite cup, but he resolved to get himself another special mug the next time he made a trip to Key West.

Ollie settled into his chair and fired up his Apple laptop. He clicked on the Macon.com site. The headline was prominent.

Former Hero Charged With Five Counts of Burglary

Ollie felt a little sick to his stomach. He knew he needed to read the article, but part of him would rather not. A dull ache was settling in behind his eyes.

Tyler Crenshaw, former Vietnam veteran, and successful business owner was arrested yesterday and charged with five counts of residential burglary. He was charged by the Macon-Bibb County Sheriff's Office after being discovered in a Lake Tobesofkee neighborhood recently victimized by similar thefts.

Sheriff Davidson said the suspect was found with evidence of other break-ins in his vehicle. He praised the efforts of his department in making the arrest and warned other potential lawbreakers that his department was always on the job to stop crime.

The charged man won several citations for his service and bravery during the Vietnam conflict in the late sixties. He currently is a resident of Crawford County, but lived in Macon during his early years.

In 1964 he was an additional victim in the infamous Elizabeth Chancellor murder case. Crenshaw's brother, Mathis Crenshaw, killed Miss Chancellor and then attacked his brother and another friend, Oliver Tucker, after they discovered the brutal crime. Mathis Crenshaw was killed during a struggle

with the other two young men. The younger Crenshaw and
Tucker both sustained serious injuries requiring medical
attention.

Ironically, the lawyer representing the suspect is the same
Oliver Tucker involved in the tragic case fifty years ago. Efforts
to reach the attorney were unsuccessful.

A bond hearing is scheduled for 2:00 today to determine if
the suspect will be allowed release pending trial. District
Attorney, Vern Crocker, said the defendant was a dangerous
criminal who should be held pending trial.

Ollie felt a little light-headed as he read the article. It
wasn't long, but it had information many people probably didn't
know or had forgotten. There were old pictures of the crime
scene in 1964 and of the youthful Tyler and Ollie from the
yearbook.

He hadn't talked to Holly about any of the stuff from those
years, and he knew she would have questions. Ollie suddenly
wished he had spoken to her about those things. He hoped she
would understand when they did have such a conversation.

***

Holly scurried to get ready for class. Law school took a lot
more time than she imagined when her dad floated the idea. She
had thought it would be a piece of cake, but having finished
undergrad over a decade ago, she realized quickly that she didn't
have the study habits she once did. The discipline she had
developed working in law related jobs was not necessarily the

same she needed to read the materials and brief the cases assigned by her professors. She was doing it though, and found she actually enjoyed the process. *Thanks, Dad.*

Dad. How strange it seemed to think of Ollie Tucker in such a way. The transformation of him being thought of like that had been remarkable for her. She knew there were many parts of him she didn't understand yet, but she was convinced her mother should've never let him get away. He had a loving heart that was hidden behind that successful single lawyer façade. The facts that he was paying for a quality legal education and had helped her find the apartment near the school proved that. Trusting Holly to help him in his office with sensitive cases showed his incredible belief in her abilities. She was determined to make him proud of her as she was of him.

As she spritzed a whiff of cologne and turned to leave the small bathroom, she heard the newscaster on the television set in the adjacent bedroom.

Our lead story this morning, the Macon-Bibb County Sheriff's Office has made an arrest in the so-called serial burglar case that has plagued the community for the last year.

Holly hurried into the room and stood in front of the TV as a mug shot of Tyler Crenshaw was shown on the screen. The picture was not flattering and had the effect of depicting guilt as many of those photos often did.

Tyler Crenshaw of Roberta was taken into custody yesterday while cruising a Lake Tobesofkee neighborhood.

Sources in the sheriff's office said Crenshaw was driving a nondescript van that contained evidence of five burglaries.

The suspect has no criminal record, but was involved in a case that was widely covered in 1964. The brutal murder of Elizabeth "Libby" Chancellor by Tyler Crenshaw's older brother, Mathis, also resulted in the older brother's death when the younger brother and his friend, Oliver Tucker, confronted him after the hideous crime.

A bond hearing has been scheduled before a magistrate this afternoon. We will report the outcome and have additional details on the news at five.

Holly was stunned. Just when she thought she had made strides in knowing her father, she realized there was plenty left to learn. She had many questions.

***

Tyler lay in his cell and tried not to think about his situation. His mind was dwelling on things of the past. It wasn't anything he hadn't thought of before. In fact, as much as he didn't want to admit it, his life was tied to all those things from long ago. Why couldn't he let it go? After so many years, they should be gone.

Things outside of his control had defined his whole life. At least, that's the way it felt on some level.

He couldn't help it. The head ramblings occurred.

Whatever happened to me was my own fault. Wait a minute; it was out of any control I held.

His mind felt like more than one, almost like it was split in two. All he wanted was the way he had felt so many years ago when he and Ollie were best buddies, and Libby kept them grounded. He knew the days were long gone, but he couldn't let the past remain there.

Salty tears fell down his cheeks as he remembered those days. Fifty years had elapsed, and he still couldn't find a way through them. He wished he could go back there. The days before it all went to crap.

He closed his eyes and remembered. She had been so pretty. He had loved her, too, of course. And she had loved him in ways others wouldn't recognize. Sure, she loved Ollie, but she always smiled at Tyler with true affection that came from the heart. Her death had torn something from him he could never find again. It had done even worse to Ollie. Now, they were joined in the pain, but they couldn't bring themselves to talk about it after all the years.

All of that pain had screwed him up even more than he had ever been as a lonely kid. He knew that, but it couldn't be helped. It had made him a stranger guy in lots of ways, and others found him more flawed as a result. The guilt he felt was the worse. Whatever, he was determined to make things right even if others didn't agree.

I've got to get out of here. When I do, I'll make this right.

CHAPTER 21

Inside the Law Enforcement Center's courtroom buzzed with anticipation and curiosity as several defendants including Tyler were led to the seats resembling church pews. The three local television networks were represented, and their video cameras were set near to one another to gather close coverage of the proceedings. There was also a newspaper reporter in attendance with another photographer beside her in the back of the room.

Ollie sat on a wooden bench on the side of the courtroom next to two men older than him. The men were civilian employees of the sheriff's office working as bailiffs. If people didn't know the lawyer, he was sure some would think of him as one of those. He had even been told by a couple of the old guys that he might want to apply for such a position when he got ready to leave the practice of law. Ollie had only laughed at the thought.

It had always amused but frightened him that bailiffs assisting the court were often put in positions that the general public would find threatening. The defendants they were charged with escorting to face the judge could more than likely swat them away like flies. The old guys, gentlemanly as they were, offered little protection if a deranged or violent offender decided to take action against folks in the courtroom. It was amazing to Ollie that he had never seen anything like that happen.

The court came to order as an armed deputy led the magistrate into the courtroom. The officer was beefy and looked fully capable of protecting the demure female wearing a full-length black robe. He positioned himself next to the small-elevated desk where the judge sat and then folded his arms while staring at the gallery. His intimidating look had the effect of encouraging respectful behavior, and Ollie instantly felt the older bailiffs were better protected than he initially thought.

Ollie had been informed before the proceedings began that the judge would handle all other matters on the docket before getting to his case. He had thought about remaining outside the courtroom until Tyler's hearing, but decided he might get an idea of how the judge conducted her business if he watched everything. Besides, he wanted to be there for his friend, and he knew Ty was nervous.

No one was present from the District Attorney's office, but the lawyer figured someone would show before Tyler's case was called. Ollie had tried to find out their thinking earlier in the

morning and to come up with a pre-arranged bond amount. His
efforts had been for naught as no one would commit to the DA's
mindset. It had caused him some unease although Ollie refused
to believe a reasonable bail wouldn't be set.

The judge called the first name on the calendar in a rather
timid voice, thought Ollie. He knew very little about the woman
running the show mainly due to never appearing before her. He
had been told she didn't possess a law degree, which was not an
absolute requirement for the job. He'd also learned she had been
a long-time employee of the office, having started as a legal
secretary and worked her way up the chain. Knowing friends
had told Ollie this magistrate knew the limitations of her
position.

A young woman showing signs of hard living got up from
her seat on the front row facing the magistrate. She shuffled
forward with her eyes cast down on her white rubber slides. One
of the elder bailiffs stood on her right side, and a youthful public
defender got close to the defendant's other side.

Body language and appearance suggested the emaciated
female had a major drug problem. Her skin was pale to the point
of translucence except for angry acne appearing on her cheeks.
The teeth that could be seen were yellow and showing signs of
decay. As she tried to stand still, her body twitched in her
orange jump suit.

Ollie thought she was probably heavy into crystal meth. He
had seen an old client's son fall into such an addiction a few
years before; it ultimately led to his death. Neither his client's

nor Ollie's attempts to help save the boy had any long-term positive effects. Tens of thousands of dollars had been spent on rehab efforts that only led to more heartache for the family. This woman had the exact look of that guy, and the lawyer couldn't help but believe her downward spiral would never be stopped at this point.

As the magistrate went over the charges, which included felony theft, misdemeanor obstruction of an officer and the possession of prescription drugs outside of their regular container, the woman began chewing on her almost nonexistent nails. Her other hand was busy twirling dirty dishwater blonde hair that hung limply on skinny shoulders.

The woman never opened her mouth throughout the brief appearance. The officer who had made the arrest was not called to testify either since the defense attorney informed the court they were waiving a commitment hearing. Bail was then set at $3000.00 and a motion to make it an OR (own recognizance) was denied by the magistrate. Ollie doubted the defendant would be able to get out of jail even with such a relatively small bond and would more than likely stay there until the case was resolved in some fashion. That could take months and exposed a weakness in the criminal justice system that those in the know often complained about.

As the next defendant was called before the bench, Ollie looked at Tyler. His old friend appeared scruffy from not having shaved. His eyes were bleary and expressionless. At least a couple of the cameras were trained on him, and Ollie made a mental note to change the way Tyler looked for any future publicity that might occur. He knew physical appearance often gave false impressions to others, and it was important to place any criminal defendant in the best light possible.

His mind drifted while the next couple of hearings moved through the process. Ollie thought briefly about the phone call from Holly after she had seen the television report that morning. She had been upset more about the events from Libby's murder than anything they had previously discussed, even more so than when they had discussed the relationship between him and her mother. Ollie had promised they would talk about it tonight at dinner since she would not be coming to the office until almost closing time.

Even with all the happiness he had found getting to know Holly, he knew it would be difficult for him to relive the memories. All the time that had passed had not erased the pain and the hole remaining in his heart. Ollie told himself he would try and might even include Tyler, if he could secure his release.

"Tyler Crenshaw, please step forward," heard Ollie as he snapped back to the present.

Ollie stood and walked to his spot beside Tyler just as the door opened into the courtroom. The District Attorney with a minion trailing behind like a puppy strode inside making a dramatic entrance. He had a grim appearance that seemed staged to the defense lawyer. The lawyer was sure the media cameras caught it on film, and Ollie thought he would see it again on the evening news and probably later in other venues.

The D.A. nodded at the old defense lawyer dismissively and then focused on the magistrate who seemed intimidated. Ollie hoped this was not a bad sign.

"Good afternoon, Mr. Crocker. The court doesn't often see the District Attorney at this stage of the proceedings," the judge said in a fawning manor.

She then turned to Ollie and continued, "And, Mr. Tucker, I don't believe I've met you before. I've heard good things about you. I appreciate both of you being here today. Have the two of you discussed the possibility of agreeing to a bail amount?"

Before Ollie could respond, Crocker turned his face so that his profile was at an angle for the TV cameras and said, "No Your Honor. Unfortunately, I have been inundated with several major cases in the office and have not had the time to meet with defense counsel. There are other factors in this defendant's case we have been trying to investigate as well. I'm here to oppose bond being set at this time until my office has more time to look into those concerns," said the DA.

Tyler reacted before Ollie stopped him, "I haven't done anything wrong!"

Ollie put his right hand on Tyler's left shoulder and then whispered into his ear, "Don't say anything else unless I ask you. Trust me, Ty."

The magistrate's face was strained as if she was caught off guard. Some of the color had left her face. Ollie glanced at Crocker before addressing her.

"Sorry for the outburst, Your Honor. My client is sixty-six years old and has never been arrested before. He's obviously upset by Mr. Crocker's statement. I want you to know I made efforts to speak with the District Attorney before this hearing, but I was unsuccessful. We are prepared to make bail at a reasonable amount set by the court. Anyone else in this position could have already been released by the preset bond list according to the Superior Court's standing order. I'm sure Your Honor is very familiar with those guidelines. Based on my understanding, the bond for my client should be set between five thousand and twenty thousand dollars," said Ollie.

The magistrate shifted in her seat and only acted with more discomfort. Ollie was certain she didn't have to face this level of argument often. Ollie didn't think it was over either.

Crocker retained his tilt and spoke again. "If it please the court, I can call witnesses to establish the seriousness of the charges against this defendant. Also, I will state in my place I am in discussions with other prosecutors in this state concerning possible charges against this defendant in at least three other jurisdictions."

All of the remaining color in the woman looking down at the two lawyers disappeared to the point that she appeared ready to faint. *This is not going well for her as well as for Tyler,* thought Ollie.

"Your Honor, the fact the District Attorney may have witnesses ready to testify doesn't change the fact the current charges are alleged burglaries without prior convictions for those charges, which are bondable offenses in this jurisdiction. The District Attorney knows if there are other jurisdictions choosing to file charges, they can file a hold with the Sheriff on my client. We don't need to hear any evidence at this point and will waive our right to a commitment hearing if we can get bond set today," said Ollie while trying not to sound as sanctimonious as opposing counsel.

Neither attorney said anything as the magistrate fidgeted with the papers in front of her. Her full-blown nervousness was apparent for everyone in attendance, and Ollie was sure it would be noticeable on the television screen later.

"I agree with Mr. Tucker. Bail will be set at twenty thousand dollars. Since this is the last case of the session, court is adjourned," she said barely audible. She then left the bench at record speed before anyone else had a chance to say anything.

The District Attorney nodded again at Ollie with an icy glint in his eyes. He then walked toward the reporters who called out to him after the judge left the room.

Ollie and Tyler faced one another. Tyler had a smile resembling a grimace. Ollie breathed a sigh of relief.

"I'll have you out of here in an hour unless they pull some kind of shit, Tyler. I suspect they won't or they would've already. We'll talk more then," said Ollie.

The Adam's apple in Tyler's throat moved up and down as he swallowed. "Thanks for looking out for me again, Ollie. I would be dead for sure without you."

CHAPTER 22

The staff was gone and Ollie was alone with Holly in his office. It had taken longer than expected to secure Tyler's release and then even longer to get his van returned from the impound lot, where it had been held since the arrest. Tyler had only wanted to go home after all that finagling, and he declined the offer to have dinner with Ollie and Holly. It was completely understandable under the circumstances.

Holly had gotten to the office in the meantime and had taken the opportunity before her father's arrival to use the desktop computer in the vacant office. She used a couple of search engines to find old articles about the tragic murder of his childhood sweetheart. She felt a little stupid for not having found out the information before since she was supposed to be such a crackerjack investigator. Holly had searched before ever meeting him the first time and had discovered loads of information about him as a lawyer, but she guessed the sheer number of years that had passed since the killings served the purpose of burying that event.

Now they were quiet as each was lost in private thoughts. Ollie loosened his tie and unbuttoned the top one of his shirt. He slumped in his executive chair behind the desk and rocked back propping his right foot on a drawer handle.

Holly quietly stretched her neck and rolled her shoulders forwards and backwards to ease the tension caused by too much time sitting before the computer screen. She watched Ollie's tired expressions with concerned looks of her own.

"You know, Dad, I've heard experts say you shouldn't keep stuff inside," said Holly.

Ollie's mouth turned downward and his face showed a sour expression as if he was sucking a persimmon. "That's easy for you to say, baby," replied Ollie without looking up.

"I can't imagine what you've gone through, Dad. I never knew any of that stuff in the media. I'm sure it's opened old wounds."

Holly figured he was trying to block the memory out, but that wasn't working. She thought too many things were cluttering his mind, and now she was adding to the mix.

She watched as he got up from his chair and walked around the desk to a corner cabinet. A collection of single malt scotches appeared, and the lawyer studied the bottles even though he had barely touched any of them in months. He finally selected the standby that had accompanied him faithfully in the past and kept it in his hand as he closed the door to the furniture.

"I need a drink before I try to do this, okay," he said turning away.

Holly got up and followed him as he left the room headed toward the small kitchen area. She watched from the doorway as he grabbed a cocktail glass and added a few ice cubes.

"Do you want one, too?" he asked as he poured the glass half full of liquor and added a splash of water from the faucet. He then swirled it with a stirrer pulled from a container near the coffee pot and then stuck the piece of plastic in his mouth.

"No, thanks," she said and paused before finishing. "I'm not judging, Dad, but are you sure you want that?"

"I'm not sure whether I do or not. All I can tell you is that it seems to have helped me in the past during times of crisis. I need it right now, and I need you to cut me a little slack," he said with some irritation.

She said nothing in response as he took a large sip from the drink. He picked up the bottle in one hand and the drink in the other and walked back to his office. Holly trailed behind wearing a worried look and slight frown on her face.

He sat down heavily in an overstuffed chair within the space reserved for more intimate meetings and placed the bottle on a nearby coffee table. After taking another sip, which reduced the remaining drink to less than a third of the glass, Ollie set the beverage on a coaster. He removed the plastic stirrer and began chewing.

Holly waited until he was situated and then took another chair facing her father. He stared at something she couldn't see. His age showed through the lines in his face, but it still had a pleasing appearance. She thought he was the epitome of a handsome older man.

When Ollie began to speak, the confidence that usually came through the timbre of his voice was muted. At least, that's the way it seemed to Holly.

"It's not that I don't remember things from that part of my life, it just seems like it happened to somebody else, not me. I'm sure there's a psychological term for that like the other character faults I've developed over my lifetime," he started.

Holly resolved to remain quiet and let him do the talking. It was a tactic she had taken many times before in her previous career. Although she wanted to know as much about him as he was willing to divulge, she was afraid he would clam up the minute she started asking too many questions. Being the private person he had been for so long was not going to change with ease.

"That young boy was carefree. He loved games and could play all day long. He liked to learn and probably enjoyed school as much as summer vacations. His life only got better when he met Libby. They added Tyler to the mix, and he became a friend to both," Ollie said referring to himself in the third person.

He stirred the drink with the chewed end of the plastic straw and then replaced it in his mouth. After gnawing another few moments, Ollie continued his narrative.

"The happy-go-lucky kid became an even happier teenager. It was a lot simpler back then. Not so many distractions as there are today. He spent the necessary time to do his schoolwork, but found time to play sports and still have plenty of time for girlfriend, Libby and his guy friend, Tyler. While his life was not perfect, it sure seemed that way.

"As the teen grew, so did his love for Libby. Everything he did was colored by their deepening feelings toward one another. First love, true love, as trite as it might sound, enveloped his heart. It consumed him like nothing else, and it made him happier than anything.

"He and Libby made lots of plans, not just for the immediate days and nights, but also for the future. In a few years they would be out of college, and then they could get married. She would start teaching, and he would go to law school.

"After he finished getting his law degree and started making money, they would have three kids, two boys and a girl. They would probably spoil them, but they would be smart and cute and bring lots of joy. The boys would be stars on the baseball team, and the girl would be the first female president. Their lives would be full and they would live happily ever after, just like in the movies," continued Ollie before finishing the drink.

Her dad's face sagged as Holly watched him pour another drink over the rapidly melting ice. At least he didn't make it as big as the last one. It was difficult to watch him struggle with the memories and the associated emotions.

"I still miss her. After all this time, I still miss Libby," he said changing to first person.

Ollie took a big swig of the second drink. He closed his eyes and was still. Holly wanted to cross the space and hug him, but she didn't.

When he opened his eyes, they contained a fire not seen before. Her dad was frightening for a moment, and Holly witnessed murderous intent.

"I would've given my life for her. She shouldn't have died like she did. That son-of-a-bitch had no reason to kill her and slice her up. She never hurt anything or anybody. Part of me blamed God for letting her die, especially like that. I think I still do, almost as much as I blame myself."

Holly felt hot tears in the corner of her eyes. To see her father in such torment made her almost as mad as he seemed.

"I was so stupid that night. I never even thought she might be in trouble. I could've saved her. I should've saved her. I felt responsible for not being with her. Then I thought Tyler could've even been part of the problem, too. It was so screwed up in my head when I thought about it. I'd given Matt a ride that evening to place my Libby in danger. He was Ty's brother, too. It was a screwed up mess that night, and I've never been able to get over it.

"It never made any sense from the moment I saw her lying on the ground. She had been violated by that animal and then stabbed and slashed over forty times. It looked like some kind of frenzy, blood everywhere.

"I remember him screaming at me and Tyler before he attacked us. He looked crazy, but I didn't care at that point because at that moment I wanted to die, too. And then he stabbed Ty and instinct took over to try and protect him. I fought with every ounce of strength I could muster and didn't even realize I'd been cut a few times until it was all over. He was so strong that it took Tyler and me working together to make him stop. All three of us had a hold on the knife before it went into his heart.

"I'll tell you this. She deserved to live a lot more than me. I'd give up whatever I've gotten in my life to let her live. She was the best person I've ever known."

Ollie drained the second drink and there was very little ice left. Holly wondered if he would pour straight scotch into the glass.

"Dad, maybe we should get some dinner. It's been a long day, and I'm kinda hungry. How about you?" asked Holly.

Ollie looked at his empty glass as if contemplating another drink. Holly hoped he was done with the liquor tonight. The emotions shown while he had spoken made the air in the room seem heavy, yet Holly felt a new level of closeness developing. More alcohol might blunt the progress.

"Yeah, maybe that would be a good idea. Your choice, but I'll need you to drive," said Ollie.

"No problem, Dad. I've got your back tonight."

***

The Viewer felt pretty good. Things were going like he thought they should. Nobody would ever suspect him or his motives. He was smarter than all of them. None of them had a clue who he was or why he did what he did.

His life had been jumbled throughout. It didn't matter, though. He had sorted it all out. Being a Crenshaw carried certain responsibilities. He would make things right so that Matt didn't die in vain.

CHAPTER 23

O llie decided to walk the few blocks from the office to the courthouse. Two weeks had passed since Tyler's arrest with no developments in the case. The lawyer's efforts to find out what evidence the DA's office might have in their possession had been stonewalled until now. A phone call had just informed him he could look at what was available courtesy of the Chief Assistant District Attorney.

The autumn weather was ideal for strolling. The cooler temperature and the leaves that showcased a full palette of colors helped Ollie's feelings as much as the exercise. Since he had opened up to Holly, there was a certain amount of relief felt he wouldn't otherwise have believed. The stress of representing his oldest friend was affecting his sleep patterns, though.

He took in deep breaths of fresh air as he sauntered down the sidewalk and let his mind wander. A meeting with Tyler the prior week left unanswered questions. His friend was adamant that he was innocent of the charges leveled against him. He claimed it was a setup, but had no reason why. Tyler could think of nobody with a motive to do such a thing. The undercurrent of anger Ollie had seen in his friend before had caused an element of uneasiness in the meeting that still bothered the lawyer.

Ollie wanted to believe Tyler, but he had secret doubts not shared at this point. He knew it shouldn't matter whether his friend was guilty. A lawyer needed only to represent his client zealously whether he was at fault or not. What little information he had, seemed to point toward guilt, and it would have to be as Tyler described to make the situation different. That would mean someone had an agenda against Tyler. Ollie couldn't imagine why.

His mind shifted to Holly as a breeze fluttered the golden leaves on a ginkgo tree. Even though Ollie was experiencing confusion in one area of his life with his friend, he continued to prosper in his daughter bonding. He knew it had changed him, and he thought for the better. He was determined to make up for not being there all the years she spent growing into the woman she was now. Hopefully, he wasn't going overboard helping her go back to school and providing her a job. He didn't want her to feel smothered or that he was interfering too much in her life.

To his knowledge she hadn't even had a date in the time he had known her. He was bothered by that fact, and it made him worry she would end up like him. Whenever he broached the subject, she only laughed and said she didn't have time for a man in her life right now other than him. He was flattered initially, but his concern for her to have a more normal life than his had been nagging him lately.

She had a lot going for her other than a cover girl face and a body made hard by the disciplined exercise classes she did religiously. Holly had an inquiring mind that Ollie thought was perfect for the law, and her work ethic was superb. Every task he had assigned to her she had completed competently and on time. She was the antithesis of most of the employees he had hired over the years, and he was convinced Holly was the full meal deal. He wished he could tell her mother what a fine job she had done raising their wonderful daughter.

As Ollie neared the courthouse, he recognized Leo Berry running toward him in the direction of the Health Club. They knew each other as not only occasional opposing advocates in the State Court, but also as friends from the club. It was a Macon establishment having one time been the local YMCA. Now it was affiliated with the Medical Center and counted among its members many of the movers and shakers in the community.

Berry was a prosecutor known for his fairness and was universally liked by defense lawyers. He had not quite reached forty years of age, but he was quickly making a name for himself in the legal community. In the last year he had been hailed as a hero for helping to bring down a major drug operation, and it was rumored he might be a candidate against the sitting District Attorney as a result.

The prosecutor slowed down his pace, as he got closer to Ollie. The older lawyer stopped walking and smiled in response to the broad grin the younger attorney wore.

"Afternoon, old-timer. Forgive me for not shaking your hand; I'm a little sweaty at the moment. Haven't seen you in the club the last few weeks. Feeling okay?" asked the prosecutor after removing buds from his ears and pressing a button on a small MP3 player attached to his Mercer tee shirt.

"That's Mr. Old-timer, to you, kid. I see you're still running with devil music blasting through your brain. Didn't you learn your lesson about that last year?" asked Ollie, referring to a near-miss the prosecutor had experienced with a car in the recent past.

"I always face the traffic when I'm running now, and I keep the volume turned down a lot lower than I used to do. I learned that lesson for sure, counselor. Just don't mention it to my wife if you see her at the next Bar party. She'll give me a lot of crap if she thinks I've reverted to old habits," said Berry.

"Okay, but it'll cost you, Mr. Prosecutor. Next time I've got a DUI case in your court, I'll take a reckless and we'll call it even," said Ollie with a chuckle.

"In that case, you'd better go ahead and tell the wife I'm the reckless one," laughed Berry.

"Hey, it was worth a try. Everybody knows how hard it is to get you to compromise a case, Leo. What's the rumor I hear about you running against Crocker?" said Ollie.

"Now, Mr. Tucker. I know I've agreed to a reduction of charges for at least one client of yours in the past. I only do it when the facts or the law require it. You know that. As for the gossip about me running for DA, I'm neither confirming nor denying. For grins, would you support such an effort?" replied Berry with a smirk.

Ollie pretended to ponder the question while stroking his chin. "Hmmm, I wonder what kind of deal I could get for that kind of promise," he said snickering into the hand that he had been using on his face. "Let's just say I'm not a particular fan of the current district attorney."

The young prosecutor simply nodded in response. He glanced at his watch and told Ollie he needed to hit the showers before getting back to work. When the older lawyer added he was on his way to the DA's office to see Jessica Mooney, Berry told him to tell her to be careful and not fall off her shoes. After both laughing at the known fact that she wore the highest heels in the courthouse, they parted ways in different directions.

***

The Macon Circuit District Attorney's offices were located on several floors of the Macon-Bibb County Annex and the historic Grand building adjacent to the main courthouse. Ollie had long lost count of the number of assistant district attorneys, investigators and other support staff the offices now accommodated. He figured it had to easily be four or five times larger than it was when he first started practicing law in the dark ages of the early seventies. Back then there were only a half dozen or so prosecutors and a handful of other staff. Everyone knew everybody else working in the criminal justice system, and for the most part they were all congenial to one another. It was quite different now and not nearly as pleasant.

For someone who had practiced law nearing a half-century mainly as a sole practitioner, he couldn't imagine being a cog in such a large operation. Ollie had found it difficult during the times he had hired associates because none of them seemed willing to do things like he wanted them done. He only realized he was probably too hard on them after they quit to go work elsewhere, or when he would get fed up with what he called incompetence and sent them packing for other pastures. Ollie had heard more than one former associate tell him they couldn't stand the micro-management he subjected them to. It would drive him crazy to think he had to supervise such a cadre of lawyers now working in the DA's office. He was much better off working by himself.

He arrived at the receptionist's desk only to find it empty. Because of the configuration, Ollie was unable to see into the office suite beyond. He gave it a few minutes before trying the door, but he discovered it was locked. There was no bell he could ring to draw attention or any other way to let someone know he was waiting. He rapped on the door, but no one answered. Irritated, the lawyer pulled his cellphone and punched the DA's number from his contact list. He got a computer-generated response directing him through a maze until he could connect with Jessica Mooney. When he tried that extension, the call went straight to voice mail.

"Ms. Mooney, this is Oliver Tucker. I'm standing outside the front door of your third floor offices. No one is at the front desk. I came as soon as I got your call informing me I could see the file on Tyler Crenshaw. If you're available, could you please let me in," Ollie said into the phone with a clipped voice.

As he ended the call the door opened, and the long-legged chief assistant appeared wearing a lopsided smile. Ollie, still frowning, couldn't help his displeasure.

"I can't believe an office this big doesn't have someone on the front desk at all times," he said.

The prosecutor cocked her head slightly, but maintained the uneven grin. Ollie thought her attractive in an unorthodox way. She wore a stylish gray pantsuit and white blouse with a bright scarf tied around her neck. The spike heeled shoes made her three inches taller than her already statuesque height. Her short brunette haircut was pumped up to add even more tallness. At least she wasn't taller than him, which provided some degree of comfort. Tall women had always been intimidating for some reason.

"Most visitors are required to report to the second floor reception area first before coming up here, Mr. Tucker. We're skipping a step. I'm your personal escort to the inner sanctum today, Honey," she said.

The older lawyer was taken aback momentarily. He didn't know Ms. Mooney very well at all, and he felt she had already disarmed him. It only led more to the annoyance he felt. He made an instantaneous decision to change his approach.

Ollie tried to look as suave and debonair as he could muster. Although he was certainly old enough to be the prosecutor's father or maybe a dirty uncle, two could play the game he suspected she was using to make him feel uncomfortable.

"Sorry, for the outburst of attitude, Ms. Mooney. I don't get over here as often as I once did and wasn't aware of the changes. I really appreciate your phone call and the willingness to meet with me today. By the way, I hope you don't mind me saying you certainly look fetching, and I would let you escort me anywhere."

The chief assistant's face flushed slightly, and she laughed nervously. Her stance shifted on one hip, and Ollie remembered the earlier conversation with Leo Berry. She turned and started walking inside the suite of offices with the defense lawyer following close behind.

"By the way, I was talking with one of your colleagues a while ago about your choice of footwear, and he asked me to warn you not to fall off the stilettos. I know he was trying to be funny, but I think you handle them rather well. As my youngest employee would say, 'You rock them shoes, girl.'"

She reached her corner office, and Ollie could see her shoulders were hunched while she laughed silently. When he asked if she was okay, the prosecutor responded with a snort.

"Come into the queen bitch's lair, Mr. Tucker," she said through a girl's giggle trailed by another sound coming through her nose.

He went inside the workspace that he hadn't seen since Mooney had become the chief assistant a couple of years ago. The two immediate predecessors had been long-serving members of the office, the last passing away suddenly after retirement and the one before him now working for the feds.

"Other than a few feminine touches, it looks like it has withstood the tales of time," said Ollie.

He walked over to the window overlooking Mulberry Street and surveyed the view. Leaves were falling from some of the trees forming a colorful array on the ground, which served as a divider between the one-way traffic on opposite sides of the street.

When he turned back to Mooney, she was watching him with appraising eyes as if trying to figure out what kind of opponent he would make. At least, that's what he thought.

"Has anyone ever told you that you look like James Brolin?"

Ollie was taken off guard, but replied, "The actor?"

"Yeah, I don't know another one, silly man. You're about the same size and height. Your hair is more salt and pepper than his, but you have very similar facial features."

"Thanks, I guess."

"Well, hell yeah! I was just wondering if you have a single son about my age and does he look like you. I mean you're a little too old for me, but I would love to have Josh Brolin standing where you are now. That Brolin kid would suit me just fine," said Mooney.

Now it was Ollie's turn to snicker. It was infectious enough to encourage the prosecutor to join him with a couple more snorts. Both began hooting like owls and they had tears in their eyes as they laughed more at one another than the subject.

The mood of the meeting was thus changed. The old defense lawyer and the younger prosecutor sat and discussed things other than the case that brought them together. Ollie learned she had an adolescent son from a previous marriage who she doted on, and she found out he had a daughter a little younger than her in law school. While talking about their children, they found an easiness with one another that usually took a lot longer, and it had started with a humorous exchange.

"So, what can you share about the case without me filing a formal request for discovery?" asked Ollie when they got around to business.

"You'll find this out about me, Mr. Tucker, I don't try to hide anything I have. And, I don't mean just evidence," she said with a big wink.

He grinned again and said, "You're a bad girl, Ms. Mooney. I'll take you at your word. Show me what you got."

The lopsided smirk reappeared and she got up from her chair. She walked over to a cabinet and pulled out a cardboard box. Sauntering over to where Ollie sat, she set it before him.

Written in black magic marker on the outside of the box were the words, *Crenshaw evidence.*

There were several plastic bags inside the box with evidence tags attached to each one. The tags, presumably filled out by the collector, listed the contents, even though the interiors were visible.

Ollie looked at the bags one by one and what was contained therein. He guessed this was what had been confiscated from Ty's van. He saw several of what he thought to be inexpensive items that didn't appear remarkable at first blush. A couple of the articles had to be costume jewelry at best. There was also a stack of something looking like business cards with an artfully rendered eye in the center. He couldn't see any writing on the cards and wondered about their possible significance. The last thing he saw in the box of items was his insulated coffee cup that had been missing for months.

Shit.

CHAPTER 24

The basement was customized to suit his taste and contained three rooms. One was his gym that contained a state of the art treadmill, a well-used exercise bike and a set of weights. There were mirrors on all the walls so he could watch himself work out, and he did so faithfully for at least an hour every day. He was not muscle-bound, but he was hard as steel. Not many people knew it because he didn't flaunt the body and kept it tastefully covered at all times when he was around the public.

The second room was used for storage. There were several items he had used in various jobs he had held over the years since he left the service. He was handy and had developed those talents well. The tools of the various trades were kept down here in case they were ever needed again. Among other stored articles were a number of electronic devices that allowed him to indulge in activities that thrilled him more than anything else in life.

The third room was the largest, and it held his most prized possessions. He had built a cabinet on one wall that held two hundred and forty individual compartments roughly the size of shoeboxes. There were less than a dozen without something in them, and he supposed it was almost time to build an additional storage cabinet. Each one represented a conquest, a successful entry into someone's private space, resulting in a trophy for his efforts.

The Viewer spent countless hours in his prize room, as he thought of it, and that's where he was now. He had the compartments arranged and catalogued in chronological order so he could pull the first one and know that enclosed within was the first trophy he had ever collected. He had studied and admired them so many times over the years that he could name and describe each item in detail. He could also recite the location of the home where he collected the award.

He had various kinds of things gathered in the prize room. Very few of them had much value in terms of money. There were a few jewelry pieces, but most of them were costume variety bangles. There was an old Timex watch that was unremarkable except it reminded him of one that his grandmother had worn. There were also a couple of inexpensive tie tacks that had caught his eye and ended up in the collection. One of them was a crossed miniature knife and fork that he had seen worn by his preacher.

Some prizes had belonged to males, and others had belonged to women. He was sure a shrink would have a field day trying to figure out why he took some of the things. The Viewer thought everyone of them was special in some fashion.

He was rather irritated at losing a few of his more recent acquisitions, especially the coffee mug belonging to the King Asshole, Ollie. However, he was confident he could replace anything he lost by simply returning to the sites and selecting substitute prizes. He planned to do that very thing in the near future.

What he had once thought of as a hobby had become more of an obsession during the last several years. When he first began collecting, it was a casual process that occurred, as an opportunity would present itself. Typically, he would be on a residential job and the prize would jump out at him begging to be taken. Now, the process included much more planning and was rarely spontaneous as it had been when he started. It made the whole practice challenging and the reward even greater after secured in its own compartment.

He opened the first compartment and pulled out the hairbrush. It was old-fashioned and had stiff bristles, just like the one his mother used when he was a kid. He would watch her stroke her long hair after she took it down and it was mesmerizing. Those memories flooded back when he saw the first prize, and it brought a certain peace.

Holding the handle gently in his hand, he admired the smooth finish. He rubbed his other hand over the spines and felt a shudder of pleasure course through his body. He had known women during his lifetime, but none had ever brought the sensations he encountered when fondling one of his prizes.

Almost with a reverence akin to holding a rare artifact, the Viewer replaced the brush to its spot. He then opened the last one in his collection so far. It was a bracelet taken from Holly Lee's apartment. He loved the feel of it in his hands.

CHAPTER 25

It was a Friday night, and Holly wanted to wind down from a long grueling week with some live music. One of the things she loved about downtown Macon was she could always find a place to enjoy some act she had never heard before. After a full week of classes, studying late every night, and work at her dad's office, she felt the need to relax.

She slipped on some well-worn jeans and a comfortable sweater that accentuated her curves. The shoes she chose were casual three-inch peep-toed cork- heeled wedges. Her long brunette hair was casually twisted up and held by a tortoise jaw clip. She spritzed some Jimmy Choo at the base of her throat and on her wrists and then lightly rubbed them together.

She put on her favorite Brighton earrings and fastened her heart-shaped matching necklace around her neck, and then looked for the bracelet that completed the set. It was not in the place she normally kept it. After searching for a few moments, she decided to substitute her Alex and Ani wrist wear, which completed the ensemble to her liking.

Some of her classmates were going to meet her at the club at ten o'clock, but she had an hour to kill before then. All dressed up and ready to go, she decided to head to the place ahead of them. She could enjoy a drink and get a head start. She was older than the rest anyway, and would more than likely want to get back home before them.

Holly arrived at the place on Cherry Street and looked around. There was a decent crowd made up of an older and younger mixed bag of folks. The band was rocking and some were swaying on the postage stamp sized dance floor. As she watched, it made her thirsty and a little horny if the truth were told.

She walked up to the main bar, found a seat, and ordered a Top Shelf Margarita. It was her favorite drink and had been so since a trip to Mexico after graduating from college. The problem was that tequila could make her crazy if she wasn't careful. She had been extra cautious for a while, but she was feeling antsy tonight.

Holly stirred her drink and took a sip. It was cold and made her mouth pucker. The main thing it did was to make her smile.

"Hey, that must be a good drink. That's the biggest smile I've seen tonight."

Holly looked to the source of the comment. He was a nice-looking guy sitting two seats from her. Maybe a little older than she was, but at first glance she liked what she saw.

"It is good. Want a sip?"

"I'm not much into Mexican liquor. Thanks, just the same."

"So, what are you drinking?"

"Scotch, single malt," he said holding up the small rocks glass.

"That's what my dad drinks."

"He's got good taste in alcohol."

"I wouldn't know, but I'll take your word on it."

He looked at her appraisingly. She returned the gaze. There was an attraction, at least physically. Holly's internal temperature was rising. She hadn't felt this kind of heat in some time. Was it the alcohol or due to the man giving her a little attention? She hadn't been involved with anyone since the breakup with her boyfriend over two years ago.

Holly sipped her drink and thought back to the last time she saw Steve. The relationship had lasted longer than any to that point in her life. Three and a half years was an eternity in her dating experience. He had wanted to get married and have kids. She didn't want the same things out of life, at least at that moment in time. Now she was marching closer to forty, and it looked like maybe she might never want the traditional family structure. She wondered if growing up in a single parent home was responsible for that way of thinking.

"Lost in your thoughts?" asked the stranger.

"Um, sorry. I'm just a little tired I guess," replied Holly.

"No need to apologize for being beat. That's what the weekend is for, right? Nothing wrong with getting out, having a drink or two and listening to a band. At least, not in my mind," said the man.

"My thoughts exactly," said Holly. She paused and then introduced herself, "I'm Holly Lee, what's your name?"

"Nice to meet you, Holly. I'm Shawn Matheson. Mind if I join you?" he asked with a smile.

She only thought about it a moment and then gave a slight nod toward the spot beside her. He moved from his stool and took the one immediately to her right.

"I'm a little new to this scene, so I hope this doesn't sound too much like a line, but do you come here often?" she said.

He chuckled pleasantly and replied, "No, my days of hanging in bars are long gone. I came out tonight because I like Randall Bramblett, and I heard he was playing. Are you a fan, too?"

"I've heard of him, but I have to admit I'm not familiar with his music. One of my friends meeting me here later told me he was great. I was ready for a break from studying, so I thought it would be good to check him out," she said.

"I think he's not appreciated nearly enough for his talent. Been around making music since the seventies. I became a fan when he was a member of Sea Level. Always admired the way he played the sax. And for some reason I've always loved his gravelly voice. He's played with a lot other artists, too. Like Bonnie Raitt and Steve Winwood, just to name a few, but I prefer when he plays with his band," he said.

He paused and took a sip of his drink before continuing, "Sorry, didn't mean to gush like that. Guess you can tell I like the guy. So, you said something about taking a break from studying. You go to school?"

Holly laughed and said, "I guess I look a little old to be in school, right? The fact of the matter is that I'm at least ten years older than most of the other people in my law school class."

The man looked at her and nodded. "I would definitely want you as my lawyer. If the judge was a man, he would rule with you every time."

She blushed and took the compliment. Not too many of those had come her way in recent times, and it was nice. Her appraisal of him was escalating more as they talked.

"How about you, Shawn? How do you spend your time when you're not hanging out in bars?"

He smiled again and looked at Holly directly. She liked his rugged face more by the minute.

"I'm in business for myself. I do a little bit of everything. I guess you could call me a glorified handyman. If you ever need anything done around your house, I'm your man."

"Hmm, never owned a house of my own. I've been renting ever since I left home, so I don't need a jack-of-all-trades to fix my place up. If I did, I'd definitely consider you for the job. That is, if you've got the right references," she said.

Immediately, she was sorry she had said that. It sounded too much like a come on. She didn't want him to think that, at least yet.

Shawn stared at her as if trying to decipher her inner core. She couldn't read him at all.

"I'd be happy to oblige your every need, Holly."

For some reason, Holly thought it sounded a little creepy the way he said it. But, he looked sincere and his rugged good looks made the difference.

"Well, you never know what the future brings until it happens. I'll keep that in mind," she said.

Before either could say anything else, the band took the stage. The music started and before the end of the first song, Holly was hooked. This guy was as good as described. When the song ended, she looked at Shawn and gave thumbs up.

He smiled and reached over and patted her hand. When she looked into his eyes, she knew this was a guy she wanted to get to know better.

CHAPTER 26

Ollie sat at his desk awaiting Tyler's arrival. Since the lawyer's meeting with Jessica Mooney the previous week, he had grappled with the implications of finding his coffee mug included in the evidence taken from his friend's van. So far, he couldn't figure it out.

First, why would Tyler steal anything? He had done very well for himself over the years. He had owned several successful businesses, and Ollie was aware he had plenty enough money to live comfortably the rest of his life.

The thing about these thefts, though, was the motive didn't seem to be about stealing for value. It indicated to him that the culprit had some kind of mental or emotional problem. There had to be some kind of damage to the psyche that led to wanting to take somebody's coffee mug.

To his knowledge, Tyler was a normal guy. Could it be his friend had suffered psychological or emotional harm from his brother's death so many years ago? Or maybe, he had some issues remaining from his Vietnam experience. And if he did, why in hell would that lead to stealing stuff that was pretty much worthless? Ollie couldn't remember anything about Tyler that caused him to think that way although he had been more than a little quirky when he was a kid.

Ollie was conflicted more about this case than any other one he had ever handled. He was loyal to Tyler and wanted to help him. But, no matter how much any defense lawyer claimed not to be bothered about the client's guilt or innocence, it usually sank into your consciousness at some point. When he had represented someone he knew in his heart was guilty, it had haunted him when he got that person off. Ollie didn't want to feel anything like that, especially when his client was his best friend.

He remembered a day from their teen years. Ollie hadn't thought about it until now. They were walking home after getting off the bus.

"I wish I could be like you, Ollie," said Tyler.

"I'm nothing special, Ty," replied Ollie.

"That's where you're wrong, Ollie. You are. You've shown me that you are for as long as I've known you. I've always known I was different, but it never mattered to you. You like me no matter what," said Tyler.

"Y'all are two weirdoes, that's why I love you both," said Libby.

They all had laughed. It had been a good day. Most days had been before she died.

She had been right. Both Ollie and Tyler were weird in their own ways. Ollie couldn't hold that against his friend.

The immediate problem required him to remain as open-minded as possible. If he were going to find a solution to Tyler's mess, he would need to draw upon his experience.

His phone rang and Red announced Tyler's arrival. Ollie told her to bring him in along with a fresh cup of coffee.

A few moments later, the receptionist entered the room holding a steaming mug with Tyler following a couple of steps behind. Red had an exaggerated frown on her face and cut her eyes in such a way Ollie could tell she was referring to his friend. When the lawyer glanced past Red, he saw that Tyler wore almost an identical scowl, and it nearly caused Ollie to laugh out loud. He looked back at her to find her grinning like a jackass eating briars, as his granddaddy used to say.

"Anything else, Boss?"

"No, that'll be all, Red. Just make sure we're not interrupted, please."

Tyler sat down stiffly, and Red left the room. As she did, she turned back to Ollie and stuck out her tongue behind Tyler's back so that the lawyer was the only one to see her juvenile antics. He stifled a laugh again and coughed into his hand to cover it. The girl was always funny and often helped to lighten the mood, but he was going to have to warn her to stay professional.

The two men sat in silence while Ollie sipped his coffee. It was hot, strong and just what he needed.

"How are you, Ty?"

The scowl became more intense. His face was devoid of any sign of happiness. The steely gleam in his eyes spoke of deep emotions that included anger in the forefront. Their bloodshot nature bespoke of suffering sleeplessness.

"I'm so pissed about all this, Ollie. I can't sleep and I don't want to eat until I figure out what's going on. It makes no sense. I've been spending every minute going over my life wondering what I've done to cause someone wanting to destroy me. I'm sure I must've really offended somebody along the way, but damned if I know who or why."

"It's good to work on that, Ty. It's counterproductive if it's causing you to breakdown, though. Maybe you should try a different tact. How about using a process of elimination? I mean, start by looking back over recent jobs you've done and work backwards to see if any of your former customers were upset with the quality of your efforts. Maybe one of them didn't like the color you picked for their remodeled bathroom."

"I've already been doing that, Ollie. That's the first thing I thought of. Maybe I screwed over a customer by cutting a corner or two, right? But, honestly I've never done that, at least, not that I remember. I've gone over every file for the last fifteen years and I can't find anything."

"I need to show you something, Ty. It's the evidence that was taken from your vehicle. I want to know what you recognize."

Ollie pulled out several printed copies of pictures he had taken with his cell phone. They represented all of the items of evidence Jessica had shared with him. He wanted Ty's honest reaction without his influence.

"These are pictures of items taken from your van. I want you to look at each one and tell me if you recognize any of them."

Tyler slowly scanned each picture. He squinted at a few of them. He shook his head slowly and then said, "No, I don't know any of these things."

Ollie watched as Tyler studied the pictures. He couldn't detect any recognition in his friend's face. It only added to his indecision about Ty's involvement in the crimes.

"Look, Ty. Anything you might be able to give me about this stuff would help. Be honest with me. Do you see anything that looks familiar? How about the coffee mug?"

"I don't think I've ever seen it before. It looks like something you could find in any beach town or on the Internet. Why in hell would somebody want to steal that?"

"It's mine, Ty. My mug that I've drunk from for over fifteen years. I got it in Key West. I don't know how it got in your van."

Tyler glanced again at the picture and then said, "You think I took it, don't you, Ollie?"

"I don't know what to think, Ty. All I know is that is my cup that was found in your van."

Tyler screwed his mouth into a small shape. He looked around the office before staring at Ollie. "I didn't know it was your mug, and I didn't take it."

"Look, Tyler. I'll represent you no matter what. I just need to know the truth."

"So, you don't think I've told you the truth? You don't believe me, Ollie? Why would I ever lie to you, huh? Haven't we already been through the worst?" asked Tyler with a rising voice.

Tyler's eyes were haunting and accusatory. Ollie couldn't maintain the staring contest and dropped his eyes to the pictures scattered on his desk. There was something that nagged at his brain, but he just couldn't put his finger on the cause.

Ollie glanced back at Tyler and now saw hurt on his friend's face. The lawyer's protective nature took over at that moment.

"I'm sorry, Tyler. Of course, I believe you, man. I know you wouldn't lie to me. I admit I've doubted you a little since the arrest. There's been something bothering me about all this even more than having those doubts about you, though. Not only is somebody messing with you, they're screwing with me as well. That's the only logical conclusion I can come up with, even if it seems irrational. So, why the two of us? We've got to figure this out together."

Tyler tried to smile although it came across more like a contorted twist of lips and teeth. "That's the best thing you've said to me in a long time, Ollie. If anybody can, we will."

CHAPTER 27

Ollie had been eating lunch at The Rookery since the seventies and still enjoyed their food as much as he ever had. Its central location on Cherry Street made it a destination for employees of all downtown businesses, and the variety of choices on the menu kept them coming back often. It had an old feel that he liked. As he did on many occasions when a trip to the courthouse was necessary, Ollie decided to have his mid-day meal at the eatery and had arranged to meet Holly between classes.

Upon arrival at the restaurant a little before one o'clock, the lawyer saw there were a couple of empty sidewalk tables available. Normally, he opted to dine inside where he could enjoy his meal while seated in the privacy of a wooden booth. Because it was a sunny and cool early fall day, Ollie decided to request one of the colorful blue metal outdoor tables. It conjured

up memories of locations other than Macon, Georgia where he
had consumed food and beverages in outside venues. It wasn't
Key West, but it was a great idea for the hometown, and Ollie
hoped more restaurants would try the concept when the weather
allowed.

The hostess escorted him to his table and left two menus.
He shifted in his chair so he could see in both directions of the
street. He saw Holly farther up the sidewalk near the Greek deli
where he also regularly dined. She walked toward him, and the
closer she got the more beautiful she became. Her hair was
pulled back in a simple ponytail, and it bounced with every step.
She wore an orange and black ensemble that would make any
Mercerian proud. Ollie thought she appeared happy.

Holly broke into a big grin the closer she got to her dad.
The single dimple was prominent and gave her a unique charm.
She gave a little wave with her left hand accompanying the
exposure of white teeth. A group of men working on one of the
downtown facades stopped what they were doing as she passed
by and one of them made a wolf whistle that could be heard a
block away. She gave them a friendly nod, but never broke
stride as she neared the restaurant.

Ollie stood up as she entered the seated area blocked off
with a black metal railing. They embraced and Holly kissed him
on the cheek.

"Well, you look like you're a Mercer student, and I think
the local construction crew approves of how you're dressed,
too," said Ollie as they sat down.

"Yeah, I can pass as an older one or maybe an alum like you. I can't believe how much I've gotten into this student thing again. And, I'm really into all the team sports. All of our teams are good. Now, as for the whistling workers, I guess I'm flattered that somebody still notices," replied Holly with a laugh.

"I'm glad you're enjoying the experience, Holly. The last few years, I've rediscovered the teams, too. The basketball team had me pumped when they won the conference and then made the NCAA tournament. When they beat Duke in the first round, I literally shed tears. The football and baseball teams have been great, as well."

"I know you've said you played sports when you were younger. Did you ever hope to play at the college level?" she asked.

Ollie slipped back into the past when he was a star pitcher on his high school team. Those had been good times that ended way too soon. There had been some interest from a few different colleges back then. The days slipped away after that fateful night, and he never played competitively again. He had thought it would be too painful not to see Libby in her favorite seat near the dugout.

"Hmm, I was like a lot of kids, I guess. I wanted to play as long as I could, but other things got in the way. I like to think I could've played."

The waitress appeared and asked for their drink orders. Ollie asked for sweet tea, and Holly ordered unsweet tea with lemon. She also asked that the spoon be left out of her glass.

"I bet you could've played for the Bears. One thing I've decided about you is that you're modest. I wish I could've seen you play," said Holly.

He felt his face flush at the compliment. "Thanks, I'll have to see if I can round up some old eight millimeter film my dad shot back in the day. We transferred it to DVD. There's some footage of me playing in a few games, and one of me when I threw a no-hitter. Anyway, that's enough about ancient history. I haven't seen you in a few days. Everything okay?"

She beamed. "Everything is so good, right now. No kidding, I think it's the best time of my life. I like my classes, even the boring ones like contracts. My professors treat me well because I'm not intimidated. I've made some good friends, although most are at least eight to ten years younger. And, ta-da, I've met somebody I find promising."

Ollie sat back in his chair. He brought his hands before his face and formed a triangle with his fingers. There was a smirk on his lips.

"Last thing, first. Particulars, please," said Ollie.

"You mean, you don't want to hear about my contracts class?" she giggled.

He grinned and said, "Offer, acceptance, consideration, contract, right? No, silly young'un, I want to hear about this someone you've met."

The waitress appeared and asked if they were ready to order. Neither had opened the menus, but both knew they wanted one of the signature burgers the restaurant was known for. Ollie opted for the Classic City Cheeseburger with bleu cheese crumbles, and Holly chose the Allman Burger that came with Swiss cheese and sautéed mushrooms. The lawyer also got onion rings while the student chose battered fries. Hardly a low calorie meal, but Ollie and Holly had both skipped breakfast and were starved.

"So, let's resume our conversation," said Ollie.

Holly's dazzling smile was even brighter in the sunlight. "Well, his name is Shawn Matheson. I met him over the weekend, and we really hit it off from the start. I'm not sure of his age, but I think he's a few years older than me. He's nice-looking and is in good shape. Loves live music, like me, and he's already turned me on to Randall Bramblett. Have you heard of him? I know how much you like singer-songwriters."

"Sounds like Shawn has turned you on more than to just music," said Ollie with a raised brow.

He continued, "Yeah, I've been a fan of Randall for a long time. He's never received quite the recognition I think he deserves. If Shawn likes him, I approve of the guy already."

"I think you'll like him. He's a gentleman, like you are. He's not pushy either, like a lot of guys I've been around. Oh, and he drinks single malt scotch."

"What does he do for a living?"

"As I understand it, he's an entrepreneur and works in construction. He told me he's working on some of the renovation work in downtown. I wondered if the two of you had ever met, but he said no. Shawn knows who you are, though. He said he would like to meet you," she said with some excitement.

"His name doesn't ring a bell with me. If you like him so much, I'm pretty sure he'll be fine with me. You're a grown woman with a good head on your shoulders, so I trust your judgment. You seeing him again soon?"

"We've set a dinner date for Wednesday, so maybe the boss will let me off early that day, you think?" she said with a wink.

"I expect so, I hear he's got a soft spot for you," he replied.

The waitress returned with the drinks, and the two of them sucked the cold beverages through straws. The conversation turned from her new friend to some of the cases she had been working on for her dad. They discussed different strategies over bites of the juicy burgers that were cooked to perfection. Ollie appreciated the freshness of her observations as much as he did the food.

"What's new with Tyler's case? I know you met with the DA and then he came in afterwards, but we really haven't talked about it," said Holly.

The lawyer slowed his chewing not wanting to discuss the matter with his daughter. He had deliberately taken that case off the table with Holly for reasons he wasn't exactly sure how to describe, but had not told her. He trusted her completely, but his friendship with Tyler didn't allow him to share the complexities of their relationship or the fears he felt until he had at least asked his friend for permission to include his daughter's input. Ollie felt she could help, but he needed to talk to Tyler first. He couldn't help but remember she had been investigating him as a potential burglar while she was employed in her former job, and that fact would have to be disclosed.

"I've seen some of the evidence. Mostly, the items taken from the van were not things you would think of as the typical burglar's targeted booty. It doesn't make a lot of sense to me at this point as to what motive Tyler would have to commit such a series of thefts. He denies involvement, and I have to believe him," said Ollie.

Holly had a funny look on her face. "Why do I get the feeling you don't want me working on this case? Is it because I told you he was a person of interest in a case I was investigating? I can probably help with the investigation if nothing else. You do know I'm loyal to you, right?" she asked.

Ollie sipped his drink, swallowed and cleared his throat. He toyed with an onion ring before responding, "Of course I know you're on my side, but, I must admit I've been torn by something in the case. Makes me not to want you caught up in the middle. Until I can talk again to Tyler about you getting involved, I'd really prefer you staying out of this. There's already a predicament, and I don't want to add anything else to it. Trust me on this, and I promise I'll tell you more later."

She studied Ollie's face for clues and then said a simple, "Okay, Dad."

He was relieved for the time being. He was afraid it would be tricky going down the road, however.

CHAPTER 28

Ollie was in the middle of a dream. Part of him knew if wasn't real, but he couldn't quite accept it because he was so content in the vision.

He was flat on his back gazing at the azure sky dotted with fluffy clouds. Extending his arm into the air toward a patch of whiteness, he cupped his hand so that it framed what now resembled cotton candy. Ollie smiled at the thought of pulling the sweet confection from the air and letting it dissolve in his mouth. He closed his fist around the cloud and then quickly pulled it inside pretending to eat it. When he looked back to the spot, the one he had consumed was no longer there, and he somehow felt lighter in his stomach.

Libby was angled at his side and laughed at his antics. She placed her hand on his belly and began rubbing it like Aladdin's Lamp.

"Was that a good dessert?" she asked.

He turned on his side so that he faced her less than a foot apart. They stared into each other's eyes, and Ollie felt as if he were diving into her soul. The blanket they lay upon was soft, and the vibrant green grass underneath provided extra cushioning. The kiss that followed was long and deep with urgency both felt. He actually experienced an ache in his chest as their mouths parted.

"You taste a lot better than a cloud. I think I could eat you alive," he whispered.

She teased him with a nip on his bottom lip and then kissed him once more before turning on her back. She sat up and began surveying the scene from Coleman Hill. The spot was popular as a place to enjoy a picnic and the Macon skyline.

He remained on his side for a few moments and studied her profile. Nobody could tell him that a sixteen year-old was incapable of feeling true love. At that moment in time, he would've done anything for the beautiful girl sitting beside him. He wanted to spend the rest of his life with her. *Please don't let this end,* he silently prayed.

Ollie rolled over and tried to sit up, but something strong held him down. Terror seized him as the bright blue sky swirled above into a dark soup. He tried calling out to Libby that they needed to leave, but his efforts came out as an inarticulate croaking sound.

The happy fantasy was changing into something completely the opposite. The part of Ollie's consciousness that knew this wasn't real now wanted out of the situation. There was an evil presence not letting him go no matter how hard he tried.

When he looked to where Libby had just been moments before, Ollie discovered she had disappeared, and teenaged Tyler occupied the spot. A chilling wind was starting to blow, but his friend didn't seem to care. His fair skin contrasted against the darkening sky changing everything in the dream to be black or white. He was hunched over with something in his hands that Ollie wasn't able to see.

"You know she loves me, too," said Tyler barely audible over the moaning wind.

Ollie still had trouble speaking. "I know, but it's not the same kind of love, Ty," he finally managed.

"If you weren't around, I bet she would love me like you," he replied.

"Maybe, but I don't think so. What've you got in your hands?" asked Ollie as Tyler kept playing with the object.

He turned to Ollie and showed him. It was a tortoise shell barrette that Libby had worn as a kid.

Ollie was having trouble breathing now. It came shallow and ragged from his heaving chest. He watched in horror as Tyler morphed into his maniacal brother. The barrette changed into a knife dripping with blood. Malicious intent shone from the dark eyes, and Ollie thrashed as he screamed.

The nightmare was over, and Ollie was wide-awake in his bed. He was twisted in the sheets and damp with sweat. His heart was beating like a drum that he could hear in his head. He couldn't remember having a bad dream like this since he was much younger. Did it mean anything?

As he was trying to block out imagery from the nightmare, Ollie heard a board creak in the hallway near the bedroom door. Normally he wouldn't give such a sound a second thought in the old home, but waking up after the dream had his nerves on end. He knew he had to get up and check it out if he was going to get back to sleep.

He began extricating himself from the covers while letting his eyes adjust to the darkness. When he was completely unwrapped from the sheets and comforter, he swung his feet and legs over the side of the bed and found his worn slippers.

His first step toward the door after putting on his shoes caused a muffled crack underneath his foot. Ollie stopped in his tracks and listened. Silence followed for what seemed an eternity. He began the journey again at a quicker pace until he reached the door that was slightly ajar. Holding his hand on the knob, he hesitated when his heart skipped a beat.

Tightness gripped his heart, and the pain made it difficult to breathe. Now the sound he had heard earlier was forgotten and not the main problem any longer. He needed to get to a hospital instead. Fast.

CHAPTER 29

The last night and following day had been hectic to say the least. Ollie was propped in the hospital bed feeling relieved not to have doctors, nurses, technicians and other related medical personnel cloying around with never-ending prodding, poking and pricking parts of his body. Thinking back, it was the first time since the deadly fight fifty years ago that he had faced death, and it had shaken him to his core.

He had realized he was in the throes of a heart attack, and Ollie had known the next step was to get to a phone and call for help. Being alone made it a requirement that he take that responsibility before he was incapable of doing so. His very survival depended on getting medical help immediately.

He had retraced his steps across the room to the stand beside the bed where a phone was located. Each step brought additional anxiety, as the discomfort in his chest didn't subside.

After reaching the landline telephone, Ollie had experienced another disquieting moment, as he didn't initially hear a dial tone. The flat sound had finally engaged though, and he punched 911. The operator asked the nature of the emergency, and he had paused because his voice had disappeared during his ragged breathing.

My name is Oliver Tucker, and I think I'm having a coronary. Please send help.

The conversation had been mainly one-sided since Ollie wasn't sure he could speak any further. The operator had stayed on the line talking in a calm manner and telling him help was on the way. Maybe it was due to the hospital being less than two miles away, or maybe to the early morning non-busy hours, or possibly to her assurances, but the paramedics had made it in mere minutes. There had been surprise when they didn't have to force entry, as the front door was unlocked. Valuable time had been saved as a result.

Everything was pretty much a blur for the next few hours. He only remembered bits and pieces. The ride in the ambulance, the blaring siren, and being wheeled on the stretcher etched his brain like the event from another time. There was little doubt in his mind that the emergency medical services team that worked on him from the first moment of their arrival and the continued efforts of the professionals in the hospital had saved his life.

Before he had been taken to the hospital, EMS had administered oxygen, aspirin and nitroglycerin to Ollie. There had been drawing of blood and an EKG confirming Ollie's prior self-diagnosis. He knew the quicker the treatment began the better his chances for survival and the less chance for serious damage to his heart.

Within the first hour after getting to the cardiac care unit, Ollie had been prepped and taken for a heart cath that showed two arterial blockages. Using the latest techniques, balloon inflation occurred and stents had been inserted to repair the arteries.

At some point after the procedure, one of the nurses had asked him for his next of kin's name and phone number. Holly had appeared shortly thereafter and was allowed a brief visit. He had not talked with her but a few moments and had seen the level of her emotions through the tears welling in her eyes. He tried to assure her he was going to be fine and had asked her to let the office staff know his status.

Ollie didn't consider himself an introvert, but he had tried to remain a private person for most of his adult life. He had never been a patient in a hospital since the few days he spent after the long ago attack and had not had any major health issues in the subsequent years. Now, it seemed like every few minutes someone was standing over him asking him questions, some of which he would prefer not to answer. All those things led him to feel as if he were under a microscope and not much in control of the situation, and he didn't like it even a little bit.

Periodically, Ollie would watch the heart monitor. *At least the ticker's still working,* he thought.

He wondered if he should reassess things and think about retiring. He didn't believe he was living very stressfully even though the case against Tyler was something weighing heavily on his mind. Ollie knew he was able to leave the practice behind if he needed or wanted to, but to do so now might cause him even more stress knowing his friend depended on him. He also would worry about his employees being without a job. Besides, he had really begun enjoying the work again and helping his clients since Holly had come aboard. She provided a new purpose, and he didn't want to squander it.

He had to do what his doctor had instructed in order to optimize the remainder of his life, whatever choices he made regarding work. The doctor's directives had been specific. Ollie had suffered permanent damage to his heart, but at least the loss of muscle was listed as less than ten percent. The cardiologist warned that Ollie would need to go through rehab for at least a month, watch his diet and follow the exercise program that was recommended by his cardiac care team. A cocktail of medications would now be required for the duration of his time on earth, and the doctor had also told him that he might experience increased anxiety and even depression. He was going to endure changes, and it was up to him to make them happen, if he could. Otherwise, he was not going to be around for long.

CHAPTER 30

Holly was experiencing a range of emotions directly related to recent activities. Happy that her dad was now home, relieved he wasn't suffering any pain, yet sad that he seemed to be withdrawing inside himself, she wanted to somehow bring him out of the funk into which he was sinking. She had only been involved in his life for a relatively short period of time, but already loved him with a ferocity she had reserved for her mother.

She thought of her mom and the emptiness caused by the loss. Mom had always been her best friend before death claimed her life by the bitch called cancer. Holly couldn't bear the thought she could now lose her dad to the bastard named heart disease.

She remembered one of the last conversations with Mom. It had been tortured and ragged as her mother battled through pain and the drugs that only helped some.

I want you to live your life without regrets, Holly. You shouldn't make the same mistakes I have.

Mom, I don't know what you're talking about. You've been the best parent anybody would want.

I should've been honest with you about your father. I've been stupid for not telling you about him before now. I'm sure he would've been good to you. So sorry he's not been in your life. Doesn't even know you exist, and that's my fault.

Holly recalled being surprised by the revelations from that dialogue. Her mother had told her for the first time her dad's real identity, something she had not done before because of reasons Holly couldn't understand.

I think he's a good man. Mixed up, but I guess we all are. Oliver Tucker is his name. And, God, was he handsome! Probably still is. When I met him, he took my breath away. You've got his eyes. Hair, too.

Why didn't you tell me, Mom?

At first the reasons made sense to me, Holly. You see, we only knew one another for a little less than three months. It was love for me, but it never was the same for him. He could never give it back like I wanted. Held back his feelings. But I found out he had loved another, and that it had ended when she died. Said he didn't want to ever feel that way again. As soon as I knew you were inside me, I had to get out of town. Didn't want him to feel responsible. I felt like it was my fault for getting pregnant, but there was no way I was going to lose you.

I moved back to midtown Atlanta near your grandparents because I knew they would help, but not judge me too harshly. They never did, and it made being a single parent a lot easier.

After you were born, I thought several times about letting him know. But, you kept growing up and were a happy kid. I couldn't tell that you were suffering by not having him in your life and with the passing of time; I thought it would only complicate things for everybody.

Holly thought about how ironic it was that neither of her parents had ever married. They had each retreated within themselves over doomed love affairs, and that was just too sad to think about. She couldn't help but believe they could've found some happiness together if efforts had been attempted.

The fact of the matter was she couldn't say a lot about their failed love affair because she was no spring chicken herself, and yet she felt like she had never been in love. Holly had been involved with guys at least since her senior year in high school, but no one had ever been "the one."

She couldn't explain adequately why that was so. It wasn't due to any demanding aspect of her personality, or at least she didn't think that was the case. She had spent more time than a lot of women she knew trying to make a name for herself career-wise, but it had ultimately proven pointless since she was no longer an investigator. However, at least those skills were now proving valuable working toward a law degree as well as employed in her dad's office.

Maybe, she had finally met the right man in Shawn. Of course, it was too soon to know, but he was unlike anybody else she had ever dated. They had only been out a few times, but he was attentive to her without being annoying, confident without being cocky, and just the right amount of open and mysterious to be interesting. She liked the way he listened to what she said and always looked her in the eyes when they talked.

They had kissed the first night after the concert and she had felt like putty. He had not made any efforts to pressure her into anything further, but they had exchanged phone numbers, and he had promised to call her for a dinner date.

Since then they had been to lunch a couple of times, dinner three times, followed by breakfast after the last date. She was no prude, but it had been the first time she had been intimate with a man in quite a while. She had thought it had been well worth the wait because he was such a skilled and patient lover.

His downtown loft was tastefully decorated and had provided the perfect backdrop for seduction. The view of the city, the softness of the couch and the taste of pinot noir on her palate had enhanced her expectations of pleasure. She shivered involuntarily remembering the coarseness of his fingertips rubbing on the bare skin of her neck just before she kissed him. It had provided the invitation for him to take action, and she hadn't been disappointed in the night that followed.

Yeah, she liked him a lot, but she had other things to consider at the moment that prevented her from taking a deeper emotional plunge with Shawn. Primarily, she had to help her dad get back on an even keel. She hoped Shawn would understand she might not be able to see him as often over the next several weeks.

For the short term, Holly resolved to put in more time at the office. It would be difficult balancing her law school lectures and the study obligations it took to be ready for the classes. Very few freshman law students had part-time jobs, as they were frowned upon by the administration.

She had to help her father, though. He had given her hope for future happiness that had only recently been imagined. She had dared to allow a dream of becoming his law partner one day. The first step to helping him be less stressed was to resolve Tyler Crenshaw's case. She decided that would become her primary goal. Everything else would shift down the priority list for now.

CHAPTER 31

Tyler puttered around his home without any definite plans. He carried a Budweiser in his hand and sipped absentmindedly as he wandered. Since his arrest and release from jail, his mind had been jumbled, and he had not been quite himself. He had always been handy and kept a list of projects in his head that he would complete when he had time. Now that he seemingly had plenty of free time to work on any of the tasks, he couldn't find the needed motivation to get started.

He walked out the back door of the house and slumped into one of the Adirondack chairs located on a large attached custom made deck. It was an area where he generally loved to spend time because it held a spectacular view of the rear of his property. Tyler had always enjoyed nature, and from this seat he could watch all sorts of natural activity. It was like having a personal copy of National Geographic on a grander scale. He often saw deer and other wildlife in his backyard, which brought him a sort of peace he couldn't find in other aspects of his life.

When he first bought the acreage in one of the adjoining counties from where he grew up, Tyler was still in his twenties. It was the seventies and property was a lot cheaper back then. Tyler had worked hard after getting out of the military and saved most of what he made. Along with the inheritance he received after his father's death from an automobile accident, he had more than enough money to buy the place that was still his home after almost forty years.

He had wanted to build a house that he designed and in an area that was undeveloped. He still remembered loving the woods near the Macon neighborhood where he grew up, and had made it a requirement that any property he purchased would have as much forest as he could afford. The initial ten acres he bought had now grown to eighty. With the exception of the cleared area where the house, garage and his large shop stood, the rest of the property was heavily wooded and as natural as you could find this close to civilization. The nearest house to his was at least a half-mile away.

As Tyler sat and drank his beer, he saw a silver-haired fox at the edge of the tree line. The animal was focused on something that Tyler couldn't see in the tall grass closer to the house. In a way, the fox was a lot like he was. He watched and studied the surroundings before deciding his course of action.

His mind drifted. *It was all so fucked up. How did it ever get this way?*

When he was a kid, he had always felt different than everybody else. He didn't even have a friend he could remember before he got to know Ollie and Libby. They had made him feel normal. He was even able to become friendly, at least to some degree, with other people although it was never completely the same with anyone but them. He had felt closer to those two friends than to even his family.

The few years he had with his best friends had come to an abrupt end, and then everything had changed forever. It was all because his brother had gone off the deep end over a girl. On some plane in his brain he understood how a woman could make you lose your way. Libby had made him feel sort of like that when she smiled at him, and she wasn't even his girlfriend. But, why would Matt go so far? It was too crazy. He wished that he had tried talking to his brother about what he had been going through, but they had never been that close.

What was the name of the girl Matt had dated? It had been so long ago he couldn't remember. He thought it was a common name like Mary Smith, but he really couldn't recall. For another fleeting moment he wondered whatever happened to the girl.

The fox had shifted and moved closer in the grass. It was almost as if it didn't need to use its feet to change positions. Whatever it was following was in mortal danger and probably didn't realize the threat.

So many years had passed since the tragedy, yet the event lingered. He had found his way in the world the best he could. Ollie was still there for him, but his friend had other problems to deal with. Tyler knew his old friend would never let him down, no matter what. He had proven it so many times. But, it seemed unfair to depend on him now. Ollie's recent heart attack had been unexpected, and the risk of losing him troubled Tyler. The last conversation they had left him worried. As a result, he felt it was necessary for him to take more responsibility and clean up all the mess.

The predator pounced and from Tyler's vantage point the prize in its mouth appeared to be some type of rodent. For the first time since he had spotted the fox, the animal looked toward him. It didn't look afraid of the man and went into the woods a few moments later.

Yep, I need to become a fox, thought Tyler, *to catch a rat.*

CHAPTER 32

It had been a few days since Ollie's release from the hospital and though he wanted to reestablish his routine like it had been, he had found that he just couldn't muster enough energy. Part of it was physical because that tired feeling had not gone away and even climbing the stairs felt like a challenge. The larger part of it was mental because of the fear and anxiety that had crept inside his soul threatening his emotional control.

His doctor had warned him of such, but he made short shrift of those cautions. He was a survivor and had gone through a knife attack as well as the recent heart attack, so he thought he understood.

Only people going through stuff could know about it, right? You only truly understand what you experience, he thought.

He was having more trouble with motivation this morning, and he attributed the problem to the medications the doctor had prescribed since being released. Whether it was true or not, he knew he was going to have to live with it from now on. Therefore, he had to get over it and start counting his blessings.

The first one was having his office downstairs because it provided the opportunity to be nearby at a moment's notice if needed. He could easily stay in his upstairs living quarters and rest as much as he thought was necessary. He wouldn't normally stay there during office hours, but these weren't normal times.

By 9:30 a.m., he still had not taken a shower or thought about getting dressed for work. Ollie remained in cotton pajamas while ensconced in his recliner. Remnants of a toasted bagel with strawberry jam were on the table beside his chair as was a half-cup of now cold coffee. Mindless chatter came from the television set as some talk show host gushed about a movie star and her latest film. He didn't care anything about what was being said, but it somehow helped keep his mind from slipping into panic mode again.

Ollie flinched when the telephone rang. It seemed the most routine things now caused him to stress.

"Yeah," he answered.

"Boss, no pressure down here, but we've had a few clients wanting to see you. Do you want me to make some appointments later today?" asked Red.

Ollie found himself chewing on his bottom lip as he contemplated his response. He had never felt this way before.

"Who wants to see me?"

"I've had four calls from former clients. Mrs. Clements wants to talk about revising her will. Tony Bussey needs to see you about some trouble his daughter has gotten into. John Anthony thinks he might want a divorce, but he wants to discuss it with you first. Hack Thomas said he couldn't talk about his problem over the phone."

Ollie sighed audibly. He was familiar with the mentioned clients and had counseled with all of them on numerous occasions over the years. In many instances they had met with him and only needed a little hand-holding through some imagined problem. It was part of the job, and he didn't mind most of the time. He liked all of those people and seeing any of them professionally or otherwise.

"Okay, set each of them up this afternoon if they're available. If not, tomorrow morning will work. I need to get a shower before I come in," said Ollie with his voice trailing off.

He was feeling a little better because people needed him. That was a big part of being a lawyer.

What if he couldn't help? Would it be better if they found other representation?

Ollie had never second-guessed himself before and part of him knew this wasn't right. *I'm losing my grip,* he thought.

"Boss, are you still there?" Red's voice showed concern.

"Yeah, I'm here. I'll be down in a little while," he answered before hanging up the phone.

He glanced back at the television as the host, guest, and audience were all laughing at something Ollie hadn't heard. It didn't matter because nothing seemed funny to him at the moment. He clicked the remote to mute the sound and watched the screen in silence. For the first time of the morning, a smile crept to his face and then he actually laughed out loud at the silliness of the situation. The show was funnier as a silent feature.

This time he didn't cringe when the phone again rang, and the smile remained as he recognized Holly's cell number on the caller id. "How's the budding young lawyer this morning?" he said answering the call.

"Glad to be in between classes at the moment. Thought I'd check in to see what's shaking at work, and Red told me you hadn't been in yet. So, I thought I'd call the man himself to see if he's okay."

"I'm moving a little slowly this morning, but otherwise I'm fine. I'm about to jump in the shower, and then I'll make a grand entrance," he replied with what he hoped wasn't false confidence.

"Good, I'll be through with class early and plan to be there to help as much as possible this afternoon. I've even been thinking about the Crenshaw case and wanted to talk about that some, too, if you're up for it."

"I need all the help I can get. Maybe you can sit in on some client interviews after lunch. It'll be good practical experience for you."

"Really? I'd love to do that, Dad. I promise I'll keep my mouth shut and take good notes."

"Of course, I'll have to let the clients know you're my assistant, and if they shouldn't want you in the meeting, I'll have to ask you to leave. I don't think any of them will mind, though."

"I can't wait. I bet I'm the only freshman that gets to meet actual clients! I'll see you about one, Dad. I've got to run for now. Glad you're feeling better," she said before hanging up and Ollie could respond.

He cradled the phone and looked back at the television. The diminutive female host was waving her arms wildly and had an odd expression on her face. It made him start snickering again and finally got him out of his chair.

***

Holly bopped into her father's office just as he was finishing home-cooked vegetables from the Bear's Den. Red had brought him the Styrofoam container laden with the tasty food after she had enjoyed her mid-day meal from the establishment located near the Mercer University campus. Ollie often ate there and had asked his receptionist to get him a plate to go when finding out her lunch plans.

"That smells delicious. Heart healthy, I'm sure," said Holly with a raised eyebrow.

"Hey, give me a break. I'm only eating vegetables and didn't even touch my cornbread," Ollie said pointing to the yellow square still wrapped in cellophane.

He shoved another bite of turnip greens into his mouth as she said, "I'm betting those pieces of ham I just saw disappear wouldn't qualify as produce. What's left of your squash and black-eyed peas was probably seasoned with some of the same hog, too."

"Okay, I admit I'm a southern boy through and through, so I like some pork-flavored veggies. I'm going for little victories, girl. I think leaving off the country fried steak, rice and gravy qualify as an improvement. Cut me some slack, please."

She laughed and said, "Okay, Dad. You're right, that's a little victory for you. I hope you'll keep it in mind every time you eat to at least delete some of the bad stuff from your diet. It would even be better if you would substitute something healthy. I'm counting on you being around for a while."

"Deal," he said closing the lid on the container. "Let me take this to the kitchen, and we'll get ready for the first client of the afternoon."

When Ollie got back to his office, Holly had taken out her laptop and was doing legal research. It was something the old lawyer didn't really like to do, and he was glad she seemed to enjoy the process. He still did most of his research the old fashioned way by using his substantial collection of books, but she preferred the speed and convenience of a computer.

"You look really deep into something," said Ollie as he sat back down at his desk.

"Yeah, I've been looking at some cases we might could use to challenge the search of Tyler Crenshaw's vehicle when he was arrested. I was going to surprise you by trying my hand at drafting a motion to suppress," she replied.

Ollie showed initial surprise and then thought about other instances when Holly had taken the initiative to work on something he had not really asked her to do in advance. He realized he shouldn't be shocked by the efforts, but he couldn't help but be impressed.

"I'm a little overwhelmed you would undertake such a project especially since I haven't even asked you to look into it. That's pretty advanced for a first-year law student."

She stopped tapping on the keyboard and looked at her father. "I can tell this case is causing you the most strain right now, so it's the one I want to help with more than anything else. It makes a lot of sense because of my criminal law background. After my years in investigation, I think I'm a little more advanced than the typical freshman," Holly replied with an edge in her voice.

"Of course you are; I didn't mean to sound like that. You don't know how much it means to have your help," he paused before continuing. "I'm going to tell you something in all sincerity that has nothing at all to do with you being related. You are doing an incredible job here. In the few months since you started, you've shown more ability in the shortest time than anyone I've ever employed. I'm including everybody. I'm convinced you're going to be a great lawyer."

Holly's mouth fell open. She had rarely heard him give compliments, which made his words that much sweeter to her ears. Before she could say anything in response, the phone rang on Ollie's desk announcing the arrival of Francine Clements. He asked Red to bring her back to his office.

"Mrs. Clements is one of my oldest clients. I think she'll be fine with you sitting in, but she's quite a character. Try not to get too tickled," said Ollie with a twinkle in his eye.

Red escorted the client into the office preventing Holly once again from making comment. The lady's presence took over the room and everybody in it. She was barely five feet tall dressed in a tailored black Gucci pantsuit and a white Oscar de la Renta blouse. On her feet and contrasting somewhat with the rest of her outfit, she sported Merrell Avesso black suede flats. The total cost of her outfit was more than the average Maconite's monthly mortgage. The smell of her dated perfume permeated the space, causing the others to want a gas mask.

"Okay, baby. Thank you for bringing me back here. I know you were just being kind to an old woman you probably don't think has any sense left. You just remember what I said about that man of yours. He needs to go ahead and marry you before your looks start to fade. You're a precious girl and pretty as a picture, but we all start losing it after a while. You wouldn't believe how good-looking I was when I was your age, and look at me now. Not that it matters that much. I've had more men than I knew what to do with. Maybe that's why I got married so many times. If that guy can't make up his mind pretty soon, you go find you another one. Tell him Frankie told you so."

Red had been trying to make her exit, but Mrs. Clements held on to her hand like a vise during the monologue. When she finally let go, Red almost ran from the room as the milky skin of her face turned scarlet.

Holly had risen from her seat when the client entered, as had her dad. He made his way to the doorway where she still stood with the use of a pronged cane.

"Well, hello handsome. You're the one who got away. How are you, Oliver? You appear a little peaked to me."

"I'm doing pretty well, Frankie. Probably better than I deserve," he said as he hugged her. "How have you been?"

"Bad and bawdy, you sexy thang," she said with an exaggerated wink.

Ollie shook his head side-to-side and said, "Some things never change. Frankie, I want to introduce you to my legal assistant, Holly Lee. She's a student at Mercer Law and doing a great job for me. I'd like to have her sit in on our meeting, if it's okay. Holly, this is a long-time client, Mrs. Francine Clements."

The two women appraised one another for a moment with Holly taking the lead. She walked forward and held out her hand and said, "It's very nice to meet you, Mrs. Clements. I love your outfit. You have great taste in clothes."

"Well, aren't you a silver-tongued devil. Pretty, too," Mrs. Clements said taking Holly's hand and holding on to it. "You look a little old to be in school. You must be special because Oliver has never asked to let anybody working for him be a part of any meeting I've had with him."

Holly smiled at the older woman and replied, "I can't say special, just fortunate to be in the same office. I'd be honored if you would allow my presence, but I understand if you'd rather be alone for your consultation."

"I don't have a problem with you being here. However, I do have a problem with this damned hip. If you don't mind, I need to sit my old ass down now," the woman said.

Ollie pulled out a chair for her to sit down while suppressing laughter. Holly couldn't help but let out a short giggle. Mrs. Clements had an amused look on her face while watching them both.

Holly took a seat a discreet distance from her father and the client. She picked up a yellow legal pad and took out a pen to use for notes. Ollie sat down directly across from the lady as she stretched the leg that had been favored with the cane.

"Frankie, I haven't seen you the last couple of years, but you haven't aged a bit. The only difference I can see is the walking stick."

"It's been three years and I'm not sure I believe you, but I guess there's not much difference in how you look between eighty-five and eighty-eight. As for the cane, it's better than a fricking walker, wheelchair, or hip replacement surgery. I'm fighting like hell against any of those alternatives. How about you, handsome? Are you sure you're okay?"

Ollie's smile faded a tad. He hated talking about himself on a good day, and he didn't want to say anything about his recent problems with his heart. Francine Clements knew half of

Macon, and he didn't want any news of the health issues to be spread to anybody else from her or anyone else. He always avoided telling lies, but he didn't want to blab about personal issues either.

"I could stand a little sun and a maybe some rest and relaxation. I might make a little trip to Long Boat Key in a couple of weeks if work slacks off a bit. That brings me back to you, Frankie. What can I help you with?"

Francine Clements was an astute woman. She seemed to sense her lawyer pretty well since he had represented her since the seventies and that he didn't want to talk about his physical wellbeing. They exchanged a moment. She let it drop and said, "I want to change my will."

Ollie gazed at his old client and said jokingly, "Again?"

This was a private joke that Holly didn't know anything about. She watched the two of them as they laughed good-naturedly.

Francine finally quit laughing and turned to Holly. "Ollie is trying to be funny, Sweetie. Actually, he's made me laugh, so I guess he succeeded. I've changed my last will and testament quite a few times over the years. But, you've got to understand. I don't have any children of my own. My beneficiaries are nephews and nieces who piss me off on a regular basis. Therefore, as a mature woman of means, I exercise my privilege to cut them off when I need to."

"Who's made you mad this time, Frankie?" asked Ollie.

"Don't you even try to get all judgmental on me, Oliver. Whenever I've changed my will, I've had good reasons. I don't do this without good reason."

"It's not my job to make value judgments on any of your beneficiaries, Frankie. You know your wishes are my commands. I've got a thick file to prove it," he said holding up the client folder.

"I'm curious, Oliver. I know you've never married, and I guess you don't have children of your own. I also suspect you've done very well financially over the years. So, in some ways disposing of your estate is like my situation. Have you changed your will over the years?"

Ollie tried to keep his face blank. Frankie had always been brash and never seemed to mind putting him on the spot over the course of knowing her. Once again she was digging at his personal life.

"You want to know something about me, Frankie, that you don't already know? I never tell client's confidential information any more than I tell my own."

Francine Clements grinned. She first looked at Ollie and then at Holly. It was almost as if she knew more than she was letting known. "God, I'm glad you're my lawyer, handsome," she said.

Everybody was silent for a moment, and then Francine continued, "Do you know that I had your friend Tyler do some work for me?"

Ollie struggled not to show emotion. This woman was trying him way too much, and he was beginning to feel agitation toward her. She stared at him as if observing for a reaction.

"What? You didn't know? Tyler Crenshaw has done several jobs for me over the years. Anything to do with a construction project, no matter how big or small, I call him. By the way, I'm counting on you to get him off the charges filed against him. There's no way he's guilty of a crime."

"Frankie, I can't discuss another client with you," Ollie said with a disapproving glance.

"I'm not asking you to discuss just anybody, Oliver. He's our friend, first. Sorry, I don't mean to interfere. I guess growing old makes me speak my mind a little too freely sometimes. I'll change the subject to why I'm here. I want to change my will. Are you going to help me or not?"

Ollie let out a breath through his nose and breathed deeply before speaking. It was a method he used when trying to calm himself.

"Of course, Frankie. You're one of my favorite people as well as a client I hold dear. Let's discuss what you have in mind," he said closing the subject of Tyler.

Over the next thirty minutes the lawyer and client reviewed the changes to be made to the will. There was only one major modification dealing with a nephew experiencing a drug problem. Rather than leave him a substantial amount of money upon Francine's death, it was decided to set up a trust to provide him a monthly income. The other alterations dealt with acquired items of jewelry since the last will had been drawn and how to divide them between various heirs.

Since there was time before the next appointment and to save Francine another trip to Ollie's office, he called Joyce and asked her make the changes to the document. Her known efficiency as an executive assistant made the lawyer aware she could get the job done in a minimum amount of time. She kept all documents she completed saved on her computer hard drive, and it was relatively easy for her to do. While Joyce worked on the revised document, Francine focused on Holly.

"You've been quiet as a spider spinning its web over there. Why don't you join in the conversation and tell me a little bit about yourself?" she asked.

Holly cleared her throat and laid down her legal pad. The top page was completely full of notes she had made during the course of the interview.

"Well, as you noted earlier, I'm what's called a non-traditional law student since I'm somewhat older than most. Still a thirty-something, as they say, but I feel younger most of the time. Law school's different than when I was in undergrad at UGA, and I'm studying a lot more now than I did back then.

"Before I moved to Macon to start school, I lived all around Atlanta and worked in law enforcement for awhile and then for the District Attorney's Office as an investigator, so I've got some training in criminal law," she said.

"Interesting. Of course, it's a lot different than when I was your age. Women now do a lot more jobs that men did exclusively back then. Most of us going to college back in the forties were studying to become teachers. At least that's what it seemed like when I went. Not that I regret my education and early career choices, but I bet yours has been a lot more interesting. How about your love life? With your looks, I bet you stay busy as a bunny," she said with a twinkle in her eye.

A little nervous laugh fell out of Holly's mouth. She shot a glimpse at Ollie who appeared amused that he was no longer the subject of Francine's digging.

"Generally speaking, I'm not one to kiss and tell, Mrs. Clements. Let's say that school and working here are more important to me right now. I'll let you in on a little secret about my private life. I do have a guy I'm seeing. His name is Shawn Matheson, and he's hot, but that's all I'll say on that subject."

The old woman seemed pensive for a few seconds and then replied, "Okay, Sweetie. No more prying if you'll call me Frankie."

They chatted a little longer before Joyce reentered the office with the finished document. It was quickly signed and witnessed. The client decided she would have it filed for safekeeping in the Probate Court rather than take it with her, and Ollie told her he would take care of everything.

"As always, Oliver, I appreciate you looking after my affairs. I hope I won't need to ask you to change my will again before I check out of this world."

"You'll probably outlive us all, Frankie, but you know where to find me if you need me," answered Ollie with a smile.

Francine left, but as she did, she walked by and whispered to Holly. "Tell Shawn I said hello, and he better treat you right or he'll have to deal with me."

Everyone watched the old woman limp away, and they all had smiles on their faces.

CHAPTER 33

There was a chill in the early morning air. Leaves rustled around the shadowy figure concealed within dense shrubbery near the residence. A dimly lit lamp close to a window at the rear of the house allowed the man to peer inside partially opened blinds. No activity was detected as was expected. He had seen the owner leave previously carrying an overnight bag and knew no one else lived there.

The Viewer had backed off his favorite activity since the close call inside the lawyer's home office. He thought back to that night. The old squeaky floors of that structure had alerted Tucker the last time he had entered and might have resulted in detection had not the medical emergency occurred at an opportune time.

It hadn't mattered to him on that occasion that the man was inside when going in because he was always careful whether an

owner of the place he chose was there or not. He preferred that
no one be around so he didn't feel rushed when looking for his
trophies, but it wasn't the primary concern much of the time. It
only added to the rush when he knew the owner was there asleep
and clueless the Viewer was walking around.

It didn't matter either whether there was a burglar alarm
installed since he was familiar with such devices and could
avoid or disarm as needed. He knew Tucker had an older model
alarm system, which he hardly ever used, but it was easy to
bypass anyway if armed. That last time the old lawyer hadn't
even turned on the system, and the Viewer had easily picked the
lock to obtain entry.

He had suffered major disappointment at not having
completed what he had set out to do that night and had been
getting more restless with each passing day since. The Viewer
knew at some point he would have to go back there and finish
what he started. He wanted a replacement for the cup he had lost
and to leave his Ispy calling card. It would be a stretch to go in
for the third time, but he had no doubts he could do it without
problem. He had other things to do beforehand, and that trip
would have to wait for a while longer.

First things, first, he said to himself. He gave one last look
at the surroundings and headed to the front door.

Oddly enough, the one thing that gave him the most trouble
when he explored was the presence of an inside dog. Over the
years of practicing his hobby, nothing was nearly as challenging
as a yipping canine that he wasn't aware of until inside. Usually

his advance scouting alerted him to such potential danger. There had been a time or two when it hadn't which necessitated changing plans.

Unless the owner had gotten a pet in the last six months, there shouldn't be a problem for this foray. In fact, the Viewer foresaw no issues at all since he knew the cancel code for disarming the alarm, and he knew the layout of the house well enough to probably not even need a flashlight. He even had a copy of the key to the front door that he had made when he had been there before. *I am golden, no doubt*, he thought to himself as he prepared to enter the house.

It never ceased to amaze him at the trusting nature of a lot of people. He had a wide collection of keys that were catalogued in case he found a need, or special desire to make a trip back to a place he had been earlier. Typically he didn't go back more than once after finishing a job, and this shouldn't be any different.

He was dressed as he always was. Dark clothing, including a full mask covering his face, adorned him. Even if somebody were to see him, identification would be impossible. He felt like some kind of secret agent on a dangerous mission.

The Viewer unlocked the door with the key he obtained earlier and immediately heard the alarm tone begin. He walked deliberately to the keypad and punched in the code to disarm. It didn't work. He tried again thinking he had hit the wrong numbers. Within a second or two, the alarm started a piercing sound that broke through the night. Lights began flashing as well. He couldn't be sure because of all the noise and his growing disorientation, but it sounded almost like cameras were clicking as well.

Something was wrong. It was time to get the hell out. The Viewer had never encountered anything like this before, and for the first time he felt threatened. He turned from the noise and ran. His heart pounded as he headed toward his van.

CHAPTER 34

Ollie sat in the courtroom beside his client, Tonetta Bussey, with her father, Tony, on the other side of her. For not the first time, the lawyer wondered what parents were thinking when naming their children. It had always bugged him when kids were saddled with a junior, or a Roman numeral after their name. That was bad enough taking away what he considered the individuality of another human being. However, the names he saw today bestowing some sense of distinctiveness were often ridiculous in their own way.

Tony was a long-time client and had come to see him the same day as Frankie. His daughter had a sullen presence in that initial meeting that Ollie had seen several times before with lost young people. It was one of defiance and a form of apathy that the lawyer found hard to understand. Her dad was a hard-working, salt-of-the-earth type who only wanted a better life for his offspring than he had experienced. His daughter wasn't buying it, so it seemed. Bad attitude sprang from her pores like too much greasy food on a hot day.

She came to the first meeting showing her piercings, one imbedded in her right eyebrow, one through her left nostril and several in both ears. The jet black eye liner and matching fingernail polish accentuated her black leather pants. A flimsy semi-sheer blouse indicated at least one dark shoulder tattoo. Shiny combat boots completed the ensemble.

Tonetta, also known as Netta to her friends, was seventeen going on thirty. She liked music that sounded nothing like anything her dad had ever heard. She hated school with a passion and felt like she didn't belong with those people. Only a select few could ever hope to understand. It didn't help that her mother had run off with another man when she was fifteen leaving the girl in a lurch at a confusing time in her life. Anger at convention ruled her emotions.

The problems had been compounding over the last year as she became entwined with a circle of friends who gave even less of a shit than she did. Nothing criminal had occurred until a couple of weeks ago. Now she was charged with one count of shoplifting and another of simple battery on the clerk who saw her commit the theft and tried to stop her from leaving the store with the merchandise hidden in her purse.

Ollie had told Netta and her father that he would represent her and thought he could work out a favorable resolution, but it required them to take his advice. Tony was readily agreeable, as the lawyer had never let him down in the past and had always charged reasonable fees for his services. His daughter looked a lot less so when Ollie told her she would first have to lose all the face hardware and wear clothes that were more appropriate for a courtroom. She had an even more sour expression as Tony told her she would be reimbursing him for attorney's fees and for any other costs incurred.

Perplexing as such behavior was to Ollie over the years, he was concerned as much for her father as he was for the newest client. He had seen parents devastated as their kids got started on the wrong road and then seemed unable to stop the spiral that eventually resulted in dropping out of school, prison, illegal drug abuse and other undesirable consequences. Ollie knew this fork in the road was vital to Netta and her father. He and Tony could only hope for the best.

The lawyer had handled cases in the State Court of Bibb County many times over the years and liked the people who worked there. They were efficient prosecutors and thousands of cases were resolved in the court's operations. As he sat watching the various participants, he marveled at the sheer number of people included in the setting. When he began practicing in the early seventies, the court calendars were only a fraction of the current size.

Law practice had changed as well. In some ways it had become like the practice of medicine. Everybody was a specialist. All the legal advertising only added to the impression. The days of the general practitioner were practically gone leaving Ollie feeling like a dinosaur. He only knew of a handful of attorneys like him who felt competent enough to handle more than one or two types of cases.

Ollie had been sitting on a pew near the front of the courtroom for about ten minutes when he saw Leo Berry come into the courtroom through an entrance located behind the bench. He knew the doorway led into what doubled as the jury room for trials and a conference room on arraignment days. When the prosecutor noticed the older lawyer's presence, they both nodded to acknowledge each other as the defense attorney mouthed an indication he wanted to talk. Ollie expected they would discuss his case as soon as Leo had a few minutes.

Since Netta's court date was a first appearance, he knew he could postpone the date by opting to place the case on the next trial calendar. Ollie's experience had shown this was a good course of action sometimes because of the transitory nature of some witnesses. If a key witness disappeared prior to trial, that often resulted in the dismissal of an otherwise prosecutable case. It was also helpful to have additional time to investigate the matter or to get the balance of attorney's fees from the client. He also knew if he could work out what he hoped to for his client, that wouldn't be necessary. Since Ollie preferred clearing cases as soon as possible rather than keeping them open, he hoped to resolve the misdemeanors today.

The judge would occasionally ask for the people in the courtroom to keep the noise down, but discussions abounded in the large area as he steadily accepted negotiated pleas while others were being worked out between prosecution and defense. The environment was different than the majority of settings he had been in, but Ollie had seen the process work so many times before and knew it saved time in the long run.

As the clock marched toward ten and the time when the judge would begin a recitation of rights to the masses in the courtroom, Berry motioned to Ollie to meet him at the rail separating most people from the bench. Ollie told his client and father he would be back momentarily and then joined the young prosecutor. They shook hands and spoke in soft tones.

"Hey, Ollie. How 'ya doing? I heard you had a heart attack," said Berry.

"I'm okay, Leo. A couple of stents fixed me up. Other than feeling a little tired, I'm making it. I'm rehabbing and plan to get back to the health club real soon," replied Ollie.

"Well, take it easy and don't push yourself too much. What 'ya got this morning to cause you to be a part of this thundering herd?"

"Tonetta Bussey is her name. I've already seen the police report that I had faxed over to my office. Shoplifting and simple battery are the charges. I know the security chief at the store, so I know he's going to be around and not be a disappearing witness. It's a clear-cut case, and I don't see much of a defense. She's seventeen without any prior arrests. I was hoping to get her in the youthful offender program and try to keep it off her record," said Ollie.

"Sounds like she meets our criteria. I assume you've let her know what's required," said Berry.

"Yeah, but I was also hoping you could go over the guidelines with her and her dad beforehand and impress upon her the importance of successful completion. I get the feeling she might accept your warnings better than mine. You know, you're more contemporary than me," Ollie said with a smirk.

The lawyers were aware they were being watched and didn't want to appear that this was just a big joke or some kind of conspiracy between them. The younger lawyer stifled a laugh and then asked Ollie to take his client and the father down the hall to his office.

When all were present, the prosecutor went over the details of the proposed disposition of Netta's case. They included a requirement that she admit guilt by signing a guilty plea, but the adjudication would be held open for at least six months pending the completion of behavioral counseling and classes. She would also have to do forty hours of community service during the period of supervision. Any failure of the terms could result in being kicked out of the program and subject her to sentencing by the court of up to twelve months in jail and a fine of up to a thousand dollars on each count. The carrot being held out to her was a promise that the successful completion of the program resulted in dismissal of the charges.

"You might not believe it at this moment in your life, but this is a huge opportunity for you. I talk to people almost daily that were not given such a chance when they got in trouble, and now they have a hard time finding a job. Do you ever think about what you want to do in life?" said Berry.

"I just want to be on my own," Netta said while looking down at the floor.

"Not a bad goal, but you'll need a decent job to pay the rent, buy food and other things you've probably never thought about. I bet you don't realize how much money it costs just to get the necessities much less the extras most people want," Berry said pausing.

"Look, I'm not here to preach to you about how to get ahead in your life, because ultimately you're the one who'll be living it, not me. You can continue to make bad choices like the one causing you to be here today, or you can make up your mind to learn something constructive from this bad experience. Negatives can be turned into positives, but it's going to be hard," said the prosecutor.

The girl didn't appear convinced as she replied, "What if I don't want to do all that stuff?"

"There's always the option of doing some time in the jail. Did you like the time you were there after your arrest," answered the prosecutor.

The teenager brought her face up and looked at the young lawyer. Some of the hardness had left and tears brimmed in her eyes. She changed focus and turned to her father.

"I'm sorry, Daddy. I don't want to go back to jail. Learned that lesson. I'll try not to let you down."

"It's okay, baby. I feel like I've let you down since your mama left. I only want the best for you. We can get through this together," said Bussey.

The old defense lawyer had a lump in his throat. For the first time since meeting Netta, Ollie felt like she just might make it. At least she had a chance that a lot of folks didn't get. It made him feel good to be a lawyer.

***

Ollie was leaving the courtroom after formally entering his client's plea into the pre-trial diversion program and feeling pretty good about his work when he noticed Jessica Mooney standing in the hallway speaking to another assistant district attorney and a young defense lawyer named Jon Cartwright. Jessica flashed a slightly bucktoothed smile in his direction, and Ollie headed that way.

The other ADA talking animatedly to the group was recognized as Sally Robertson. She was known first for her love of dogs and second for beaches everywhere. Her reputation as a trial lawyer began when she represented criminal defendants and handled multiple divorce cases with strange twists. She had recently become a prosecutor and now specialized in some of the worst cases imaginable.

It was hard to believe this otherwise fun-loving tomboy who had the moniker "Judge Kiwi" could be tough as nails when it came to sending sickos to prison. A lot of good criminal lawyers started out as prosecutors and then switched to the defense, but Sally had taken the opposite road. Ollie had represented clients in domestic cases against her in the past and knew she was a good lawyer no matter what side she was on.

"Well, if it ain't Ollie Tucker, a bad mutha----", said Sally leaving off the rest of the expletive.

The three lawyers chuckled at Sally's funny introduction. She was known for her irreverence that rivaled Jessica's bawdiness in some measure.

"Shut yo' mouth, you talking about Shaft," said Ollie.

The group started laughing again with Jessica making snorting sounds. "You're pretty cool for an old fart," said Sally.

"I'm surprised any of you kids know anything about such an old movie," said Ollie.

"I'm surprised you're calling yourself "Shaft" at your advanced age," said Jessica making an obscene gesture with her fist clinched and her arm pumping that brought on another raucous round of laughter.

Ollie's face flushed slightly before he deadpanned, "That's just a nickname a select few can attest to, present company excluded."

The other lawyers were laughing like high school kids while the old attorney tried to remain a certain amount of decorum. Part of him wanted to be their age again, but he felt secure in the moment that he had grown older and hopefully wiser.

"Cool, man. You're my hero. I've never been able to get the last word in on these two," said Jon.

Ollie winked at the younger guy and spoke softly, "Just let them think they're in control."

Jon's law partner, Andy Forrester, motioned for him that he was needed in the courtroom. They were both contract criminal defense attorneys for the court, which kept them busy along with their private practice that included representing the Department of Family and Children Services. Ollie had been involved with cases with both and found them knowledgeable and competent even though Andy was a diehard Phillies fan making him a source of endless ribbing in Braves country.

As he left Jon whispered to Ollie, "Give 'em hell and never surrender."

"I'll do my best, JC. Hey, and tell your partner the Phillies still suck," Ollie said with a nod and a smirk.

Ollie turned to each of the prosecutors and said, "So, what are you two doing on this floor anyway? It must be trouble for somebody when two of the best trial lawyers in the DA's office are lurking in this hallway."

The assistants stole a glance at one another and Sally grinned. Her sandy hair that was close-cut in a casual style made the old lawyer think she had recently been in the sun, as it contrasted against tanned skin untouched by any makeup. She wore a light-colored tailored pantsuit and flats that fit her personality perfectly. He knew her Judge Kiwi nickname had been born for reasons related to her love of the beach.

Jessica, on the other hand, was the polar opposite with her choice of attire. She looked as if she were ready for a fashion runway with her navy designer pants and matching jacket complimented by her signature stiletto heels and scarf. Ollie doubted she ever left the house without making sure every hair was in place, sprayed and coifed, with enough makeup applied to cover any imperfection she perceived.

"Actually, we were looking for you. Your office told us you had a case in state court, so we thought we'd brighten your morning," said Sally.

The big smile on her face made Ollie think of the Cheshire Cat. Maybe that's why he felt like he was about to fall down a rabbit hole.

"And why might y'all be looking for me? I'm sure you're not going to ask me to breakfast at the Market City Café, even though the corned beef hash is to die for," he said.

"Sounds good, but bad for my curves," said Jessica pausing. "But, Robertson might be interested since she can eat anything she wants and never gains an ounce."

"I've told you, Jess. You need a dog or ten. They'll make you get off the couch and take 'em for a walk. You gotta move more, woman," said Sally in her southern drawl while sporting a plastered grin.

"Uh, no to both those ideas," Jessica said to Sally and then turned toward Ollie who watched the two women with puzzlement.

"Seriously, what can I do for you two besides being a source of your amusement?" asked Ollie.

"Just like a man, not into foreplay," said Jessica to Sally precipitating another round of snickering.

The old lawyer was only slightly annoyed, if the truth was told. He really wanted to continue in the humorous exchange, but he had more appointments scheduled and work to do.

"Okay, Mr. Tucker. Here's a news flash for you. Headline number one reads something like; *Serial burglar strikes again and leaves his picture.* In slightly smaller print, *District Attorney moves to revoke bond.* How do you like them apples?" asked Sally.

Ollie felt the blood drain from his face. He thought he'd better call the office and let them know he might be late for his mid-morning appointment.

CHAPTER 35

Holly sat across from Shawn at a small table for two inside Satterfield's. The intimate barbeque restaurant, hidden away from the other downtown eateries by a few blocks, was known for its varied menu and all kinds of pig paraphernalia strategically located in every available space. A steaming bowl of boiled peanuts sat in the middle of the quaint wooden tabletop, and the couple was digging in while waiting on their lunch.

The restaurant was full and hummed with conversation around them. It suddenly occurred to her that she had been chattering nonstop since they arrived and that Shawn seemed preoccupied. He was absently eating what her granddaddy had called goobers while she prattled about her morning classes. When she quit talking for a moment, he was staring at something she couldn't see.

"Earth to Shawn. Are you still here?"

He shook his head slightly side to side and replied, "I'm sorry, I guess I've got a lot on my mind. What were you saying?"

"Nothing very important, just what I was proposing to do to you all weekend. I take it that you're not interested in me chaining you to the bedpost with my old service handcuffs."

His smile was more of a leer as he picked up another soft peanut, cracked it open with his fingers and slurped the insides into his mouth like an oyster on a half-shell. He closed his eyes, munched and purred, "Umm, just like you. Soft with a hint of saltiness."

"Don't try to redeem yourself by throwing around compliments now, you smooth-talking devil. You've already crushed my fragile heart by your inattentiveness," she said with a mock frown.

"Pardon me, milady. I shall endeavor to never let another distraction enter this cranium again when I am near you," Shawn said in a faux British accent while holding his tea glass with his pinky finger held out from the others of his hand.

"And don't pretend I'm a pretentious character on some British soap opera either, sir," she replied with arms folded in a haughty look.

They gazed into each other's eyes for a moment before both started laughing. His sense of humor was one of the qualities Holly found attractive, and the moment was just one of several they had shared since getting to know one another better.

Holly wiped her fingers on one of the extra napkins that had been brought with the appetizer and reached across the table to first pat and then rub Shawn's arm. She could feel the sinewy strength underneath his worn chambray shirt and remembered how she felt comfortable when it was wrapped around her. He was an average-sized man, but all of his muscles were toned to a pleasant hardness she admired.

"What's got your mind so cluttered you don't want to hear about my exciting morning in class?"

"Just work and stuff, nothing for you to be worried about."

Holly regarded Shawn's face as he spoke, but didn't determine that there was any reason to be overly concerned. She decided to let it drop unless he brought up whatever might be bothering him.

The waitress brought their food and the two of them didn't speak until well into the meal. She got busy with her smoked turkey salad while he stuck with the traditional pork.

"I'm glad you brought me here. This is delicious," said Holly.

"Yeah, I like everything on the menu. One of the best things about Macon is all the good barbeque around town. I hit just about all of them at least once a month because I can't make up my mind which one I like the best. Stick with me kid and I'll take you to the original Fincher's next week, Tucker's the week after that and we'll finish at Fresh Air. Then I'll see if you can pick the best barbeque in middle Georgia," he said.

"That's what I worry about. You're not trying to fatten me up for the kill are you?" she replied.

"I do like meat on the bones, but you've got enough for me just the way you are," drawled Shawn.

She giggled like a schoolgirl as he reached across the table and kneaded her triceps with a gentleness that belied the power in his hand. There was a certain sexuality about his touch she had never quite felt before.

"You know, I could get used to how you make me feel, Shawn. I'm sorry I've been busy the last couple of weeks and not able to spend much time with you. I'm glad you're in my life right now."

As soon as the words came out of her mouth, she was afraid she had said too much. It was the closest thing to words of love that she had spoken in a long time.

Expressionless initially after she spoke, Shawn's face gradually softened into one denoting pleasure. "That may be the sweetest words ever said to me, Holly. That makes me very happy," he said.

She smiled back at him and thought, *This guy might just be the one.*

CHAPTER 36

Ollie felt like he was being swallowed by quicksand as he trudged back toward the office. The morning that had started with promise for a young client had turned into early afternoon and now threatened his closest friend with new dangers. He hadn't fully processed the revelations the two women prosecutors had laid on him yet, but the old lawyer knew he would have to immediately. Otherwise, Tyler could be looking at additional charges and revocation of his bond.

It was lunchtime, but he didn't feel hungry. A wave of nausea crept from his gut as he remembered bits and pieces of the meeting with Jessica Mooney and Sally Robertson.

He had followed them back to the DA's office where he was ultimately led into a conference room. There he was shown a series of still photographs purporting to show a burglar in the act of entering a residence. Though the prosecutors said none showed the face of the criminal, they alleged it was Tyler Crenshaw.

Ollie had studied the photographs closely and thought to himself that the body type certainly looked like his old friend. It was impossible to know for sure though, because the face of the perpetrator was completely hidden by a mask covering the head of the person shown. The photos only depicted one thing for sure to Ollie; the offender went to great lengths to hide his identity.

The defense lawyer had made no comments other than to tell the assistant district attorneys he failed to see how anyone could say beyond a reasonable doubt the pictures were of his client. He had challenged them to show any other corroborating evidence such as fingerprints that would indicate his client was involved in the attempted crime. He knew that was a safe bet since the images showed someone wearing what appeared to be surgical gloves. The prosecutors had been noncommittal when challenged, but Ollie got the impression they were trying to rattle him, and he was determined not to show any concerns he might have about his client.

Ollie couldn't help but let doubts about his friend sneak back into his brain. No matter how much he had tried since the whole mess began, he couldn't divorce completely his fondness for Tyler from evidence that indicated his guilt. His professional side knew it shouldn't matter in the least, but his relationship with the man over decades clouded his judgment. Either way, guilty or innocent, Tyler needed his help, and Ollie remained determined to give it.

The lawyer was still a little uncertain what his strategy needed to be unless he could get rid of the presumption of involvement that followed from Tyler's recent possession of stolen property. That, in and of itself, was enough to get his friend convicted. He would get with Holly after she got in today to see where she was in the drafting of a motion to suppress. That was a key, and if they were successful with getting rid of the evidence taken during the traffic stop, that should be the end of the prosecution.

His mind shifted away from the case as Ollie thought of Tyler. They had known one another since grammar school, and there was a history they shared that was unique. Over fifty-five years of friendship should qualify him as being an expert on a person, thought Ollie, just as Tyler would qualify as an expert on Ollie.

A memory jumped in his head as he walked. Ollie was in law school, so it had to be in the late sixties or early seventies. He couldn't remember exactly the year, but knew he hadn't graduated or started practicing law yet. It had been one of those rare times during the three years of graduate study when he needed a disruption from the routine.

Tyler had just gotten out of the service and was home for good. They hadn't seen one another in over a year, but they had swapped a few letters while Tyler was fighting in Vietnam. It was a weekend, and both were ready to break loose and celebrate Ty's safe return.

He remembered how proud he was of Tyler although many people were less than nice to the returning veterans. They had ended up in a bar with a lot of young folks who opposed the war. Little did they know or care that both Ollie and his vet friend didn't think much of it either. It didn't matter to a couple of the patrons who kept baiting Tyler accusing him of killing innocent villagers including women and children. The vitriol that was being spewed seemed not to bother his friend as much, but Ollie couldn't let it go.

Ollie had finally had enough of the assholes and the one too many drinks he had consumed talked him into confronting them. It was the only time in his life that alcohol resulted in Ollie wanting to fight. It was so stupid and unlike him and could have resulted in his suspension from school.

Thankfully, Tyler had gotten him out of harm's way before the police arrived. It was one night that Ty had taken care of Ollie rather than the other way round. They had made it back to Ollie's apartment unharmed and then spent the rest of the night talking about their dreams of the future. Now that he thought about it, neither spoke of marriage or children that night. The main thing he remembered about the time together was the sense of closeness he felt to his friend. They swore to each other they would remain friends forever. It was something he couldn't forget.

Despite the fact Ollie and Tyler had not been quite as close the last few years, it always seemed when they got together that it had only been a few days since they had seen one another, even if it had been months. It was the nature of their friendship that allowed them to pick up right where they left off. That's why if bothered him so much that he now had doubts about his friend when he had never had any before.

He had to work all this out, soon. He was too old not to.

Ollie arrived back at his office and went inside. Red was talking animatedly on the phone to someone probably not a client. They were discussing a movie the lawyer hadn't seen, much less heard of. What he heard only made him grumpier and more apt to complain.

"I got to go. The boss is here and he ain't looking happy," Red said as she hung up the phone.

"I don't think that sounded like a business call, Red. You know I'm not tickled about private phone calls on work time."

"I'm sorry, Boss. My friend Missy was talking about that new vampire movie, and I told her it was stupid. We got to fussin' about it. I promise it won't happen again, Mr. Tucker."

"You know I don't care what you do on your private time, Red. This isn't your private time when you're here. I don't want to hear that kind of conversation anymore," he said with irritation showing.

The cute redhead's face showed signs of distress as she lowered her head, and for a second Ollie felt she might cry. He was instantly mad at himself for taking out frustrations that he was feeling over the latest developments in Tyler's case on Red. She was a good employee undeserving of chastisement over such a petty issue.

"Look, I'm sorry to sound so harsh. You do a nice job for me, and I appreciate it. Mark it up to me being an ornery old cuss, but remember this is a business," said Ollie.

Red broke into a smile again, and it was contagious. "Don't sweat it, Boss. You're still the best boss I've ever had even when you act like a Meany cat. I promise I'll keep the phone calls with friends down, at least while you're in the office."

"You won't do, girl," he said while shaking his head. "Can you tell me if I'm still clear for the afternoon?"

"Yup, you're free to take the afternoon off to do what you want."

"And leave you to talk to all your friends about vampires and werewolves on my time? I don't think so. Just let Holly know I want to see her when she gets here, and see if you can find something to keep busy that resembles work," Ollie said with a sly grin as he walked toward his office.

***

Ollie was focused on reading a case in a book from his collection of Georgia Court of Appeals decisions. Legal research was a necessary part of being a good lawyer, but it was something he often complained about and didn't like to do. He frequently put off doing such work until the last moment. The old lawyer's brows were furrowed as he studied the ruling and didn't notice as his daughter entered his office.

He finished reading and removed tortoise shell half-glasses from the lower portion of his nose. As he pinched the bridge, Ollie sensed rather than saw someone had joined him and turned to the doorway.

"Hey, Dad. Red said you wanted to see me," announced Holly.

Not for the first time since becoming a part of his life, he admired the freshness of her face and the understated way she seemed to always brighten his office. It was something he hoped would continue for as long as he lived, and the thought made him smile.

"It may sound trite, but I always like seeing you. At this stage of my life, you make my day more than anything else I can imagine. I was thinking we could work on Tyler's case this afternoon since I don't have any appointments."

"Sounds like a plan to me, Dad. I've finished drafting that motion to suppress, and I was going to show you today anyway if you had the time."

She appeared excited while bounding into the room. She set her well-worn Coach purse and an expandable folder on the large conference table and began pulling out the contents. Ollie recognized printed copies of opinions, what looked like a couple of prepared legal documents and the ever-present yellow legal pad Holly had whenever she worked.

"What I've done is of course a rough draft because I've never tried writing anything like this. I looked in a couple of formbooks and checked some motions you had in a file that Joyce maintains in order to get the format," she said as she handed the manuscript to Ollie.

"I printed out some decisions that discuss the issues we've got to address when the hearing on the motion is set. I also have prepared a memorandum that examines those same topics. I didn't think you had done much research yet, so I may have some information in the memo you already know. I hope you'll find what I've done helpful," she continued.

Ollie nodded approvingly as he glanced over the work product. A quick perusal of the motion didn't show any glaring errors. He would want to study the cited authorities, but he had seen much worse efforts from lawyers already in practice for years. This young woman was way ahead of the level of study she had completed, and he couldn't help but be proud.

"First blush, this looks impressive. I want to read the cases you've found for my own edification before we talk about this in more depth, but I really like what I see developed in the motion to suppress as well as the legal memorandum. I'm pleased, to say the least."

Holly beamed at the compliment and replied, "Thanks, I've seen these kinds of documents when I worked in the Fulton DA's office, but never thought I'd be writing them one day, myself.

"I know you'll need to read the cases for yourself, but I think one of the keys to challenging the search and seizure in our case centers on the analysis of the tip that was called into the Sheriff's Department. The arrest report that was filed in the case doesn't identify who made the call other than to say it was by a concerned citizen. At this point, I don't see how the State can prove the credibility of the tipster. I guess they might be able to show the caller's identity and possibly prove he or she had provided reliable information in the past. Maybe it was just an oversight by the officer to not include that in the report, but I suspect he didn't know the person calling in the information.

"As I'm sure you know, the general rule is information from a tipster of unknown credibility does not provide reasonable grounds upon which to detain a person for investigative purposes. I cited the *Tiller* case, but there are many others we can use as precedent," she continued before Ollie interrupted.

"But, there are exceptions. If the information is detailed enough that it can be corroborated, that could provide the required credibility," said the old lawyer.

"Yes sir, but once again nothing in the filed report shows enough details of the information. As I recall from reading the report before preparing this memo and motion, all that's mentioned is that a white van was driving through the neighborhood in a suspicious manner. That is about as vague as can be, in my humble opinion, and if that's all that was said, it is insufficient. It's a generalized description that wouldn't have allowed the arresting deputy to verify that the information was inherently reliable," said Holly.

"You're making good points and valid legal arguments, young lady. I believe you have a rosy future ahead as a lawyer," he said and paused.

"There are other things we'll need to contemplate as well. You bring up a quandary I've come across in other cases over the years. That is, when an officer fails to mention something in his report, do I try to talk to him ahead of time to see if he had additional information he relied upon and will testify to in court? Or do I wait and spring it on him when he's on the stand and then beat him up by asking him was it an important fact he left out and why? Usually my inclination is to take the latter tactic, but a good prosecutor will recognize the potential problems of an incomplete report and coach the witness ahead of time how to blunt anticipated questions of that nature. At this point, I know the two assistant district attorneys involved in the prosecution are excellent trial lawyers, and I would expect the officer will be ready for a tough cross," continued Ollie.

"Actually, I've already thought about that, too. I was thinking maybe I could interview the deputy and pick him a little bit. Obviously I didn't want to do that without your blessing, Dad," she said.

"You've more than shown me your expertise with investigations already, and your most recent work makes me confident you can handle anything we have ahead. Use your skills and see what you can find out, and we'll go from there. In the meantime, I'd like to thoroughly study what you've brought me today before we discuss it further," he said.

Holly got up from her seat and walked to where her father sat. She hugged him with affection and whispered in his ear, "I won't let you down, Daddy."

CHAPTER 37

Francine Clements knew she didn't have abundant time left in the world. She didn't care very much at all because her faith in the hereafter had only gotten stronger the last few years. The confidence she felt of something better awaiting on the other side sustained her and brought peace to her aging body, mind and spirit. God had given her a wonderful life, but when her soul joined those already there in paradise, everything would come full circle and she would be complete. She was ready to go whenever The Man in Charge was ready for her to cross over. Not that she was in a hurry, mind you.

She was on her side in the king-sized bed trying to fall back asleep. The bad hip was screaming unpleasantries at her, and she couldn't get comfortable any way she tried. A glance at her clock told her it was a little before three o'clock a.m. *It's a good thing I never needed a lot of sleep*, Frankie thought.

The old house she had lived in for over fifty years was spacious and filled with memories and mementos. She had kept it pristine throughout her time there including the marriages with her last two husbands. Altogether, Frankie had been married three times and had outlived them all. Each one had been different in a lot of respects, but every one of them had loved her and left her a little better off financially. She had known another lover, too. It left her grateful although now lonely in the residence.

For some reason, it had not been her lot in life to have kids of her own. If it had, she thought at least one of them would be with her right now as she struggled through the final phase of her life. Not that she would've put that guilt trip on anybody, but it would be nice to have a blood relative nearby if she needed him or her.

As it was, she depended on the kindness of a friend or two and the occasional nephew or niece to help as she required. For the most part, she still took care of herself and was damned proud of the fact that she could. When she couldn't, Frankie would put herself in an assisted living facility, at least that's what she told herself.

She thought she heard something fall in another part of the house. Frankie had been by herself all night, so it couldn't be someone staying with her to give a helping hand. She could be hearing things or letting her aging mind play tricks on her, but she didn't think so. After listening for another minute and not picking up another sound, she decided to get up and check out

the situation for herself. At least while she was up she could go
to the bathroom and get something for the pain in the hip.

It was an effort to get out of bed and the old woman
grunted as she began the process. She had gone through physical
therapy a few years ago and knew tricks to help, but it still
wasn't easy. As she rolled to the side of the mattress, Frankie
was glad to reach and touch the nearby walker that she used as
needed. It provided a level of comfort that little else did at this
point in life. She often referred to the thing as her new best
friend as opposed to her cane that she also sometimes called her
stick.

Frankie shuffled on bare feet and leaned on the walker for
support as she pushed out of the bedroom. The old woman
wasn't scared, she was merely curious. If anyone had dared to
invade her space, woe would be upon the poor devil. Her initial
thought was that drugged-up nephew of hers had gotten in and
was rummaging around for something to steal. He had already
done that a couple of times prompting her to change her will.

She was surprisingly quiet as she made her way down the
hallway. It probably helped that she barely weighed ninety
pounds, and the wheels on the front of the walker were freshly
oiled to keep down the squeaks that drove her nuts.

There was movement ahead as Frankie entered the living
room. A small lamp she kept lit cast a shadow that danced on
the farthest wall. She watched for a moment before continuing
her early morning trek. The fascination she felt to find out who
might be in her house kept her moving forward. Only a handful

of people knew her security code and had a copy of her key, so it had to be somebody she knew.

On she trundled until she was positioned between her front doorway and the intruder who was busy looking inside a massive cabinet containing old books, ceramic figurines and other assorted what-knots. Frankie observed the person picking up various items and studying them like they were artifacts from some Egyptian dig. She noticed he had on gloves, but fondled each item with special attention.

Frankie watched as the guy placed one of her prized heirlooms into his pocket and then saw him put something onto the shelf where the item had been located. She didn't recognize who it might be, but she was pissed.

"What the hell are you doing?" the old woman barked.

The figure standing at the cabinet turned rigid and didn't turn around. He slowly reached up to his head and appeared to be smoothing the mask that covered his face. Frankie moved a few steps closer.

The old woman studied the guy with a critical eye. Even though he didn't turn around, there was something familiar about the way he stood. At least Frankie knew it was not a relative, but the thought that someone else was in her house uninvited made her even more confrontational.

"What are you stealing from this old woman, douche bag? There aren't any valuables in here. You're such a dumbass. Can't you get a job? No matter, you're going to jail. I'm taping you right now, asshole. What do you think about that?

The figure still didn't move throughout the old woman's directed comments. Then he slowly coiled, and energy radiated from his body as he turned.

Frankie gasped as the man darted in her direction. Her location in between the burglar and the front door placed her in direct danger as the cat-like movements he took caused her involuntarily to take her hands from the walker. She felt her hip give as pain shot down her leg, and she listed to that side of her body.

The man dodged by her and the walker just as she toppled over on her side. Frankie's right wrist grasped unsuccessfully for the aluminum handle as she fell. The last thing she felt and heard before her head crashed into the hardwood floor was the snap of the delicate bones of her wrist as her new best friend pressed there under the weight of her body. Then she was still as blood spread on the floor from her head.

The intruder stopped at the doorway and turned toward the body laying only a few feet from him. He looked at her for only a moment and then swiftly opened the door and disappeared into the dark of night.

CHAPTER 38

Ollie was feeling better after a good night's sleep. It was amazing what it could do to change his outlook on everything. He even smiled at the sight of his own face in the mirror and thought he looked more like himself than he had since the heart attack.

The lawyer thought back to the evening before and remembered the pleasant dinner with Holly at Natalia's. It was a delicious meal as always in the signature restaurant, but just being with the remarkable young woman made the time special.

He was so proud of her, and the love he now felt made him want to shout it out to the world. Until now, Ollie had been reluctant to share the fact Holly was his daughter. He had worried that others wouldn't understand the relationship or question why it had taken so long for it to be revealed. He could understand that kind of thinking because he had struggled with those issues, too. Bottom line however, the decision had been made over dinner the two of them would start acknowledging their kinship. They had agreed it was a big step for both.

To seal the deal, Ollie had introduced Holly to some of his colleagues who happened to be at the restaurant having dinner with their spouses. One of them, Tim Hines, had been practicing law as long as Ollie and knew him well. When Ollie made the introduction, Tim had shown instant surprise.

Ollie Tucker, you old rascal. Why would you keep such a beautiful daughter hidden away?

You may have just answered your own question, counselor, he had replied.

Holly had interrupted the two older lawyers by saying; *I haven't been in a nunnery for the last thirty-something years.*

They had all laughed before Ollie had explained; *Actually, neither of us knew the other existed until earlier this year. It's taken a little while for us to work out our relationship, but it's all good now.*

Ollie smiled again at the man in the looking glass. He knew the next person he wanted to tell. His best friend. Tyler. He only hoped Ty would be as happy about his daughter as he was.

***

As Ollie drove to Tyler's house, he tried to remember how long it had been since he had last been there. It had to be a lot of years. When he had called his friend to see what he was doing, Ty had sounded more than surprised to hear that Ollie was thinking of coming to see him. He had commented something about 'Hell must be freezing over.'

It was Ollie's intention to put Ty at ease while they discussed things, and he thought the easiest place to make it happen would be in his friend's natural environment. He wanted to review the upcoming motion hearing as well as letting him know about Holly.

He listened to the sixties station on the satellite radio, and soon he was back in the decade when he was growing up. It had been a period of time that brought him to the pinnacle of happiness and then the very depth of sorrow. As he thought about the loss of innocence that accompanied those years, Ollie couldn't help but feel an ache that had never gone away. Music could do that to him when he least expected it.

One minute he was grinning as he remembered holding Libby's hand while listening to the Beatles singing about wanting to do just that. The next minute tears were falling as he listened to "The Big O" describe the pain in his heart. There had been so many changes Ollie had seen and gone through before the seventies finally hit, and the music of the time seemed to mark each event.

The country road he travelled reminded him of times gone by as well. He could remember being with his folks as they journeyed to nearby farms that seemed much farther away than they were. Back in the fifties Bibb County still had many rural areas and more than a few dirt roads.

Owners of family farms and other truck farmers leasing property would offer for sale their homegrown produce at the local farmers market or from roadside stands advertised by crudely made signs. His parents would buy many of the fresh vegetables by the bushels and spend time and effort to wash, blanch and freeze butterbeans, tomatoes, okra, corn and various types of peas. Of course, he and his brothers were expected to help, and Ollie had spent his share of time shelling peas and beans as well as shucking corn. Their Kenmore storage freezer was always packed by the end of the growing season and would provide fresh tastes during the winter months. The old lawyer still loved the flavor of fresh vegetables more than anything else he could think of eating.

Ollie arrived at the driveway that led to Tyler's house. The acreage surrounding the house provided a natural setting that perfectly complimented his home. There were a few oak trees in the front shading the evening sun, and in the back was a forest line that looked dense and seemed to extend for miles. Ollie liked the custom made mailbox that resembled an old farmhouse located at the end of the pristine poured concrete drive. The picturesque view was a scene worthy of a magazine.

The house was a combination of old and new. In some ways, Ollie thought of the timeworn television show, Dallas. There was a certain stateliness of the structure, and the white paint of the columns on the front spoke of the past. On the other hand, it was a modernist's version, obvious by the satellite dish that stuck out like a sore thumb on one end of the roof.

When he drove the length of the entranceway and ended up at the rear of Tyler's house, Ollie parked the expensive sedan near the huge attached deck. His friend sat in an Adirondack chair with his dog nearby. The well-behaved Border collie didn't move as the lawyer got out of his car and made his way to where his friend sat sipping a beer.

The coolness of the morning air greeted Ollie as he walked toward Ty. The dog assessed him when he finally made it.

"This is indeed a momentous occasion," said Tyler as he took a pull from his Coors Light.

"Whatever," replied Ollie.

"Grab you a beer from the cooler," Tyler said as he nodded toward a Styrofoam ice chest near the chair he reclined in.

"It's 10:45 in the morning, the only time I drink this early is at the beach," said Ollie.

"Pretend," said Tyler.

Ollie walked over to the cooler and picked out a beer. Twisting the cap off, he flipped it into a nearby trashcan and took a seat beside his friend.

Neither spoke for a few moments as they looked toward the rear of the property. The heavily wooded area was ablaze with autumn colors. Some leaves were falling as a slight cooling breeze blew through them. A vintage United States flag run up a metal pole on the opposite side of the deck rippled slightly, and the sound of the flapping cloth was soothing as a sail on open water.

"I'd forgotten how relaxing it is to get away from the city," said Ollie.

"I was beginning to think you'd forgotten other stuff as well," answered Tyler.

"Maybe I did for a minute or two," said the lawyer.

The two men looked at one another for a moment before Ollie broke into a childish grin. He raised his beer and reached across to clink it against Tyler's.

"Here's to remembering the good and forgetting the bad."

"Forward and not backward," replied Tyler as they each took a swallow.

"You've really made this place into something special, Ty. I was thinking on the way over here that I couldn't remember the last time I was here."

"I remember. It was a barbeque I had for Labor Day back in ninety-six, so that's been eighteen years ago. You showed up with some hot-looking babe whom every man here couldn't keep his eyes off of. You were tan from some trip to Key West or somewhere in the Caribbean, sporting Wayfarer sunglasses and a Tommy Bahama shirt, and were driving some fancy sports car that all the guys drooled over as much as the woman you brought. I thought you were a little late in the game to be middle age crazy, but you played it cool like you always have," replied Tyler.

Ollie looked pensive for a moment and then said, "Yeah, I loved that car. Can't remember the girl's name, though."

Tyler laughed and said, "I bet you can't remember the car either, buddy. You know Ollie, that's one of the things that's always amazed me about you since we've grown up. You'll change some things at a whim, whether it's people or property. Not everything, mind you. You've stayed in your hometown all your life and your home office has been a constant, too. Women and cars though, you change almost as often as your underwear."

Ollie had to laugh and admit to himself that he had gone through a lot of cars. He had purchased many over an endless time frame when he had a rule to trade every two years no matter how much he liked the vehicle he was driving at the time. It had been a crazy affectation that he no longer subscribed to, and it had been a rule that he could never adequately justify.

While he was coming clean with himself, he had to confess many women had come and gone through his life, too. They had not been as numerous as the automobiles, but if he dared to try and think about all their names, he would probably fail miserably. That didn't say much for his success with women as far as he was concerned, but he was sure some guys would think just the opposite.

"Cat got your tongue, Ollie?" asked Tyler.

"I was just thinking how right you are, Ty. I've been a fool in so many ways. I'll say this, it seemed like fun at the time. Now, I'm not so sure."

"I understand," said Tyler with a touch of sadness in his voice.

"It's one of the reasons I wanted to come see you, Ty. There are some things I want to let you know about my life. There's other stuff about the case I want to talk about, too. I know I should've told you about it before now, but I've had problems dealing with it all. It's way past time for me to deal with everything."

"I'm glad to see you, Ollie. No matter the reason."

"Me, too. But, I've got to let you know something I never knew until a few months ago. I'm a father. Can you imagine that?"

Tyler got out of his chair and walked around the deck. He rubbed his face and then took a drink from his beer.

"I'm surprised if you don't have more than one, buddy," said Tyler.

Ollie laughed half-heartedly. "I've practiced safe sex, most of the time. I guess I didn't at least once."

"Yeah right, maybe just one time."

"Well anyway, I found out I have a daughter. It's pretty incredible when I think about it. You've met her, and I want you to get to know her. Holly is her name, and I have to say, she's amazing. She's pretty and smart and makes me want to be a better man."

Tyler didn't say anything at first. He appeared to be studying his friend's face.

"Ollie, I'm glad you've got somebody special in your life. I think that's the greatest thing I've heard in a long time. I totally believe whatever you say about her, too. But, you should know you're already a good man. If anybody were to ask me, I would say you're the best one I've ever known."

"You flatter me way too much, Ty. I've made plenty of mistakes in my life, and I'm sure I've hurt people along the way including you in recent times. I have to include Holly's mother in that mix, and I can't imagine what damage I did to that woman to make her want to keep that girl's existence a secret from me. I want to spend the rest of my life trying not to be as selfish as I've been in the past. One way I plan to do that is by helping Holly, and another is by being a better friend to you."

The two men continued talking for the next hour as guys reconnecting after an absence. They discussed Ollie's revelation at length as the lawyer found relief in having someone he could finally unburden the fears and hopes he had felt for the months since Holly had come into his life. It was a cathartic experience for both.

As Ollie described the good work his daughter had been doing for him in the office, the conversation turned to Tyler's case. It was another main topic and reason for the lawyer wanting to visit with his friend.

"She's really done a nice job on a motion to suppress I'll be filing with the court on Monday. I didn't have to change much to the draft she prepared, and the research was solid. I don't think I could've done better myself. I'm feeling pretty good about our chances of prevailing when we have a hearing on the motion," said Ollie.

"I'm not an attorney like you, but what I understand about something like that is you'd be trying to keep evidence out of the trial, is that right?" replied Tyler.

"Yeah, the basis of the motion is that the items taken from your van were illegally obtained by the arresting deputy and should therefore be excluded as evidence. If we win, that should be the end of the case."

"But, that doesn't really prove my innocence, Ollie. People would still think I'm a common thief. They'll just think I got off on a technicality because of my clever lawyer. It's important to me that all those people I've done work for know I wouldn't do anything like they've charged me with," said Tyler and paused.

"By chance, have you seen some of the comments written about me anytime there's publicity? I've been called everything but a Christian, and I don't like it. I don't want to be known as the sick weirdo who got away. You've got to help me, Ollie."

"Look, Ty. My number one priority is to see you acquitted and make sure you don't end up behind bars. I understand wanting to prove your innocence and clear your name, but I'm going to take advantage of every available legal argument. We will cross the bridge of restoring your reputation when you are free. The first step will be having the court rule with us that the state gathered evidence as a result of an illegal search and seizure."

Tyler had a sour look on his face as Ollie stopped speaking. He drained the remainder of liquid in the bottle he held, and then got up from his chair. After depositing the empty container in a nearby container for recyclables, he walked to the back end of the large deck and began staring in the direction of the tree line.

Ollie watched his friend and studied the body language of the man as he moved and then stood still. He remembered the photo that the two prosecutors had shown him was the subject of a botched burglary. He did notice a similarity of body types and stances, but thought it impossible to say the pictures were of Tyler.

Once again, nagging doubts crept into the old lawyer's brain. He shook them off as he silently promised himself to stand by his buddy no matter what.

CHAPTER 39

Monday morning was shaping up into a busy one. Ollie knew he had at least two or three appointments scheduled, and he wanted to finalize the motion to suppress and get it filed in Tyler's case. The weekend had been relaxing and had left him feeling rejuvenated and ready to seize the day.

The hook-up with Tyler had been good medicine, and his heart felt strong again. He even planned to get back to the Macon Health Club and go for a walk before lunch. It was nice to have more energy, and he knew the exercise would help him recapture additional amounts when the endorphins kicked in.

He glanced at his watch and saw that it was almost nine o'clock. He had already been working over an hour rechecking the legal authorities cited in the motion, and everything looked in order. There were only a couple of cosmetic changes for Joyce to make before filing it. Ollie wanted the hearing to be set as soon as possible, and thought it likely since the current presiding judge of the Superior Court Criminal Division was someone not liking of delays. Judge John Walker was a man who believed firmly in the legal maxim of, "Justice delayed is justice denied."

The phone on his desk interrupted his thoughts about Judge Walker as he answered an unidentified transferred call from Red, "Hello."

"Mr. Tucker?" an unfamiliar feminine voice asked.

"Yes, this is he."

"I've never met you before, but I'm Francine Clements' niece, Jamie Stewart. Great Aunt Frankie has always told me I should call you if anything ever happened to her."

A sense of doom passed through Ollie before answering with a question, "Is your aunt okay?"

"She's had a bad fall and in the intensive care unit of the hospital. The doctor told me it doesn't look good. I haven't been able to talk to her because she's unconscious. I didn't know what else to do except to call you," the young woman started crying.

"I'm sorry to hear that Frankie's not doing well, but I'm glad you called, Jamie. You should know she's been a favorite client of mine for a long time. I'll try to get to the Medical Center later today and check on her. In the meantime, you probably know you have her power of attorney to help conduct her affairs until she's capable of resuming those activities," said Ollie.

"Yes sir, she showed me where those papers are in her house. I'm not exactly sure what I'm supposed to do, but she's told me you would help. I'm afraid she won't make it through this, Mr. Tucker."

"Don't worry, Jamie, I'll help anyway I can. Don't give up on her. She's about as tough as they come. Do you know what happened?"

"I'm not exactly sure. I tried to call her Saturday morning 'cause I was supposed to take her to the grocery store. When I didn't get an answer I went to her house and found her on the living room floor. I thought she was dead until I got close and saw that she was breathing. She had a cut on her head from falling down, and blood was all around her. I guess her knee gave away 'cause her doctor says it's shot. Now he says she's also got a fractured hip to go with the worn out knee on that side. She also broke her wrist when she fell. I bet she'll be mad at that walker and probably won't think of it as her best friend, anymore. She'll probably blame it, if she wakes up," she said and sniffed.

"I'm really sorry you had to go through all that by yourself. I'm sure that wasn't easy. I'll tell you what; I'll give you a couple of choices. One, come by my office at your convenience, and we'll talk about the steps to take for using the power of attorney. Or two, I'll meet you at the hospital this afternoon, and we can talk about it. Whatever works best for you. I'll help you get through this, I promise," said Ollie.

"Thanks, Mr. Tucker. I see why Aunt Frankie likes you so much. If you don't mind, I'd rather wait at the hospital until I find out if she's going to make it. I'd really appreciate it if you would meet me here."

"No problem, Jamie. I'll see you about mid-afternoon."

The two exchanged cellphone numbers and agreed on a location to meet inside the hospital. The young woman seemed relieved as Ollie hung up.

Ollie was saddened by the news of Frankie's situation and hoped this was not the beginning of the end for her. He knew of several people in similar circumstances who had not recovered from such a serious fall. Mrs. Clements held a special place in his heart, and he would have to do something to show her if given the chance. He thought of sending a unique and beautiful flower arrangement from Lawrence Mayer's florist shop, but then thought they might not allow such in the ICU. He made a mental note to check with the hospital when he visited to see if it would be possible. He was sure Frankie would love to see some color when she woke.

Ollie suddenly thought of Tyler and remembered that he and Frankie were close and had been since Ollie had recommended him for some work to her home many years ago. They had just talked about her when the two old friends were together over the weekend. The lawyer knew Ty would want to know that she was in the hospital.

Rather than use the landline on his desk, Ollie picked up his cellphone and looked in his contacts list for Tyler's number. He never could remember telephone numbers anyway and liked the convenience of touching an icon for a quick connection.

"Hey, Ollie. Calling to tell me how much you enjoyed seeing your old pal on Saturday?" Tyler said as he answered the phone.

That was another thing the lawyer liked about the phone technology now prevalent. Receiving a call gave a heads-up to the person before answering. Ollie often used the device as a screener when deciding if he wanted to talk to the person.

"I did like getting together over the weekend, Ty. I hope we can do it again real soon. I'm afraid that's not the reason I'm calling."

"The tone of your voice ain't very reassuring, buddy. Is it about the case?"

"No, it's about Frankie. She's had a bad fall and is in the intensive care unit. I just got a call from a great niece of hers. She's one of her caregivers and found her on the floor on Saturday, probably about the same time we were drinking a beer and talking about her."

The other end of the connection was so quiet that Ollie thought the call had dropped. He asked, "Ty, are you still there?"

He then paused, and asked again, "Tyler?"

"Is she going to be alright?" Tyler answered barely audible.

"I don't know. I understand she's in some kind of coma possibly due to a head injury, and she's got some broken bones including her hip. I'm going to the hospital later today and try to find out more."

"Oh. That doesn't sound good."

"It doesn't to me either, Ty. That's why I'm calling. I know you and Frankie are pretty close," said Ollie.

"Yeah," was all Tyler said in response.

Ollie wished he could be with his friend. Even though he couldn't see him, Ollie could tell that Tyler was upset.

"Look, I'm sorry I had to give you the bad news over the phone. If you want to, I'll go with you if you want to see her," said Ollie.

"No, that won't be necessary. I've got some things to do today, anyway. If you don't mind, just let me know when you find out more about her condition. Okay?"

"Sure, Ty. Don't worry, man. As you know, she's a strong woman and if anybody can snap out of this kind of mess, it's her."

"Yeah, I know. Thanks for calling, Ollie. I'll talk to you later," Tyler said and abruptly hung up.

Ollie sat at his desk and laid the smart phone down. He hated giving bad news, especially to a friend about another one.

CHAPTER 40

The Viewer was in the trophy room of his house, but was not enjoying it nearly as much as usual. A renewed wave of nausea swept through him as he placed the recently taken tiny porcelain figurine in the spot that was reserved just for it.

The events over the weekend were fresh on his mind and still made him want to alternately throw up or scream with joy. He didn't particularly like violence, whether intended or not, but he loved winning and claiming the prize that success brought. The accident he had witnessed while securing his latest collectable was the perfect example.

He was confident that if he had to, he could break bad. It was part of his persona that he had never been quite able to completely lose no matter how hard he tried at various times over the course of his life. Part of the reason was due to his experiences growing up, and the other part sprang from his years in the military. He might be a little older, but he was in great shape and could protect himself if need be.

He had many emotions running through his head this morning. He couldn't believe how sloppy he had gotten recently, and there had to be a reason. Maybe he was spending too much time with people he thought he knew, and it had gotten him off his game.

It seemed like just about every place he had gone into lately there had been some kind of a problem. He had never believed too much in luck because he thought you had to make your own. That's why he had always prepared so much before making the decision to go into someone's place.

Even though there was a little bit of unease based on the last few entries, he was thrilled by it all. Self-contained excitement came from everything he did, and he felt invincible, most of the time.

The last foray into the old woman's house had provided the most unique encounter of his Viewing career. He knew she was home alone, but had felt that would be no problem for him. It was supposed to have been a simple look and see. He had intended to grab one of the many little pieces of interest she had and then leave for the sanctity of home before anyone knew. He had everything he needed for an easy entry before she had shown up. He couldn't believe he never heard her before she rolled into the room.

He had just picked a nice little trinket and replaced it with an Ispy card when she surprised him. It had been the first time he had ever been seen, in person at least, by anyone while he was enjoying his art. *Imagine the odds of an old crippled woman slipping up on me like that,* he thought. He was much younger and more experienced in the skill of sneaking than she.

The thing about Francine Clements was he really liked her more than most folks. She was a classy woman who took no shit. He had done work for her, and she had been appreciative. He hadn't wanted her hurt, but when she fell, he knew he had to get out of there as quick as he could. He had been certain she was dead when he saw all the blood.

He probably needed to back off for a while with his ultimate plans for revenge. Otherwise, he might put himself in jeopardy. He just needed to be patient for the time being.

CHAPTER *41*

Ollie and his daughter arrived at the Medical Center a little before three o'clock with dark skies threatening a downpour. They found a parking place in the deck across from the front entrance of the hospital complex providing protection from the elements and giving them the option of crossing via a walkway above the street.

As the two exited the car and started toward the main building, Ollie couldn't help but remember his recent stay after suffering the heart attack. He also had a flashback to the first trip as a patient that had changed his life forever. The changes to the facilities that had occurred during that fifty-year span had been staggering.

Now the hospital was the second largest one in the state and a designated Level I Trauma Center. Ollie knew the care provided there was first class and served a significant portion of the nearby population, not to mention had given him the superb treatment during his two stays. It had come a long way from the humble beginnings when it was known as the Macon Hospital.

"Dad, thanks for letting me know about Ms. Clements and letting me come along," said Holly as they walked.

"I'm glad you were able to make it. I could tell you and Frankie bonded when she was in the office. I don't know if we'll be able to see her. She's been one of my favorites over the years, and I wanted to check on her personally. By the way, I'm happy my text got through. I had a good teacher," he said.

They both laughed as he referenced the recent lessons she had given him in the art of texting. She had insisted in them communicating one afternoon exclusively in that fashion after learning he had never sent one despite owning the most updated smart phone on the market. He found that he liked the feature that allowed him to speak into the microphone, and then displayed his words to be sent. He also discovered it could be pretty funny when autocorrect got some of the words wrong.

Holly had shown him funny outcomes that she had pulled up on the Internet when she was teaching him how to perfect his text technique. The old lawyer was laughing so hard after reading the different lists his daughter had Googled, he had been afraid he would need a bottle of oxygen before he could breathe or speak again.

"I recalled the need to review and edit before I sent it," Ollie added when they got through snickering.

"That's good to remember, Dad. It's too late to change or delete once you've hit that send key. Anyway, I was happy to see your message when I got out of class, but was sad to hear the reason you sent it. I know how much you like her."

They walked in silence through the main building until arriving at the set of elevators that would take them to the intensive care unit. People milled around the area awaiting a vertical ride. Some were obviously in the medical profession given by their attire of scrubs in various colors. Others had concerned looks on their faces leading Ollie to conclude they had loved ones as patients.

"This is a big place, Dad," Holly said as they waited for an open elevator.

"Yeah, almost a city in itself," replied Ollie.

A door opened and several people got out. There were more like the ones waiting to board.

The two of them entered along with a half-dozen more folks lost in their own worlds. The old lawyer's thoughts were twirling as he punched the button to take them to their destiny. As the doors closed, he could've sworn he saw Tyler get out of the elevator directly across from him. He didn't have time to call out or make further comment as his transport started ascending.

Could Ty have made the trip to see Frankie? It made a certain sense, he thought.

When they got to their destination, they found the unit was restricted to certain hours. It was understandable that visitors were limited as to when they could visit, and the two of them found seats near the entry. Holly immediately took out her cellphone and started checking her email. Her dad smiled as she started responding with furious thumb strokes.

Ollie surveyed the rather large area and saw several groups of people. One group was huddled close by with their heads bowed. The lawyer heard one of them praying for God's love, strength and mercy. In an instant, Ollie was transported to the first time he was a patient, and he heard the family pastor pray with his parents as he lay still in the hospital bed.

Our Father in heaven, please be with this family now in their hour of need. They have suffered greatly this evening as young Oliver was viciously attacked by an evil presence. We don't know the reason for this, but we trust in You and Your wisdom.

We pray for Your strength during this time so Oliver can heal completely and have a full recovery from his grievous injuries. We offer our sincere thanks for the mercy You have shown in sparing this young man's life because we know You have plans for him. May You continue to shine Your love on him and this family in the days ahead.

Ollie remembered not closing his eyes as the man continued to say words that he couldn't relate to at that moment in time. He watched the three of them with their eyes shut and knew they were imploring God for him. He didn't care. All he could think about was his beloved Libby and now she was gone forever.

What kind of God would let that happen? Until now he had believed in Him because his life had been so perfect, and he had constantly thanked the Lord for bringing him such a great girl with whom to share everything.

Ollie knew at that precise time, his faith was gone. He wanted to yell at the preacher to shut up. Nothing anyone could say would ever change his mind. He probably wouldn't tell others because they wouldn't understand, but that's just the way it was for him.

"Mr. Tucker?"

Ollie was brought back to the present when he heard his name. Standing before him was a cute twenty-something female with what he would call a pageboy or maybe a wedge haircut. He thought of a young Dorothy Hamill.

"Yes, you must be Jamie," responded Ollie.

She nodded and attempted a smile. Ollie stood and she hugged him without warning. He felt awkward for a moment and tried to hide it by patting her on the back as he put his arms around her in response. She began sobbing which only increased the lawyer's uneasiness. He had always been self-conscious with public affection and didn't know what to do next.

"It's going to be alright," he said.

She stepped back from him as tears welled in her mocha colored eyes. Ollie reached inside his coat pocket and removed a white linen handkerchief monogramed with his initials. He handed the perfectly folded cloth to the young woman, and she took it without hesitation.

"Thanks, Mr. Tucker. I'm sorry for crying on you."

"Don't worry about that at all. I can only imagine what you've been through the last couple of days. Has there been any change in Frankie's condition?"

"Not really. She's still out of it, but the doctor told me her brain doesn't appear to be severely damaged. He said they've done scans, and he's hopeful she'll snap out of it soon," Jamie said.

Holly had gotten from her chair as her dad and the girl spoke. She stayed slightly back and to the side of them not wanting to interfere and waiting for introductions.

Ollie twisted from the waist and motioned for Holly to come forward. He gently touched the back of her arm as he guided her to his side. They smiled at each other and then looked at Jamie.

"Jamie, I'd like to introduce my daughter, Holly. She works with me and is currently studying at the Mercer Law School. Holly, this is Frankie's great niece, Jamie Stewart."

Holly stepped forward with her right hand extended and then closed her other one over the shake that followed. She continued to hold the younger woman's hand in both of hers as she spoke.

"Hi, Jamie. I really enjoyed meeting your Aunt Frankie in Dad's office, and I have to tell you I love her. I like her spunk and humor. When I heard she was hurt, I wanted to come to see her. I hope you don't mind."

"Not at all. Thanks for coming and the kind words, Holly."

The three of them took seats and talked in subdued tones while waiting on visiting hours to begin. The lawyer spent part of the time discussing use of the general power of attorney Jamie held. Because Frankie had the foresight to choose her and provide the young woman with such a document, Ollie knew she would be able to easily take care of any business decisions that might need to be made while his client was unable. It seemed, however, there wouldn't be many such decisions needed since the old woman had most of her bills automatically debited from her bank account.

They also talked about another document that had been executed for decisions relating to health care. Essentially, Jamie had been named, as agent to make choices should Frankie's health decline to the point where death appeared inevitable. Frankie had made it clear she did not want to be kept alive by medications, machines or other medical procedures that by reasonable medical judgment could keep her alive but not cure her.

"Do you mean I'd have to make the decision to allow Aunt Frankie to die? I don't think I could do that, Mr. Tucker."

"You do have the right to choose not to act as Frankie's health care agent should her health deteriorate as we've discussed. Nobody can force you to do anything you don't feel comfortable with. Like I've said, Frankie made the choices contained in the Health Care Directive she signed. So, if the unspeakable happens, you could take solace that she would want you to follow her instructions. I'm not sure we need to think about it unless or until it becomes necessary. I hope you'll try and put it out of your mind right now," said Ollie.

"I'll try," said Jamie.

Several people had gotten from their chairs and gone through the door toward the ICU. Following their lead, the three of them left the waiting room to see the woman they all loved and admired.

CHAPTER 42

Tyler pulled his van as far as he could down the driveway of Frankie's house. He turned off the engine and sat staring at the old residence he knew so well. It was a place he had been to many times over the course of knowing the woman, but had only visited once during the last few months.

The trip to her home from the hospital had been one filled with memories as he again thought of the woman who lived there. She had been someone he had felt close to over the years and could talk to about things he was unable to discuss with most people in his life.

Tyler had discovered early on that Francine Clements was the epitome of an independent lady. The first meeting they had been unforgettable as was their last.

He remembered still being in his twenties and hustling for new business. Ollie had arranged an introduction to a potential client who had become a widow a few months before and was in need of some help around her house.

Upon arrival for the first time, Tyler loved the charm of the home but could see several cosmetic needs evidenced by a leaning mailbox, flaky cracked paint and unkempt shrubbery. There were noticeable shingles missing on the roof, and he wondered if there were associated leaks.

He had gotten out of an old Chevy pickup that served as his work vehicle and was inspecting some of the issues when out the front door came a hot little firecracker. The first impression was caused by the orange shade of her hair, the tightness of the clothing worn on her compact frame and the first words he ever heard her say.

"I'm guessing you're Ollie's friend, Tyler. He never told me how good you look in blue jeans and a tee shirt," she said with a sexy smile.

"Uh, hello. Are you Francine? Ollie said you'd be expecting me."

She had throaty laughter. He almost felt like she was mocking him to a degree as she let out an expression of it. For some reason he thought of Mrs. Robinson from one of his favorite movies, The Graduate.

"What are you expecting, Tyler?" she asked with a raised eyebrow.

He had felt his face turning red. At the same time, this older attractive woman playing with him aroused him like nobody ever had. It was a trait she played upon him many times thereafter.

During the years that followed, Tyler and Frankie became close friends. At times they were much closer than anyone else could've ever imagined. Their age difference kept them from being a seriously romantic couple, but they got to know each other very well.

It continued as Frankie married not once, but twice more. Her husbands seemed not to be able to keep up with the powerhouse they had married and passed on to the other side one by one. Through it all, Tyler remained close to the mighty-mite he had gotten to know by the grace of his friendship with Ollie.

With a sense of sadness and regret, Tyler got out of the truck carrying his keys with him. He then walked to the front door while twirling his key ring on his index finger. He doubted anyone would be there since Frankie had always preferred her independence. The one person he figured might be there had been spotted on his earlier trip to the hospital and would probably be occupied for a while.

He rang the doorbell and then knocked on the front door. After a minute or two passed without an answer, he selected a key on the large metal ring and slipped it into the deadbolt lock first, followed immediately into the doorknob.

Tyler continued directly to the burglar alarm keypad and punched in the code to disarm. With that task complete, he went to a hallway closet that provided storage for several coats and jackets among other things.

Separating and sliding the hanging items with his hands revealed a shelf that could not be seen before then. On the shelf sat an electronic device used for video recording. Tyler needed to see what it might show before he would leave.

CHAPTER *43*

The room where Frankie was located didn't have much available space left after Ollie and the two women entered. Along with the hospital bed containing the frail patient was various medical equipment including a monitor showing vital signs and a single uncomfortable chair that none of the three showed any interest in using.

The old lawyer watched as Jamie walked over to the hospital bed that slightly elevated her aunt's head and upper torso. She reached down and kissed her on the forehead and gently rubbed her cheek.

She was barely audible as she whispered, "I love you, Aunt Frankie. I've got some guests to see you."

Ollie stepped in closer and stood beside Jamie. He gazed down on Frankie who was unmoving and in what appeared a disturbed deep sleep. He saw the heavy gauze bandage covering her ashen and bruised forehead and the oxygen feeder tubes inserted into her nostrils. There was a cast on her wrist and her leg had been immobilized. The whole effect of her appearance left him with a sense of hopelessness. He only wanted for now the strong medications she had to be taking were keeping her stable and in a place where pain was well hidden.

"Hey, Frankie. You need to know something. I've always had a crush on you," said Ollie.

He could've sworn he saw a slight smirk form on the old woman's mouth. "I'm counting on you to completely recover. You hear me?" asked Ollie.

Just as he was about to back off, the old woman started groaning. Ollie and Jamie shared a look and she said, "That's the first sound she's made."

Everyone was frozen and then Frankie's eyes sprang open. Her mouth tried to work, but only groans came out. They were tortured and not easy to understand.

"Ty. Ty. Tywah. Tywah."

Her eyes were wild and opened wide. No one was sure if she saw anything as she looked at something not there. She reached out her hands as if she was expecting to grab something or someone no one else could see.

Then a violent seizure began to shake the old woman and the monitor must have caused concern as a nurse burst into the room.

"Ms. Clements, can you hear me? Answer me, please?" asked the nurse.

The old woman kept calling for "Tywah" and Ollie wanted to cry. Another seizure racked Frankie and uncontrolled shaking followed. Her eyes rolled back in her head before the nurse called for assistance, stat. The three of them were asked to leave as the doctors entered Frankie's room.

The end came soon after. The doctors told the three of them that she had fought valiantly. Mrs. Francine Clements left the world without explaining things she wanted to.

Ollie was left to wonder why her last words were for Tyler as the group cried together. It had to be significant.

CHAPTER 44

Two weeks had passed since Frankie's death, and Ollie was ready to get shed of Tyler's case. He was glad to be in court today to try and make that happen by winning the motion to suppress. As he had hoped, Judge John Walker had set the hearing sooner rather than later.

The lawyer had gotten to his destination early and set up at his table in the usual organized manner. He put a yellow pad slightly to the right, the case file folder in the center and had a couple of law books to the left. His briefcase was placed on the floor adjacent to the table, but it was easily reachable if he needed anything else that it contained. He took his favorite Cross ink pen from his coat pocket and laid it on top of the blank pad.

The courtroom was empty of spectators except for an old bailiff standing by the door leading to judge's chambers. Ollie watched him with some amusement as the guy fiddled with his hearing aid. There was a running joke between regular court personnel to the effect that it must be a job requirement to have significant hearing loss, and this employee was no different.

Tyler would sit beside him when he arrived, but Ollie had told him not to expect to testify. It was possible that the lawyer might change his mind about that decision, and his friend had been briefed that such testimony would be limited to the traffic stop, if it became necessary for the defense to offer any evidence.

Holly had wanted to attend the hearing, but couldn't because of class obligations. The old lawyer had told her she would have many more opportunities in the future to observe. For now, he told her she had prepared him to succeed, and he felt confident he would.

While Ollie sat at counsel table waiting on the rest of the participants, his thoughts returned to some of the events since Frankie's loss. It had been a sad time for everyone mourning Frankie's passing.

The service had been private, and not many people had attended. The old woman had left specific instructions as to what she wanted, and Jamie followed them to the letter. Since Frankie had been adamant in her desire to be cremated and in her request for a non-sectarian service, the affair had taken on a flair that was more like a party than a funeral. There was even wine served to go along with delicious hors d'oeuvres catered by Natalia's. For the most part, everyone had been upbeat.

Jamie had said a few words about what Aunt Frankie had meant to her and then turned it over to anyone else wanting to make comments. Ollie had felt obliged to take the floor first, and he found himself talking off the cuff for fifteen minutes. He got several laughs from others as he described an episode Frankie had relayed to him resulting in her hair turning green. Since everyone knew of the woman's constant tinkering with her hair color, it was easy to picture.

After Ollie's remarks, Tyler had asked to be heard next. He had never been known for his eloquence or for speaking in public, but his words brought tears to the rest in attendance.

I've only had three real friends in my life. One was named Libby and along with Ollie, they helped this shy boy come out of his shell. She was special. I think about those days all the time and what they meant to me. Then Libby died way too young, and I got lost again for a while. Ollie and I loved that girl with our hearts. I still miss her, and I'm sure Ollie does even more than me. She changed our lives.

Now, another woman has gone from my little circle of friends, and I feel like another part of me has died with her. Frankie knew me like nobody else, more even than Ollie. I could talk to her for hours, and she accepted me as I am with all my scars and warts.

So, I've a confession to make that I've never said to anyone, not even to her. I loved Frankie, and I wish I had told her before she left us forever. Now, it's too late.

It had been heart breaking to see the struggles on his face, but even more so to hear Tyler talk. His still sinewy body seemed to fold into itself as he spoke. The two men embraced afterward, and Ty had whispered to Ollie he was the only friend he had left in the world. Ollie had felt increased sorrow for his old friend and a little guilty that he at least had Holly in his life.

The lawyer had also been busy at work over the last couple of weeks. He had started the process of helping Jamie deal with the administering of her aunt's estate a few days after the private funeral service. New clients had also been signed up, and he had taken on more work than he had in years. One was potentially a large claim against a trucking company. Ollie never would've thought about it without having his daughter on board to help him. As it was, he was more excited about practicing law than he had been in a long time.

"Do I need to sit by you, Ollie?" asked Tyler.

The lawyer was snapped out of his memories by the arrival of his client and old friend. Ollie looked behind him to see Tyler dressed smartly in a blue blazer, starched blue shirt and tan slacks. He looked professional, sharp and very much unlike any burglar the lawyer had ever seen.

"Nice duds, Ty. You're looking good."

"You said to dress like I was going to church. The problem is, I can't remember the last time I was in one," said Tyler.

Ollie laughed and replied, "I know what you mean. Yeah, come up here and sit beside me."

Tyler came through the waist high swinging doors separating the gallery from the front of the courtroom. He took a seat beside the lawyer and folded his hands in front of him on the table.

"I'm a little nervous, buddy," said Tyler.

"It's going to be okay. I'm feeling good about this," said Ollie.

Ollie felt the entrance of Jessica Mooney, as he smelled the fragrance he associated with the chief assistant district attorney. He turned toward her as she strode across the courtroom toward her table. She didn't look happy.

He watched as she tossed her file onto the surface and thought it might slide onto the floor. She had a disgusted look on her face, and for some reason Ollie thought it a good thing.

Ollie didn't move at first and watched the prosecutor's body language. There was no doubt she was pissed about something. Sensing an opportunity, he got up from the chair and told Tyler he wanted to speak to the prosecutor for a minute.

"Are you alright," asked the lawyer as he approached.

Jessica took a few deep breaths and looked like she might hyperventilate. She took a few steps close to Ollie and said in low tones, "I don't like this case."

"Well, dismiss it then."

She hesitated for a moment and then said, "I probably would, but my boss doesn't get it."

"What's the problem?"

"Between us, he's more concerned with how it might look in the press if I dismiss the indictment. He thinks he'll take the flak if that happens. If the judge dismisses after the hearing, he says everybody will blame his honor. To tell you the truth, I think he's got next year's election on his mind. I don't know if you know this, but there's already talk about him having opposition next year," she replied.

Ollie nodded slightly, "I guess I can understand that way of thinking on a political level, and I have heard talk about a young prosecutor maybe taking him on, but I can't understand it on an ethical and professional level. I think making decisions of whether or not to prosecute a case based on anything other than legal principles is wrong, period. And he should be the one in the courtroom if that's the way he feels. Besides, I think it'll fall back on him either way. If you want me to tell him to his face, I will."

"I want you to know, it's not that I think your client is innocent. I just believe your motion has some validity. It's well written, by the way. Also, Judge Walker can rip another butthole when a cop or a lawyer screws up. I don't want my witness to end up that way. He's basically a good guy," she said.

Ollie glanced in the direction of the judge's door into the courtroom and noticed that the bailiff was plodding in their direction. The wall clock indicated they were supposed to start in ten minutes.

"How about this? I'll ask that the indictment be nolle prossed, and I've got another six months to see if anything else crops us before the case is finally dismissed," she continued as the old bailiff got closer.

"I don't know, Jessica. My client maintains his absolute innocence. He wants vindication, not delay. You and I know there is no case left without the evidence taken from the van. I also know from my investigation of the three victims listed in the indictment, only two could identify Tyler Crenshaw as having had an opportunity to take the stolen items. Both of them admitted to my investigator they liked him and couldn't imagine him doing such a thing. I think you'd have major trouble at trial, even if the evidence in the van was ruled admissible," said Ollie.

"Well, I could put it on the dead docket, and then I wouldn't have a six months restriction," she said with an edge in her voice.

"And I could file a speedy trial motion and force the issue," replied Ollie with an equal sharpness.

The old bailiff finally made it to their location. He reached for his ear and tweaked the bud inside again before talking.

"Are y'all ready for me to get the judge?" he said in a shaky voice.

"Not quite, Mr. Green," said Jessica.

"What, not tonight?" the old man asked.

"Bubba, we're trying to work out a resolution. If you could tell the judge we're negotiating, it might save some time," said Ollie in a louder voice.

"Oh, okay. You don't have to yell at me, though," said the bailiff as he shuffled away.

The female prosecutor let out a sigh and shook her head. She frowned as the deputy scheduled to testify at the hearing came through the doors of the courtroom followed by a female newspaper reporter.

Ollie had wondered if any press would show for the hearing. He certainly had not let any of them know of the proceeding, but he understood some reporters had contacts that kept them aware of any interesting cases coming before the court. At least he didn't see any television cameras for which he was grateful.

"Let me ask you something, Ms. Mooney. Are you handling this case yourself? Because if you are, you should make the decisions concerning what to do with it."

Jessica turned away from the defense attorney without answering and motioned toward her witness to sit on the pew closest behind her table. The reporter took a seat on the front row behind Tyler's location and pulled a small notepad and pen from her oversized purse. She flipped open the pad and scribbled something before lifting her head and smiling at the two lawyers.

When the prosecutor regarded Ollie again, there was a glint of anger in her eyes. "Let's finish our conversation over there," she said pointing to a row of chairs where attorneys usually sat waiting on their cases to be called.

The two of them sat down beside one another out of earshot from the others inside the courtroom. Jessica crossed her legs and her left leg went limp except for the slight sweep on her foot.

"You do understand I'm not the boss," she said.

"You are of this situation, if you're hanging on the line without support," said Ollie.

"I wasn't even supposed to catch this case. I never handle property, just persons. I don't remember the last time this kind of crap landed in my lap. I'm the fucking chief, right? I'm supposed to assign the cases, but Sally wouldn't take it, and then the boss laid the pile of steaming shit on me."

"All the more reason for you to do the right thing here. You think your boss is going to do anything against you, much less fire the best attorney he's got in the office?" Ollie asked with a raised eyebrow.

"Who knows? I've got a son to raise, and I've got to do what I've got to do to protect my job. I've got too much time invested to risk having to worry about looking elsewhere."

"Jessica, we need to do the right thing here. I know you've got a job, just like me. But, both of us are really on the same side. We're supposed to seek justice. It's not all about winning and losing. I hope that doesn't sound as trite as it does to my ears."

"Only to those who may be reading your words somewhere down the line, old dude. Everybody else can just suck it."

The two of them started laughing silently. Ollie liked this woman's humor and thought she was smart. The problem she had was not an easy one, and he knew she was caught in a bad situation. Tough choices had to be made. He didn't want to add to her stress, but he cared more about Tyler than her dilemma. He had his own to deal with.

Again, the old bailiff approached the two lawyers and was muttering to himself. He wrung his hands as he spoke.

"Judge Walker wants to see you two in his chambers. He doesn't seem too happy."

Ollie and Jessica stood simultaneously as they heard the news. Neither had any desire to upset the judge legendary for his gruffness and followed like puppies after the bailiff. The older lawyer gave a glance backward toward Tyler and hunched his shoulders as he entered the judge's office.

His Honor sat in a high back leather chair with an unlit unfiltered Camel stuck in the right corner of his mouth. The expansive desk in front of him appeared to weigh at least a ton and would've dwarfed a smaller man. However, John Walker was built for the huge piece of furniture and made the scene even more imposing.

Ollie had known Judge Walker during all the years of law practice. While their career paths had been different, there had been occasions when the two of them crossed the same one, and what had resulted was a healthy mutual respect for each other.

The judge had spent his time working up the ladder of public service. He had been a judge's law clerk right out of law school and after the maximum two-year stint, he was snapped up by the District Attorney to become a prosecutor. After a long stretch in that office that ultimately led to him being appointed by the Governor and then elected by the public as the DA, "Big John" Walker had been made a Superior Court judge. He had served in that capacity ever since. Altogether, he had been working for the government over forty years.

Ollie remembered back to the early years when he defended more criminal cases than at present. Walker was an assistant district attorney who was as steadfast on the job as he was dedicated to the constant cigarettes he smoked. They had battled several times, but each one had been completed with a degree of professionalism that was not always achieved nowadays. Some defense lawyers now feared having him as judge because of his background as a prosecutor, but not Ollie. Because of their history and past dealings, Ollie knew he could count on John Walker to be fair.

"Come in, counselors. Mr. Green, please close the door on the way out," said Judge Walker in a gravelly voice.

Jessica didn't speak, but smiled and nodded as she took a seat directly across from the judge. Ollie followed close behind her and remained standing as he got to the huge behemoth of a desk.

"Good to see you again, Judge," he said while unbuttoning his jacket and sitting down beside the prosecutor.

Judge Walker either grunted or growled, but Ollie wasn't sure which. His full lips with the cigarette drooping in one corner quivered in a fashion similar to what Elvis once made popular. An uninitiated person might think the jurist was sneering, but the two lawyers now sitting across from him knew that gesture was about as close as he ever came to a grin.

"You two made any progress resolving this quagmire?" he asked.

"Judge, I hope you don't mind me asking why you think this case rises to that definition?" answered Jessica.

The judge scissored the cigarette with his fingers and removed it from his mouth. The stare that followed melted the prosecutor down in her chair at least an inch. Ollie actually felt a little sorry for her and made him glad he knew better not to say anything like that.

"You're shittin' me, right? You do know I used to do the same thing for a long time, Mooney? Longer than you and those heels you wear. I can spot a stinker without having to remove the clothespin from my nose. So, I'm betting your boss knows it as well and somehow hopes this goes away without blowing his chances for reelection next year. Am I close?" he snarled.

"Judge, if you don't mind me interrupting, I believe Ms. Mooney and I both agree there are problems with this case. We've been discussing it for a little while, and I hope I'm not out of line by saying this, but there's more for her to consider. I've given it some thought, and I think I might have a solution to the problem," interjected Ollie.

Judge Walker placed the Camel back in between his lips and gazed at the defense lawyer. Ollie looked back at him without blinking. There were some unspoken words before the judge replied, "And, what might that be, Mr. Tucker?"

"I was thinking we could submit the facts to the court and you could rule on the motion without hearing any testimony. I believe Ms. Mooney and I could agree what the witnesses would say, and then you could render a decision based on that as well as the law as it currently exists. If that results in my client's charges being dismissed as I think they should be, then so be it. Bottom line, the court makes a ruling that we can choose to rely on or appeal if either side is unsatisfied."

Jessica glanced sideways at Ollie and nodded assent. "That could work," she said, emphasizing *could*.

A discussion followed in which the prosecutor and defense lawyer agreed that the traffic stop that resulted in Tyler's arrest was precipitated by a telephone call to the Sheriff's Office reporting a suspicious vehicle. It could not be verified who made the call other than it was reported as a concerned citizen in the neighborhood. The description of the van had been fairly specific, and the deputy would admit he made the stop based on that account rather than any traffic violation. The lawyers argued a bit about that making the encounter illegal before the judge stopped them.

"As you two well know, it'll be my job to determine that issue, if y'all agree on the facts. Based on what I've heard so far, it's not sounding so good for your team, Ms. Mooney," said the judge with a gruffness that made Jessica visibly cringe.

The ADA swallowed hard as Judge Walker stabbed the air so hard with the Camel that it caused bits of tobacco to come out the end. Ollie's confidence was boosted again as the judge kept gesticulating with the cigarette.

"I've got real concerns about the reliability of such a tip as you've described forming the basis of a traffic stop. A decent description of the vehicle being in the area doesn't make it an explanation for why it was suspicious, and it's a long ass way from being close to doing anything illegal. What the hell made it such?

"Furthermore, any decent cop I've ever known could find some articulable suspicion for stopping a vehicle, but evidently your officer didn't suggest anything even as innocuous as a questionable window tint, failure to signal, weaving in the roadway or having a faulty taillight. How many times have we heard those kinds of things? It's to his credit that he didn't make up any reason, and I don't doubt he thought he was doing the right thing to investigate.

"Bottom line, I think the stop stinks and anything found in the van would be the proverbial fruit of the poisonous tree. Now, I don't know if you've got other facts or evidence to help make out your case, Ms. Mooney; but I'm well familiar with the case law even without the extensive cases cited in Mr. Tucker's motion and brief, and I do believe the motion to suppress should be granted," he said before sticking the Camel back in the corner of his mouth.

Ollie couldn't help but let a tiny hint of a smile creep on his face as the judge harangued the prosecutor. He also couldn't help the pride he felt for the job Holly had done on the motion.

The judge had just confirmed what he already knew, and he couldn't wait to tell his daughter.

Jessica finally broke the icy stare of the judge by saying, "Yes sir, I understand."

Judge Walker removed the prop from his lips and his eyes softened. The look he gave the female prosecutor reminded Ollie of those his Uncle Joey gave him on occasion way back in the day when some lesson was being taught.

"I know you understand, Ms. Mooney. I've seen how you handle your cases in my courtroom for many years, and I suspect this case was dropped on your head for reasons beyond your control. For whatever it's worth, I don't fault you at all for feeling you had to bring it into this domain. You're a top-notch lawyer, and I think this disposition protects your earned reputation. I wish I could say the same for your boss."

Ollie cleared his throat. The judge and Jessica turned their attention to him. He gave his most sincere expression to each before speaking.

"I would like to be on record that I appreciate the prosecutor's willingness to handle this matter in such a manner as we have today. It reminds me of how we used to do things when I first started practicing law.

"It's the first time I've had the pleasure of having a case with Jessica, and I admire her professionalism as much as I like her, let's say, unorthodox humor. I'm sure Your Honor has seen that firsthand a lot more than me," said Ollie.

All of them laughed at the reference and the mood lightened in the room. Jessica even let out a muffled snort.

"If the court would like me to prepare an order, I will be happy to do that. Otherwise, I'm at your disposal," finished the defense attorney.

"I wish I could've dumped this case in a waste disposal. Oh, no. Did I just say that out loud?" said Jessica.

"I know you didn't just compare me to some kind of a trash dumpster, or worse," said the judge in a fake version of his famous growl.

They all laughed again and Ollie couldn't wipe the now full-sized grin off his face. He started to plan the celebration for Tyler before any of them left the room. It would be special.

CHAPTER 45

Tyler looked through his closet in search of something appropriate to wear. He had never been comfortable in dress clothing, but he felt it necessary to pick something more formal than his usual jeans and sports shirt for the celebratory occasion. He didn't want to stick out like a sore appendage at his own party. He could wear the same ensemble he had for court a few days ago, but he thought that might look like he only had one outfit to wear. That wasn't exactly so.

He finally decided to wear a long sleeved knit shirt. The temperature had turned cooler, and he wouldn't feel so bad not having a tie around his neck. There were several colors to choose from, and he finally decided on the blood red one. Along with his black wool jacket and a pair of tan slacks, he felt it was presentable enough.

After slipping into his clothes, Tyler admired himself in the full-length mirror on the backside of the closet door. Not bad, he thought. He wasn't the good looking guy as Ollie had always been, but he at least appeared fit and not butt-ugly.

He was feeling out of sorts and was not sure what he should do next. The life he had led until now was baffling in some regards. Sometimes he was in control, and sometimes he didn't think he was at all.

Tyler went to an isolated part of his closet and shifted some clothing. A metal safe revealed itself, and he began dialing the cylinder right to thirty-one, left to twenty-five and then back to seven.

When the small door clicked opened, he peered inside. There were only a few objects visible. One was a handgun. Another was a knife. The other was a dainty gold shaped heart on a thin chain.

He slipped the folded lock blade into his right pocket of his pants, and then lovingly picked up the jewelry. Tyler touched the piece as he cupped it in his left hand. It was not especially remarkable in any way except for one. When it was flipped over, there was an inscription that was worn with age.

Love always, Ollie

Tyler felt a tear slide down his cheek as he read the short message again. The necklace had been in his possession for so long, but it never failed to bring back strong emotions. Memories came back as he rubbed the object's outline between his thumb and forefinger.

***

1964.

A few months had passed since the horrible nightmare, but it was still a fresh wound in his soul.

As he had done at least a half-dozen times since that night, young Tyler walked around the scene where Libby and Matt had met their untimely deaths. The first time there had been yellow crime tape surrounding the area. That was long gone now, and no one else was around to watch.

One minute he was reliving that night, the next minute he was torn up in some future time. Neither option was optimal to the young teen. He looked for understanding that was not forthcoming. He implored God to guide him in his difficult quest.

He scoured the grounds for some reason he couldn't explain. His tortured brain wanted to understand the why of it all. No matter how hard he tried, none of it made any sense. Libby had been the only girl who had treated him as an equal much the same as Ollie had been the only guy accepting him for who he was. He didn't want to think about her never being there for him ever again. She understood.

Tyler rubbed a spot underneath his ribs. There was still a pink scar from a stab wound and the resulting stitches required to help the healing process. He had other wounds as well, but that one had punctured a lung causing him to be ineffectual during the fight. His inability to breathe made it more of a one on one combat, and Tyler knew he might've died but for Ollie's heroic efforts that night.

He continued poking around the landscape while random thoughts darted through his head. There was some knee high grass and pine straw to contend with as the teenager brushed his foot back and forth. Then in a clump of dandelions on the edge of his vision, he saw a different shade of gold hidden in the green. He reached down to see what it was and recognized it as soon as he touched it. It was a necklace Libby had worn since Ollie gave it to her as a sixteenth birthday present.

Tyler picked it up off the ground, and the bloodstained heart fell off the broken chain into his hand. The inscription side was facing him and made him whimper like a scared puppy when he saw it.

At first, he tried with all his might not to cry. Then his lips started quivering, and there was nothing he could do to stop the impending flood. He fell to his knees and sobbed more than he ever had or would again.

The grief he experienced in those moments crushed his spirit, and he felt like the strange little kid from years before. He thought that youngster had left his shell behind for good, but now he might need another to hide in.

So, Tyler cried while rocking himself in the grass. He wept for Libby and for his dead brother, too. He also shed tears for Ollie who had pretty much ignored him since that night. He hoped they could find a way to get past the hurt because they needed each other.

When he finished crying about the deceased, the teen took the corner of his tee shirt and wiped his eyes. He tenderly placed the chain and heart in the bottom of his right front jeans pocket. He would clean it after getting home and decide whether to keep it for himself or return it to Ollie. At that moment he was unsure what he would do.

***

The older and more mature Tyler continued to burnish the object in his hand as he found himself again in the confines of his closet. He knew it wasn't healthy to cross back into the past so much as he had recently. It had all become so confusing and complex, and there were other considerations in his life as well.

A recent physical examination had revealed an elevated PSA reading, and a biopsy had confirmed he had prostate cancer. Because he had avoided seeing his physician for several years, something that could have been a whole lot less serious was now a lot more dangerous to his survival. His doctor had advised surgery, but he did not want to face that as an option. He had been cut on more than he ever wanted to endure again.

At this point in his life, Tyler only wanted to make things right. He had ideas about how to do it. He just hoped that he could.

CHAPTER 46

Holly was relaxed for the moment with her bare feet resting on an ottoman that doubled as extra storage. Recently she had used the container for her materials on the Crenshaw case. She even had her old investigative notes on the bottom that had been neglected since the favorable ruling on the motion to suppress. There was no real need at the moment to try and figure out other suspects. Other fish needed frying.

Sitting in her overstuffed comfy chair, the woman felt as content as she'd ever felt in her life. It was hard to believe how different everything was than it had been just the year before. The whirlwind that was now her existence left little free time, but she loved it all.

Well, I would like to have more time for Shawn, she thought smiling to herself. *Other than that, it's all good.*

The last few weeks had been a busy time for her. Every free minute of the day she was either in class, studying or helping her dad at the office. By the time her head hit the pillow each night, she was sound asleep, and the rhythm of her breathing could be heard throughout the small apartment.

Weekends were only a little better since it seemed extra reading and studying was required for the upcoming week. It was also the only time she had to do her laundry and other chores. The few hours she could devote to Shawn and other pleasures were enough to ensure happiness in her personal life, but she would've liked more time to indulge in additional relaxation.

This Saturday was a special treat because of the planned event for her dad's friend, so she had splurged and treated herself to a manicure and pedicure. The nail technician had suggested a bright China Glaze nail polish, Pink Voltage, and Holly admired the handiwork again. The bright color suited her mood, and she looked forward to the expected comments from her boyfriend.

Not for the first time since she and Shawn had begun seeing each other, Holly thought it strange to refer to him in such a manner. The number one reason was due to him not being a boy. He was a mature man with a physique that could drive her crazy with desire one minute and then challenge her with his knowledge of multiple topics the next.

Although she knew he was several years older, he had a knack for matching her energy in any activity they tried together whether it was running, biking or anything else requiring physical exertion. Holly prided herself for being in good shape and still tried to maintain a daily spin class, but Shawn often barely broke a sweat when they exercised together. The way he moved made her think of a cheetah or some other powerful cat.

He had seemed a little distracted lately, but that was understandable. He had told her he had multiple jobs underway that were stressing him out, but for some reason she thought it might be something else. Her discreet attempts at questioning Shawn resulted in him assuring Holly that it was nothing for her to worry about. She had taken him at his word since her plate was full.

Her plans for the evening were to enjoy the party for a short time with the small group of invited guests and then steal Shawn away to his or her apartment for a night of intimacies. She figured Shawn wouldn't object, especially since he hadn't seemed thrilled to attend anyway.

Holly remembered the brief telephone conversation from Tuesday. It had been a bit rushed as both of them were in the midst of full days.

"Hey, babe. Dad's having a little gathering at his place for his friend this Saturday, and he's said you're welcome to come. Since you haven't met him yet, I was thinking it would be a great way to break the ice."

There had been a short pause and then he replied, "I was hoping to have you all to myself this weekend. We haven't had much time together lately."

"Awh, you've been missing little ole me. I know, I've been wanting to see you, too."

"What's the occasion? I'm a little leery being around a roomful of strangers."

"I know you remember the case I told you about where I helped Dad prepare a pretrial motion? Well, it got really good results for his client. The judge ruled in our favor, and the case is pretty much over at this point. Dad's using this as an excuse to have a little office get-together. I don't think there will be anybody there other than the client, staff and their dates. Of course, I want you to be mine, hot stuff."

Shawn had paused again before responding, "So, this is a celebration for some criminal's case being dismissed? Doesn't sound like anything I'd be interested in."

It was Holly's turn to hesitate as she was taken aback. She had wanted to introduce the two most important men in her life for months, and it still hadn't happened for one reason or another.

"We don't have to stay long. I really want you to meet my father. It's important to me, Shawn. And for the record, this client is Dad's best friend and hasn't been convicted of anything, so he's not a criminal."

The chill had become palpable over the phone connection. Neither spoke for a moment, and Holly had thought they were having their first fight, if you wanted to call it that.

"You're right. I guess I can share you for a little while Saturday night," he had finally said.

It occurred to Holly that they had not spoken since that phone call. She hoped that was not a sign of brewing trouble.

No, this night is going to be special, she thought.

CHAPTER 47

O llie walked through the upstairs of his residence dressed only in blue cotton boxers and a white tee shirt. He still had at least a couple of hours before the guests would arrive and didn't feel rushed to get ready. Besides, nothing spelled freedom like walking around in your drawers.

There was a serenity encompassing him that he wasn't sure he had felt in a month of Sundays. The few days since the meeting in Judge Walker's chambers had provided much needed decompression in his life. Any unresolved issues left in his head over Tyler had been buried as far as he was concerned, and Ollie was ready to get closer to his old friend than he had been in recent times.

He had been pumped scoring the victory for more than one reason, but his friend hadn't seemed so sure. No doubt, major endangerment no longer existed against Tyler, and his friend should be pleased at that prospect. The moment Ollie had informed him that the motion had been granted, however, a scowl formed on his face, and he wanted to know how that would clear his name. The resulting conversation was nothing more than a rehash of an earlier one, with the lawyer insisting the main purpose for filing the pretrial motion had been achieved.

No matter, they had been friends through worse things, and Ollie intended the planned party to begin mending fences. Knowing Tyler as he did, Ollie was convinced they could come up with solutions that would better satisfy the desire to show his innocence. The lawyer already had one idea that he would tell Ty about that night during a private moment.

Ollie's thoughts shifted to Holly and her male friend. Being a father had changed his perspectives on a lot of things, not the least of which was a paramount desire to see his daughter happy. He could tell the man she had been involved with for a few months was adding to her well-being, and therefore made him glad to some degree.

However, there was a part of him that was jealous because some other guy was stealing time with her away from Ollie. He couldn't explain why because the relationships were entirely different, but it nagged at him like an itch he couldn't scratch. Also, not being a great role model in his own right, made Ollie distrustful of other men.

Truth be told, most of the emotional discomfort was probably due to his own inability to totally connect with a woman over the course of his lifetime. Because he had never found a person who could crack that shell encompassing his heart and soul; and the fact he could never fully let go of the past, caused Ollie to be inherently suspicious of the boyfriend's motives.

Maybe, the uneasy feeling would dissipate when he met the mystery man who had become a big part of Holly's life. He certainly hoped so for her sake.

In the meantime, Ollie had complete confidence in his daughter. She had earned it with everything she had done for him. He knew he couldn't take very much of the credit for how she'd turned out, but he remained determined to make up for lost time and provide every advantage he could.

The phone ringing brought him out of his thoughts, and Ollie made his way to the nearest extension located in the kitchen. He checked the number that flashed on the identification feature, but didn't recognize it. Most of the time under such circumstances, Ollie let the call go into voice mail. It was an effort to screen away unwanted solicitations that always pissed him off. For some reason, he decided to answer.

"Hello?"

"Is this Oliver Tucker?"

"Yes, with whom am I speaking?"

"With someone wondering how you can represent scum," answered the low-timbre voice.

Ollie swallowed hard at the menacing tone. He had received threatening phone calls at various times during his career, but none in recent memory.

"I don't know what you're talking about. You must have the wrong number," replied Ollie.

"No, I read about you in the paper. You're the one using technicalities to free a stalker. I don't know how you sleep at night. You're as bad as that Crenshaw criminal you represent."

Ollie felt his face begin to flush as anger arose. He hadn't lost his temper in a while, but he could feel it about to happen. He always hated himself when it occurred because he thought it included a loss of emotional control he didn't like. He should just hang up the phone, but he couldn't stop himself from responding.

"And you're certified to come to such a conclusion based upon your training as an asshole?" responded Ollie through clenched teeth.

Laughter that was barely audible at first then became brassy as it emitted through the receiver. Just as steam was rising from his head and he was about to blow a gasket, a familiar voice was heard.

"Ollie, it's me, Tyler. I was messing with you."

The lawyer's blood pressure dropped, and his pulse slowed. He hadn't been a butt of a joke like that since he couldn't remember when.

"You're as funny as a heart attack, Ty. And, I can tell you that's not funny at all. You almost made me start cussing."

Tyler kept laughing on his end, which eventually caused Ollie to join in. Neither could recall when they had shared such a moment. It was a silly prank reminiscent of being school kids again.

"That's the hardest I've laughed in a long time, Ollie. Thanks, Buddy."

"Okay, you got me, Ty. But, why would you use such a ploy to call yourself scum, a stalker and a criminal? You're none of those things, and it bothers me to hear you say such."

"I was saying what I bet a lot of folks are thinking. I know you read the article that Telegraph reporter wrote in the paper. It made you look brilliant for your legal maneuverings, but it didn't do anything to restore my name."

"Ty, we've been over this more than once. You've got to get that feeling out of your craw. I've been giving it some thought, and we'll talk about it this evening. Right now, I want you to start enjoying your life again. Can't you at least try?"

"Yeah, whatever. Hey, do you need me to bring anything this evening?"

"Just yourself, old man. We'll have plenty of food and beverages. I'll tell you my ideas about clearing your name, too. No extra charge."

"Okay, Ollie. Look, I've been thinking a lot the last few days. I've got some things going on right now I need to talk to you about. If we can have a few private minutes tonight, maybe after everybody else leaves, you can give me your thoughts and I'll share mine. Just us. Nobody else, if that's alright."

"Sounds like a plan, Ty. We'll share a nightcap and I'll even break out a couple of Cubans. I'm looking forward to it," said the lawyer.

The phone call ended and Ollie smiled to himself. It was shaping up to be a memorable evening.

CHAPTER 48

The conference room on the main floor smelled like a combination of a gourmet kitchen and a flower shop. The food smells came from a spread provided by Kudzu Catering, and the floral scents derived from several unique arrangements set up by Lawrence Mayer Florist shop.

Ollie stood at the table admiring the fare and couldn't help but stuff one of the chicken salad puffed pastries in his mouth. The hors d'oeuvres had been making him salivate like Pavlov's dog since he arrived down the stairway, and he closed his eyes as he chewed. Since he had skipped lunch in anticipation of the party food, Ollie was starving, and it was all he could do not to fix a plate before the guests arrived.

One of the caterer's employees was standing nearby inspecting and then rolling silverware inside white linen napkins. The name pinned on his smock identified him as Zac, and he grinned as he watched the host enjoy the morsel.

"Those are good appetizers, right?"

"Yeah, and I could graze on all this stuff about right now. That would probably mess up the perfect presentation you've arranged, though," answered the lawyer as he surveyed the geometrically placed trays containing all sorts of goodies.

"Sir, I've stored some in the kitchen if you want to sample," said Zac.

"Thanks, but I guess I'll wait for the guests. Is the bar set up?"

"Yes, sir. I've got it in one of the front rooms. I thought most people might want a cocktail before getting to the cuisine."

"I like the way you think," said Ollie and paused before continuing. "Well then, Zac. How about doing the boss for the night a favor and get me one finger of Glenlivet on the rocks with a little water? A little something to take the edge off my hunger, okay?"

"No problem, sir. I'll be right back."

As the twenty-something guy walked out of the room, Ollie snagged another sample of a different pastry followed by a broccoli floret dunked in blue cheese dressing. He was still chewing on the vegetable when the young man walked back into the room holding a crystal cocktail glass wrapped in a paper napkin.

"My hero," said Ollie taking the drink.

Zac gave a half-smile and made a motion with his finger toward the corner of his mouth to let the lawyer know he had residue. Ollie removed the paper from his glass and dabbed at his mouth.

"I think you're on the way to a healthy tip when this night is done," said Ollie as he winked and walked out of the room.

He took his time walking through the office area and made an inspection of each room. Everything had been cleaned and polished and the wooden furniture smelled faintly of lemons. There were also scented candles placed in strategic locations awaiting lighting that would provide a pleasant fragrance as the evening wore on.

Bowls of mixed nuts were set on all of the coffee and end tables. Additionally, there were heavy lead glass containers holding Godiva chocolates to offset the salty treats.

This was not to be a large party, and it occurred to Ollie he was going overboard with the amount of food he had ordered. He didn't care because he wanted to not only commemorate Tyler's exoneration, the lawyer also wanted to show his appreciation to his hard-working staff who always helped him stay on top of his profession. He wanted everyone to enjoy and not leave until they had full stomachs and happy hearts.

As Ollie admired the rooms, there was a tentative knock at the front door, and he took the few steps necessary so he could open it. Red and her husband stood there with dueling smiles.

"Hey, Boss. Looks like you're getting an early start," said the redhead.

Ollie couldn't help but chuckle and saluted the two with the drink he still held in his right hand. He then moved the cocktail to his left so he could grip and shake the other man's hand.

"I'm glad you two could make it. Come in and make yourselves at home. It shouldn't be too hard for you, Red, since you spend so much time here. Y'all are the first to arrive, so you can get a head start like me. Can I get y'all something to drink?"

"Let's see what you got, Boss."

Red led her husband inside and they went directly to the bar. Zac had magically appeared behind the table that was functioning as such and gave an enigmatic smile. The guests studied the liquor brands that were all top shelf selections. There were also wine choices as well as iced down beer. As they were deciding and before Ollie could close the door, he saw Holly getting out of a shiny black pickup truck parked up the street.

He watched as the man she accompanied held the door open while she stepped down to the sidewalk. Trying not to stare, the father maintained his gaze as the couple began walking hand in hand toward the building.

Ollie's first impression was that they made a striking couple. He had long since decided his daughter was a natural beauty without much need for any enhancements. However, when she decided to kick it up a notch with a little makeup and nice clothes, Holly Lee had movie star looks.

The man complimented her appearance in an understated yet magnetic way. Ollie guessed him to be probably five feet-ten or eleven inches tall. He was shorter than Ollie and not as broad through the shoulders, but the way he strode automatically made the lawyer think of a military background. His back was ramrod straight, and there was a slight sway of the upper body that radiated controlled energy. His dark blonde hair was clipped short and was accentuated by a tanned face.

They climbed the steps leading up to the columned front porch with Ollie following their moves. Holly had a wide beam on her face while her date wore a much more subdued smile.

"Hey, Dad. Are we special or does everybody get the host's welcome before crossing the threshold?"

Ollie grinned as he stepped out from the house and greeted his daughter. They embraced and he kissed her on the cheek. "You look like a million bucks," he said.

He then stepped backwards and reached his right hand toward Holly's escort. His scotch remained in the left, and the ice tinkled as he moved.

"Shawn, it's very nice to finally meet you. I'm Oliver Tucker."

"Mr. Tucker, I'm glad to meet you, too," said Shawn as he shook the older man's hand.

Ollie noted that Shawn's grip was strong without being vise-like. He also liked that Shawn looked him in the eye as they spoke. There was something familiar about him that put the lawyer at ease, but at the same time made him wary.

"My friends call me Ollie. I hope you'll feel comfortable enough to do the same."

"Thank you, sir. I'll try to do that...Ollie."

"Holly tells me that you and I have at least a couple of things in common. I understand you enjoy a good scotch while listening to Randall Bramblett," said Ollie.

Shawn laughed. "I do. It looks like you've got at least half that covered already," he said nodding at the lawyer's glass.

"Well, come on in and I'll help you catch up with me. I might even pull out some albums later, and we can listen to some good music."

The couple entered the house and Holly introduced Shawn to Red and her husband. While they talked and told Zac what they wanted to drink, Ollie remained at the front entrance to welcome Joyce and her date followed by Frankie's niece, Jamie, accompanied by a young man who looked uncomfortable. There was no sign of Tyler as the other guests made their way inside.

It was still early, but Ollie was starting to feel irritated that his friend hadn't made it to his own party. He tried to put it out of his mind as he closed the front door and mingled with the rest of the guests.

The next thirty minutes hurried by as the host flitted around spending time with everyone. The food was eaten with gusto, and Zac and another employee were kept busy providing the guests with food and drink. The sound level was growing louder inside the house when Ollie thought he heard the front door open. Making his way through the other people, he arrived just in time to see Tyler close the door behind him.

The host thought his friend looked dapper in the outfit he was wearing and younger than his years. Ollie also thought the man looked tired and not as erect as he did normally. Tyler smiled wanly at Ollie, and it only reinforced the lawyer's opinion that his friend was fatigued.

The two old friends embraced with Tyler's head fitting snugly underneath Ollie's chin. Both patted their hands on each other's backs as if they were embarrassed by the act of affection that was shown by two men hugging. When they finally parted, Tyler spoke first.

"Thanks, buddy. I needed that."

Ollie tried to read Tyler's eyes without any luck. He then replied, "Is everything okay?"

"It will be. Let's talk later after everybody else leaves."

"Okay, we'll do that. How about a beer or something?"

Tyler's lips twisted into a grin and followed his friend over to the bar that was currently unattended. Ollie stepped behind the table and saw there were three choices iced down.

"Hiney light, Bud or Corona?" he asked referring to Heineken and Budweiser in the vernacular.

"Give me the Mexican with a lime," replied Tyler.

Ollie opened the beer and placed a green fruit slice on the lip of the bottle. He handed it to his friend and watched as Tyler squeezed it into the top and then took a healthy slug.

"Better already," he said.

"I want you to meet some folks. Come with me," Ollie said as he led the way into the larger room where most of the guests had gathered.

Ollie surveyed the room as he entered and everyone was engaged in smaller groups. There had been significant dents made in the spread, but still enough food was present to feed a small army. He walked over to the table, grabbed a spoon and began hitting the side of a half-full glass of tea that someone had left on the table. The sound softened in the room by at least a couple of decibels as the bell-like chiming continued for a few moments.

"May I have everyone's attention for a minute?"

"You got it, Boss!" shouted Red who then looked embarrassed for being so loud. "Sorry, I guess I'd better slow down on the martinis."

Everybody laughed as the young secretary's face turned slightly less crimson than her hair. Her husband shook his head side to side and followed up, "I swear, she's only on her second one," which led to another round of snickers.

"It's okay, Red. I want everybody to have a great time tonight. You all deserve some fun. It's one of the reasons for this get together. I wanted to show my appreciation for all the hard work my office always does that makes me the best I can be. If I may, I'd ask y'all to raise a glass to toast Joyce, Red and my newest addition and gorgeous daughter, Holly. Cheers to the best legal staff in Macon, Georgia, and we don't even have to advertise," said Ollie while saluting each one at a time with the now almost empty first drink.

There was a buzz generated by several people talking and whispering with each other. Ollie noted pleased expressions on all of the employees' faces.

"I'm not through. I also want to welcome all the other guests, and I hope you enjoy the occasion as well. You honor me with your presence.

"Finally, the last order of business before we kick up this party to another level is to celebrate the exoneration of the best friend I've ever had in my life, Tyler Crenshaw," said Ollie as he placed his right arm around the shorter man's shoulders.

"Most of you don't know Tyler, and those of you who do, probably don't know of the history we share. We've been friends since we were in grammar school. That means well over fifty years.

"During all that time he's never let me down when I needed him. I don't know that he could say the same about me," Ollie paused and the two friends shared a private unspoken glance.

He then continued, "The last year has been an eye-opener for me in a lot of ways. It has probably been my most stressful, yet happiest one, at least in recent memory. This year is symbolized by having Tyler standing here with me, as he should be, innocent and free.

"There may be lingering doubts with some people in our community, but I hope there are none in this room because I believe in this man beyond a shadow of a doubt. And, I want to tell y'all first what I plan to tell anyone else who'll listen. Tyler Crenshaw is a good and honorable man," finished Ollie.

At first the room was eerily quiet, and then Holly started clapping. Soon it seemed everyone else joined in.

Tyler seemed overwhelmed with emotion and his Adam's apple moved up and down as he silently swallowed. His eyes were watery as the applause subsided and he croaked, "Thanks, Ollie."

"Okay, eat, drink and be merry. I'm going to do that starting right now," said Ollie as he led Tyler to the table and handed him a plate.

The two friends heaped food onto their dishes as the sound level again rose in the house. Ollie got Zac's attention and asked him to make him another cocktail and to take it to his office. The lawyer told Tyler to follow him as they passed through the main floor to the office suite.

When they arrived, the two sat across each other in the comfortable sitting area away from Ollie's desk. Zac brought a freshly made amber colored beverage and set it on a coaster by Ollie's fully loaded plate before discreetly retreating.

It was a more intimate scene and the sounds of the party were removed enough that the two of them could talk in subdued tones and still be heard without straining old ears. Tyler blew out an exaggerated breath and took a sip from the bottle he still held. Not much was said during the next several minutes.

Ollie sat munching on the heavy hors d'oeuvres and watching Tyler pick at his. He acted preoccupied as he took small bites of different items on his plate without finishing any of them. It reminded the lawyer of a kid sampling a box of chocolates.

"Are you sure you're okay, Ty?" asked Ollie.

"I'll be alright. I'm just a little tired. Besides, we're going to talk later after the other guests leave, remember?"

Before Ollie could answer, Holly stuck her head inside the door. She gave each of the men a look before speaking.

"Am I interrupting a private conversation?"

"No, baby. Come on in and get to know Tyler," said Ollie.

The woman glided into the room and sat at the last available seat between the two men. She didn't appear in any way uncomfortable and easily held their gaze. Without reservation, she reached over and held a slender hand to Tyler.

"It's good to see you, Mr. Crenshaw. I'm very happy Dad was able to help with your situation. I know how much he thinks of you."

Tyler grasped her hand with both of his. He smiled at her words and his eyes crinkled in the corners.

"I also know how much he loves you," he said almost in a whisper.

"Ollie's told me how much you did to help me, and I want to let you know how much I appreciate it," he continued.

"It may sound a little weird to say, but I had fun, Mr. Crenshaw. I never knew how satisfying it would be to do legal research, especially when it meant justice would be found for you. It truly meant something special to me to help you and Dad," she said.

The man smiled and said, "Would you call me Tyler?"

Her reciprocal grin said it all. His acceptance of Ollie's daughter made it so.

The next twenty minutes were spent with Holly hearing stories of her father and Tyler reliving the past as kids. She laughed as Tyler told about the time the two picked blackberries and ate so many in the process that they had the runs for two days. She cried when Ollie relayed the tale of him spending his meager savings to buy Tyler a baseball glove so they could play catch together. She loved finding out things about them both that had helped build their friendships and characters.

As the sounds in the house receded, Shawn appeared in the doorway of Ollie's office. The three occupants quit their discussion, and Holly got up from her seat to greet him. She kissed him lightly on the lips and led him into the room.

"Shawn, I want you to meet Tyler Crenshaw, my dad's best friend. Tyler, this is my boyfriend, Shawn Matheson. I think you two might have a lot in common."

Tyler eyed the younger man as if he were sizing up someone he was about to get into a boxing ring with. Shawn didn't react initially, and then a smirk appeared on his face. He stepped to Tyler as Ollie's friend stood.

As Ollie watched the two men face each other, there was an odd sense of déjà vu. Both were almost the same exact height and build. Shawn extended his right hand that was unmet for a moment before Tyler gripped it with his own for a short shake.

"Mr. Crenshaw," said Shawn with a nod.

"Have we met before?" asked Tyler as he studied the younger man.

"I don't think so."

"You look familiar. Who do you work for?"

"I've run my own business for about twelve years now. Before then, I worked out of the carpenters local, so I guess you could say I worked for a lot of different contractors."

"Maybe that's the connection. You never worked for me by chance?"

"Nope, I don't think so."

Holly interrupted the conversation by bragging on a couple of the projects she had seen that Shawn had either completed or was near finishing. Ollie countered by talking about some of Tyler's work including renovations to the office and his friend's residence in the country.

"Like I said, the two of you have some things in common. I didn't mean to make it a competition," said Holly with a light laugh.

"I didn't mean to butt in on your private conversation. I just wanted to thank you, Mr. Tucker, for a nice evening. I was hoping I could steal away your daughter before it got too late, if that's okay with you, and her of course," said Shawn.

Holly blushed and peeked at her watch. She seemed to get the hint without any trouble.

"Our private time has been rather restricted lately," she said as she walked over to Shawn and squeezed his arm.

Ollie grinned and commented, "I'm sure I speak for Ty as well when I say we're not so old that we've forgotten what that's like."

Holly and Shawn said their goodbyes and left the two old friends alone. Tyler had a furrowed brow indicating he was in deep thought.

"Hey, whatever you're thinking about, save it 'til later. I need to go check on the rest of the guests before they get ready to leave, too. Can I bring anything back to you?" said Ollie.

"No, you go ahead. I may get another beer in a minute."

Ollie left Tyler to his contemplations. He had his own that were deeper than anything before.

CHAPTER 49

Holly was satiated. Beside her, Shawn was snoring without being obnoxious. She found it endearing that the man beside her was sleeping so soundly. He had said he was tired, and their lovemaking must have been the final spark sending him to la-la land. For some reason she was wide-awake, but didn't really mind since it was not even midnight. Everything in her life was just going so well right now.

She remembered the evening with fondness. The party at her dad's had been fun, and it had been special for several reasons. She had enjoyed talking with Tyler and hearing some of the old memories he shared about Ollie. Holly had really felt a part of them for a few minutes in time, like she had become part of an exclusive club.

It had also been good that Shawn had met them as well. At least, she thought so. She had probably gone on for too long on the ride to Shawn's country place about how cool she thought it was that the friendship had endured throughout the years. He hadn't seemed so excited, but was interested nevertheless.

Holly had never been to the house in the country before. Shawn hadn't even talked about owning something away from town until recently. She had wanted to see it, but it hadn't happened until tonight.

She had only seen a couple of rooms because he was hot to trot when they first arrived. He couldn't seem to get enough of her when they got there, and she was all right with that. It made her feel special when he devoured her.

Hell, I enjoyed it as much as him, she believed.

She lay there for a few minutes longer and listened to his breathing. *Yep, he's out cold. I put one on him that Ajax can't remove.*

Slowly, she extricated herself from the bed so as not to disturb Shawn's sleep. She had to move his hand from her exposed boob before getting out, but he didn't show any signs of waking up.

Holly walked directly to the bathroom adjacent to the bedroom and sat on the toilet. It felt good to respond to Mother Nature's call, and she stayed seated a little longer than necessary. She walked on tiptoes back to the bed and found her underwear. There was a tee shirt nearby as well that she pulled over her head, and it fell halfway down her thighs. Her ensemble complete, Holly decided to check out the rest of the house.

The first order of business was to get something to drink. Her throat was so dry, maybe from the wine she had consumed already. The kitchen was modern and open. The stainless steel refrigerator was in an enclave and looked huge.

When she opened the door, it was not very full but something jumped out. It was a two-liter bottle of Diet Dr. Pepper. She grabbed it and drank several gulps right from the container. A monster belch followed, and she laughed when it fell out.

Holly took the bottle of soda with her as she began her exploration. Her initial evaluation was that Shawn had gotten professional help to assist with the décor, but it was not ostentatious.

She took another swig as she walked around the house. In the great room, she found his lap top partially open sitting on the coffee table. She felt a little like she was spying, but decided to have a look. Shawn wouldn't mind.

Sitting on the comfy couch, Holly cracked open the portable machine and gazed at the screen. There was an open spreadsheet with lots of entries. She couldn't make sense of it because she couldn't understand the significance of the items listed in the document. There were over one hundred listings, none of which she recognized.

Holly gave up on the computer and decided to continue her search. The house was big, and she wanted to see it all.

Her designer pocketbook was hanging on a nearby chair, and on a whim she snagged her cellphone from it. There were no messages for her, and she decided to send her dad a text to let him know how much she had enjoyed the evening. She knew he might very well be asleep, but would get a kick out of seeing it tomorrow. He had gotten into texting lately.

Hey, Dad. I wanted to let you know how much I liked the party. I really loved hearing you and Tyler talk about the old days. You guys are hoots! I'm spending the night with Shawn at his "country place." N-i-c-e!! I'll check with you tomorrow. P.S. You rock, old man.

She took a selfie smiling into the camera, attached the photo and hit the send button. She smiled because Holly knew when he read it, he would be grinning as well. Turning off the phone to save the battery, she dropped it again in her purse and left it where it was suspended.

Continuing down the hall, she noticed a door she hadn't seen before. Holly opened it and although the space was dark as night, she saw wooden steps leading downward. There was a light switch faintly visible on the left side of the wall that she flipped without thinking. The stairway was barebones and not well lit. Holly's curiosity led her to check out the unknown even if the scene was stereotypical of some cheap Hollywood thriller.

Holly tested the first step as she grasped a wooden handrail. There was an audible creak as her foot made full contact, and she momentarily stopped her descent. After a few seconds and no further sounds, the woman continued on bare feet.

As she reached the bottom, the dim light revealed another hallway and another couple of closed doors. She opened the one closest to her and couldn't see anything at first. Groping the wall for a switch was successful and bright lights illuminated the area. The first thing noticeable was a life-sized likeness that startled her. Holly laughed as she realized she was looking at a mirrored wall.

It was a first-class workout room containing a treadmill and a stationary bike for cardio fitness. There was also a universal machine that could be used for various strength building exercises, as well as a complete set of dumbbells to finish any urge to add muscle. A large flat screen television was set on a metal and glass stand that could be watched from any vantage point you might choose to exercise. If one needed music to help motivate, there was also stereo equipment set up near the TV. The finishing touch was the wall that allowed you to watch all efforts.

Holly was impressed by the equipment and studied each item. *No wonder Shawn is in such good shape,* she thought.

After looking around the room again and trying out a couple of the free-weights, Holly mugged for the mirror. The silliness made her giggle out loud.

Leaving the home gym, she left the light on so she could see better down the hall. Holly then opened the other closed door and flipped on the overhead lighting revealing another room about the same size as the one she had just departed.

This was nothing like the last. Her first thought was it was either an old study or a storage place, and she almost closed the door without entering. Then a piece of furniture on an otherwise bare wall caught her eye. It was an interesting item like none other she had ever seen. She walked toward it with her interest piqued.

There were lots of drawers, and Holly wondered what they held. Her unchecked curiosity couldn't be denied, so she randomly pulled open one that was centrally located. When she looked inside, puzzlement washed over her.

She removed a Sony VHS tape stored in what looked to be its original cardboard container. Surely this had to be at least fifteen or twenty years old. It had someone's handwritten description, *Memories of Growing Up* on the box. Unsure what significance this could possibly mean to Shawn, she replaced it in the drawer and then opened another compartment.

The next caused a similar reaction from Holly. Contained therein was a porcelain figurine of a geisha holding a jar. The painted face on the miniature statue looked sad, and she rubbed it as if trying to take away the sorrow it portrayed. After a moment of trying to figure the meaning, she gave up and put the figure away.

Holly's confusion over the stored items was not getting any better. She wanted to understand but had no clue what they meant. If Shawn were awake, she would ask him. Instead, she decided to open another drawer.

This one was on the bottom and when Holly slid it out, she gasped when she saw what was inside. It was something she recognized at once although not seen in a while. She thought the

Brighton jewelry was lost, and she had put it out of her mind. It was not unique, but she never doubted for a moment it was hers.

What the hell? she thought.

Her mind was processing the information and finally started making connections. The document she had seen on the laptop earlier was a catalogue of the items she had found. They were similar to the things found in Tyler Crenshaw's van. A burglar for some unknown reason had collected innocuous items with meanings she and her dad had never understood.

Somehow the thief had gathered the items and decided to implicate Tyler. *Why? It made no sense,* Holly thought. *Shawn? He couldn't be involved, but this was proof he was. He must be insane or was she?*

Now fear started creeping in her mind. She needed to get out of there before he woke up.

She closed the drawer but still clutched the jewelry. Sweat had popped out on her top lip, and she wanted to run away as fast as she could.

Holly backed up a few steps and then turned to leave. That's when she saw Shawn standing in the doorway with an inscrutable look on his face.

CHAPTER 50

Ollie and Tyler sat in plastic chairs on the back deck of the lawyer's building. The night air was cool and slightly breezy causing the cigar smoke to drift away toward downtown. It was the perfect ending for the party that had ended two hours before when the last of the guests had gone home leaving the two old friends alone.

"I haven't smoked a cigar in a hundred years," said Tyler as he took a puff into his mouth and then let it seep into the night.

Ollie sat in his contentment without speaking. He sipped at the drink he held in his left hand and then drew on his half-smoked Cuban. The smoke was blown straight up and reminded him of a volcano's belch.

"This is my first one since the heart attack. My health seems a whole lot more important to me these days. Do you know this is only my third drink tonight, and the first one shouldn't count since it was so weak," he finally spoke.

Tyler glimpsed at Ollie and smiled. "I've noticed some changes. You've also lost a little weight and your color is better. Not that you've ever looked bad, old man," he said.

"Don't forget I'm only a year older than you, youngster," replied Ollie.

"So noted. Speaking of health issues, I need to tell you about something I'm facing. I've been putting it off, and I've not told anybody else, but you're the closest thing to family I've got," said Tyler without looking at his friend.

Ollie turned his chair to face Tyler and waited. Even in the muted light from the mounted fixture near the deck entrance, he could recognize an extra degree of concern on Tyler's face.

"You know I've not been one to go to a doctor very often. The main reason was I've never been sick very much in my life and didn't see any need. Part of it is probably due to my time in 'Nam because I thought if I could survive that, I didn't have to worry about too much. I guess the last reason was after our trip to the hospital that night so long ago, I decided I never wanted to see one again," he said before pausing.

"I know. Not smart, right? Anyway, I found out I've got prostate cancer and it's spread to the bones. I've got to decide what, if any, treatment I'll do," Tyler said with haunted eyes.

Ollie was speechless. *Not Tyler,* he thought.

"You'll go through whatever you have to in order to beat that demon, Ty. I'm not going to let you wither away and die without a fight. You're too strong. I'll help you," blurted the lawyer.

Tyler's eyes lifted to his friend and watered at the words. He tried to smile, but his quivering lips wouldn't form into such.

"I'll think about it, but that's not all the news I have to share," Tyler said as he reached into his jacket pocket.

"I got this from Frankie's security system after she died. I think you should watch it," continued Tyler.

Ollie studied Tyler as he brought out a disc encased in a plain paper sleeve. His interest of what was on it could not be denied.

"Okay, Ty. Let's go inside." The two men got up from their seats and headed to the doorway. Both stubbed out their cigars in a brass ashtray before heading inside the house.

As they got through the doorway, Ollie draped his hand across Tyler's shoulders. They walked in together, and the lawyer led them to the conference area. There was a television and DVD player that Ollie turned on with the use of a remote. As the slot on the machine slid open, Tyler fitted the disc inside and stepped backward. Both men waited for the show to begin as Ollie again thumbed the remote control.

The quality of the picture was remarkably clear despite the low level of light in the room, though somewhat distorted because of the wide range of view. Ollie watched silently as a shadowy figure entered the area through the front door and walked with deliberation to what looked to be a large bookcase. The darkly clad man didn't appear to be in a hurry and picked up a few items located on a shelf of the furniture. His movements indicated control and power.

Seconds ticked off a counter on the recording as dread began to form in Ollie's mind. When Frankie entered the room pushing her walker, he couldn't help the audible breath he took. He only exhaled after seeing the fall and the masked man leave without any attempt to help her.

Ollie paused the video and replayed it. He then repeated it three more times. A realization hit him like a cold shower as he watched. He knew the walk of the masked intruder. He had just seen it this evening. Ollie was convinced it belonged to Shawn Matheson.

The blood drained from his face as Ollie turned to Tyler. His friend's face still showed a bit of sadness and pain that had been there off and on during the evening.

"Do you know the man in the video?" asked Ollie.

"I didn't think so until tonight, and I'm still less than positive. He's familiar and I'm sure I've seen him before, maybe on another job site. I just brought this disc so you wouldn't have any lingering doubts about me," said Tyler.

"There is no doubt in my mind the intruder on the film is Shawn, Holly's boyfriend. The way he moves, the way he walks and the way he stands are the same. The size is the same. It's him, Ty."

Ollie left the room in a hurry searching for his cell phone. He had to warn Holly. Tyler followed as the lawyer took the stairs two at a time headed for his living space.

When he got to the head of the stairway, Ollie went into his den and saw his cell on the arm of his recliner. He usually kept it there as he had a charger attached to a nearby outlet. It was convenient and helped him to remember the need to keep the phone charged.

He punched in the passcode and right away saw there was a new message. His face turned grim as he read the text from Holly and saw her self-made picture.

Tyler stood by him without speaking as Ollie pressed the number to call her. The cheery voice indicated she was currently unavailable, but encouraged the caller to leave a message.

"Holly, it's important. Please call me as soon as you get this," said Ollie into the phone.

The two men looked at each other and Tyler asked, "Where is she?"

"Her text says at Shawn's country place, but I don't know where that is," replied Ollie.

"Let me see your phone a minute," said Tyler.

Tyler stared at the text with Holly's picture and then clicked on the photo. He then frowned and returned the cell to his friend.

"I think I know where she is. This makes no sense, but the location on the picture lists the same road where I live in Crawford County. We can go ourselves or call the Sheriff," said Tyler.

Ollie thought a minute before responding, "We don't have enough evidence to get the law involved. They would laugh at the idea of any identification from the video you have. And how would I show he's a danger to Holly? She's been with this guy for months and never had anything negative to say about him. Hell, he was a guest at my house tonight, for God's sake."

"You're probably right, what do you want to do?"

Ollie chewed on his bottom lip as he contemplated his choices. It was the dead of night, and his daughter was in the middle of nowhere with a criminal. The worry he felt at the moment overshadowed everything else. He had friends in law enforcement he could call, but he didn't see how they could help at that moment.

"I don't know what we'll do when we get there, but if you think we can find the house, I think we should go."

"I'll drive, if you don't mind riding in a work van," said Tyler.

"Go bring it out front while I get my pistol," Ollie said.

CHAPTER 51

Holly's wrists and ankles were tied connectively behind her back in such a way she could not move. The twine Shawn had used to accomplish the feat bit into her skin whenever she tried to move. He had left her on the cool hard floor of the basement that didn't help the discomfort or the fear that grew by the moment.

She tried not to feel sorry for herself, but it wasn't working. She couldn't see her watch, which only made the time creep by slower. It had to be at least thirty minutes since he had left her there. She kept going over in her mind how her predicament had progressed to this point.

He hadn't said much when he found her snooping. He had seemed disappointed yet relieved at the same time. He said he didn't want to hurt her, and that he really loved her. Then he tied her up like some calf in a rodeo after showing the wicked knife he held.

During the process he had been menacing but didn't harm her any more than she felt from being tied up. She had wanted to try some kind of move taught in self-defense classes over the years. He must have sensed it, however, and had warned her that his special forces training trumped anything she had ever learned. She believed him.

For some reason the whole scene didn't compute. She had wanted to understand and had asked questions in an effort to find answers. With her training in investigations, she should be able to figure it out. However, Shawn was vague and his answers only led to more confusion. Evidently, he blamed her dad and Tyler for his problems. He had mumbled his troubles were entirely their fault.

Her mind desperately sought a way to get out of the situation. She had to convince him she not only cared for him, but that she wanted to help him with whatever underlying problem from which he was suffering. From what she knew about the crimes he may have committed, he wasn't too far-gone to save even if their relationship would probably not survive this attack.

The wrestling match taking place in her brain led her to know that wasn't exactly the case because of what he had done by tying her up. If he loved her as he professed, he never would have done that. Nor would he have shown her the knife that made her skin prickle.

Holly was torn by rapidly diminishing feelings for him despite what she had discovered stored in his secret hiding place and even after the threat for her own safety. Her mind raced, and now she could feel some of the dilemma her father must have felt when he thought someone he loved had committed crimes.

How could I be so stupid? Why didn't I see this coming? I'm supposed to be trained to recognize psychos, and I've been played like a schoolgirl. What does it say about me that I'm so desperate not to see the signs?

I'm on my own right now, and it's up to me to help myself, she thought. *I've got to bide my time until my chance comes.*

***

Shawn marched back and forth in his bedroom. The mistakes he had made lately were a symptom of something going on inside him that he had never experienced before. He had always been cocksure of himself, and now the cheese had slipped off that cracker.

Initially, Holly Lee had just been someone he watched because she was conducting an investigation that could lead to his identity. The investigation had never gotten far enough to uncover his real name, and he had thought she had dwelled on his uncle as the prime suspect. Losing her job in the Fulton D.A.'s Office had been fortuitous for him, and he had assumed that threat was over.

Then she showed up in Macon. He had recognized her immediately from following her a few months before. Shawn could hardly believe his good fortune as he conducted surveillance at Tucker's residence, and she appeared.

When he had first found out that Holly was the daughter of a nemesis, it provided him an opportunity for additional payback. He would exact revenge on all of them as soon as he was through with his no good uncle. In the meantime, he had used his Ispy skills to learn more about her.

Something had happened along the way that had changed his plans. He hadn't planned on falling for the woman. Those kinds of feelings were not in his makeup, but she had altered that. He had even started thinking he could give up the urge to conduct his private viewings and live a more traditional life. He wasn't sure what love was, but she invaded his thoughts constantly.

He should never have brought Holly here. Before, the loft downtown had been where they enjoyed each other's company. His flawed thinking for tonight was to show off what he called his country place and then spend the last day of the weekend alone with the woman who had become the primary object in his life. She had made him want to change the path he had been on.

What can I do? He thought.

It occurred to him the first thing was to get rid of anything that would implicate his guilt. It would be hard, but his trophies needed to vanish for him to have a fresh start. Then, he could set her free, make her understand, and leave this all behind.

***

Tyler slowed the van as they drove down the dark road. His house was nearby, but he wasn't looking for it. He knew the dwelling he was searching for could only be one of about three in the area, but wasn't sure which one it was. That was the problem with the picture on Ollie's phone. It only listed Dairy Road near Roberta as being where it was taken.

Ollie sat beside him and was visibly shaking. Tyler looked at him with concern and hoped everything would work out. His friend's lips were forming words without sound, and he thought Ollie must be praying.

What a mess, he thought.

He couldn't wrap his head around the identity of Shawn Matheson as the guy giving him so much trouble. Why would the man want to destroy his reputation? The only connection Tyler could imagine was some kind of dispute over a work project since they obviously shared similar job skills.

The first house wasn't visible from the road as the night enveloped everything. An almost full moon provided some light but not near enough to make out the structure. The driveway next to a mailbox disappeared as Tyler tried to follow its path. He felt he could eliminate the house as being Shawn's, however, because the name on the box was different. It listed the occupant as S. Johnson, so he drove farther along the road.

The other two houses between the first and his offered no clues either. Neither displayed the name of Shawn Matheson. The side county road was only about a mile long, and Tyler knew there were only four houses located there, his being one of them. He should've taken the time to meet his neighbors, but it was one of the reasons why he loved the place. Isolation had always been his friend until now.

Think!

That first house had at least included the first letter as an "S" on the mailbox. It wasn't much, but Tyler decided to go back and check further.

***

Ollie's chest hurt. It was the first time since his heart attack. The pain was not as severe and was different, but real nonetheless. Maybe it was just the stress he felt.

The ride around the dark countryside did nothing to help relieve the escalating discomfort. He silently prayed as Tyler cruised at a crawl down the road he had only visited in the daylight. It appeared totally unlike the last trip to his friend's house, and the murky shadows made it impossible to discern details of other properties.

The whole episode of the evening that had been pleasurable until about an hour before, now took on an atmosphere of the surreal. It was eerie and reminded him of being a kid again watching a show by Rod Serling, only this time being one of the actors waiting for the other shoe to drop.

He shivered and wondered if the lightweight jacket he wore was enough to keep him warm. Not that the weather was that cold, but he was chilled to the bone. He slipped his right hand into the pocket and his Walther .380 handgun felt colder than the temperature. It soothed yet scared him to have it so close. He hadn't fired it in years, but thought he could handle it accurately if need be.

Tyler had a worried look as they arrived at the last mailbox. He appeared in deep thought that only led Ollie closer to panic mode.

"Ty, we've got to do something," said Ollie.

"Huh? Yeah, I know. I was just thinking either the name on the mailbox hasn't been changed to show Matheson or that's not his name," replied Tyler.

"I'm about ready to go to every front door out here until we find Holly. I'm scared shitless, Ty."

"I want to go back to the first house. It had S. Johnson on the box. Maybe that's his name, Shawn Johnson," said Tyler.

Tyler pulled the van into the driveway and then backed onto the road headed in the direction he had just come from. About the time they were a couple of football fields away, they saw an orange glow rising into the sky. It was coming from the first property.

***

Holly lay on the floor watching as Shawn methodically emptied each drawer of an eclectic set of articles. The white canvas bag he used to hold the items resembled ones she had seen in high school that had been for football equipment storage.

"What are you doing, Shawn? she asked, trying not to sound pissed.

"You're studying to be a lawyer, what do you think?" he said without turning toward her.

"I know you're getting rid of evidence. That's not what I'm asking," she said with a hint of snippiness.

Shawn stopped packing the bag for a moment but didn't face Holly. His body language indicated he was thinking.

"I'll try and explain later," he said after a moment.

He finished emptying the last of the collection into the bag and left her alone. A few seconds later she heard a door open and then close. She couldn't see that he took a gasoline can with him.

***

"Turn the lights off, Ty. He may see us coming up the driveway," said Ollie.

The van was travelling at a slow rate of speed, and now the headlights were off pursuant to Ollie's commands. Both Ollie and Tyler were scanning the scantily lit ground trying not to run into a hole, rock or misplaced tree. It had been so good, so far until the front right tire hit a gully that jarred their jaws.

Tyler slowed down to a creep afterwards as the fire flames came more into view. It looked like it was contained in some kind of big metal drum. The fire was hot and seemed fed by an accelerant.

The van came to a halt a few hundred feet from the fire. Tyler put the vehicle in park and turned off the engine. He looked over at Ollie who returned the stare. Time to check out the place.

They exited the van and headed to the source of the flame. Both became more wary the closer they got.

No one was around the fire, and their faces glowed red as they approached. Ollie tried to see what was being consumed by the flames, but couldn't tell. His best guess was that it contained cloth as he saw yellowing wisps float away into the night. There was also an acrid smell that Ollie associated with the burning of plastic or rubber.

Ollie tried to crouch as he approached, but felt stiff and old. He saw Tyler looking like a soldier nearing the area and knew he could never do what his friend did. The stealth exhibited by Tyler blew Ollie away.

They were on the backside of the house, and nobody else was around. The flames allowed them to see a back entrance. It was dicey since they had no idea whose house this was. Something told the lawyer this was the place.

Tyler tried the door, and it clicked open. He held his index finger to his lips to shush Ollie and slipped inside. The door closed behind him, and the lawyer found himself outside alone.

***

When Shawn came back into the room, he smelled of gasoline, and he no longer had the canvas sack. He walked over to where Holly was on the floor and whipped out his razor sharp knife. She cringed as he knelt down and paused over her. He cut the cord so that her legs were no longer drawn to her wrists. It was blessed relief, and the cramp she had felt in her legs slowly went away.

"I'm not going to free your hands, yet. But, if you'll wait a little while, I may. I want to try and explain, first," said Shawn.

She sat up as soon as the full feeling came back into her lower torso. It was not easy with her hands secured behind her back. She wanted to hear what he had to say and hoped it would help her understand his actions.

"I was born Shawn Johnson in 1965," he began. "My mother, Mary, had a hard life, but it wasn't her fault. As I grew up, she told me how it broke her down.

"She met my father the year before and thought he was the one. They shared dreams like lots of young lovers. He wanted to make a life for them, but he wasn't much more than a kid. They both were. A kid having another wasn't going to work. Mama told him she was going to move up to Canton and stay with relatives until they figured out what to do. Mama said she planned to get back with him later when things got better, but he couldn't handle the separation.

"She said his family wouldn't help, either. They rejected him. That's why she never told them about me.

"My father's name was Mathis Crenshaw. I never knew him because his own brother and your daddy killed him before I was ever born.

"Can you imagine growing up never knowing your father?"

"As a matter of fact, I can. It never made me break into people's houses," replied Holly.

His gaze held a glint of anger as he said, "You think he's all that, but he was a part of my father's death."

Holly's annoyance couldn't be helped. "Shawn. I wasn't there that night, and neither were you. But, you do know your father had just killed an innocent girl and then tried to kill his own brother and my dad, right?"

"You're right, you weren't there. How do you know it wasn't your dad or my uncle who killed the girl and then my father?"

It was obvious Shawn was growing more upset and agitated as he started pacing back and forth before her. Holly knew she needed to be careful in how she responded.

At that moment, Tyler walked into the room. He held his right hand down by his side holding something hidden in his fist.

The two men glowered at one another. For the first time, Holly saw a resemblance. They had similar builds and facial features.

"Well, my long lost uncle. How special," said Shawn through a sneer.

Tyler's face was pale and pained. "What do you mean? I never knew," he almost whispered with incredulity.

"Because you never tried to find out. I never knew my dad, and you're the reason. No Crenshaw ever cared about me. Not my grandparents, not you. I had to do everything on my own," Shawn's voice dripped with distaste.

"You need to know, I never met your mother. Matt didn't tell me much about her. We weren't as close back then, and it's one of the regrets I've carried for the last fifty years. I'm sure she had a difficult time raising you alone, and I'm sorry."

"You're sorry? That's not enough, Uncle. I saw Mama suffer until the day she died, and I was only a kid. I grew up in foster care, and I never knew my daddy. I spent years trying to find out who he was and what happened to him. It was all because of you and your buddy, Ollie Tucker. I've been planning what I'd do when I finally met you. You need to feel what he felt. I need vengeance."

Shawn shifted the offensive blade in his hand. The power he exhibited through the flexed arm muscles frightened Holly as she sat watching the scene develop. She couldn't believe that those same arms had held her with such tenderness just a short time before.

Holly glanced frantically around the room trying to find something she could use if the threat came too close. Tyler seemed to be in good shape, but he wasn't a match for Shawn. The two were focused on one another and didn't seem to be paying her any attention.

***

Tyler was shaken by the news that he had heard Shawn telling Holly from just outside the door.

Matt's son. Mathis's son. Matheson. The guy was messed up more than he, Tyler, ever had been.

He had wanted badly to confront the person responsible for ruining his name but wasn't so sure now. This was his nephew. The only remaining relative in his direct line was standing before him. Somebody he never knew existed. He kept talking as his mind tried to comprehend the dilemma.

"Look, I don't know all the answers. I just know this doesn't need to go wrong. I'll try to help anyway I can," said Tyler while trying not to appear threatening.

Suddenly, Ollie entered the room that was now becoming a little crowded. He had his weapon in hand, but it was pointed at the floor. Less than ten feet separated any of the four occupants.

"So, that's why you broke into people's homes, for revenge? Look, we all have problems. I've had my share with personal shit that made me a little crazy, too. All four of us have dealt with troubles more or less tied to a night that made no sense whatsoever. I think we need to forget the pain we've had to deal with," said Ollie.

Tyler walked across to Holly and showed he held a knife as well. Without saying anything, he cut the bindings on her hands. No one else moved as she shook her hands to get rid of the numbness. He then closed the blade, slipped it into his front pants pocket, and helped the woman to her feet.

Shawn shifted his stance from foot to foot while still wielding the intimidating steel. It was obvious a silent war was raging, and the tension made everyone taut with apprehension.

Holly spoke, "I care about you, Shawn. This needs to end before something else goes wrong, please. Drop the knife, and I won't press any charges in case you're worried about that. What dad said is right."

Shawn laughed and it sounded false as a hyena's. "I don't see us becoming one big happy family."

"We could try and forgive each other. That would be a start," said Tyler.

"I'm not your lawyer, but I can help you find the best one around. Things aren't necessarily as bad as they may seem," said Ollie as he kept the gun in his hand, but pointed at the floor.

"I think all of you are full of shit and will say anything to save your asses," spit Shawn.

Tyler's eyes shifted from one person to another as his mind worked overtime. Shawn held a serrated blade that could kill them all. Ollie's gun had the firepower to stop the threat, but Tyler didn't know if his friend had enough skill to use it without posing danger to Holly. He was pretty sure Shawn could attack any of them he chose and cause serious injury or death before anyone else could prevent it. There was no doubt in his mind that the younger man didn't care about other people's lives. He had already shown his callousness by leaving Frankie on the floor.

The girl had moved slightly from her previous position, and he saw she was within reach of a scrap piece of two-by-four about the length of a yardstick. The lock-blade knife in his own pocket was lethal enough if he chose to bring it out again. Weapons were everywhere, and the threat of violence permeated the room.

***

Ollie felt his chest pounding almost as hard as the night of the heart attack. The gun in his hand felt cold, but sweat ran down his spine like a day on the beach. He had chambered a round before entering the house, and he knew the pressure exerted on the trigger made shooting only a hair away.

Please, God. I don't want to be a part of anybody else's death.

He had heard the conversations as he entered the house. The surprise that hit him like a brick in the face was still fresh when he joined the group. For some reason, a humorous moment came to mind. A colleague had once called a coincidence a "cowinkydink" and the term now flooded his brain. This entire scene was a cowinkydink of epic proportions.

His life was being reduced to a few moments in somebody's basement. *I've got to protect Holly, no matter what. She deserves a chance.*

The concept of justice he had believed in since Libby's death was in jeopardy. It was part of the reason he had become a lawyer. Let the legal process decide fate, had been his mantra.

The problem with justice is that it's murky. Guilty people go free. Innocent people are convicted.

Ollie was as conflicted as he could be. He wanted justice to prevail, but just what was that?

Perhaps he could find a way so Shawn would be able to get help. Obviously, he was sick. He needed to be held responsible for his acts, but mental illness might provide an escape from a long prison sentence.

He tried to keep the conversation with Shawn going in hope of diffusing the dangerous and spiraling situation.

***

Holly was finally glad to see some possible protection. A piece of lumber was propped up within reach, and she was sure it was sturdy enough to whack somebody if need be.

She didn't like where all this was heading. Maybe it couldn't be helped at this point, but something was going to happen soon.

I'm the key. He can be saved. That's what her heart said.

Hell no! That's what her head screamed.

"I don't think you're a violent man, Shawn. Please put it down before somebody gets hurt." That's what came from her mouth.

Shawn turned his head slightly in her direction, and his eyes glazed over. His voice dripped with venom, "I did two tours in Iraq and special ops other places. You don't know what war does to a man."

"I know, son. I was in the jungle when you were just a kid. I can help you, Shawn," said Tyler gloomily.

"Let all of us help you, Shawn. You won't have to do it alone," said Ollie.

Shawn was twitching and didn't respond. Holly's feeling of impending doom kept growing. She inched closer to the board.

Holly waited and watched. Her dad held his gun down, but she saw the barrel raising a fraction. Tyler made no move to suggest he was ready for attack.

Before she could think about any more scenarios, Shawn moved with incredible speed toward Tyler. The flash of his knife took her breath.

She grabbed the board with both hands and rushed toward the two relatives.

***

Ollie raised the pistol in front of him as Shawn dashed across the room knife in hand toward Tyler. He couldn't take a shot because it happened so quickly, and Holly was following the younger man's path.

At the last second before Shawn reached Tyler, the uncle sidestepped his nephew and pushed him while sticking out a foot. The younger man's forward momentum after tripping caused him to collide into the wall with considerable force. An indention into the plaster formed around the right side of Shawn's body, and the knife stuck deeply into the wall.

The lawyer watched as motion decelerated to a slower setting. He held the gun in a position so he could fire and was reasonably sure of his target line at the moment. He could kill Shawn, and a part of him craved to do just that.

Shawn didn't crumple, and after a few moments yanked the hand and knife from the wall to face the others. Tyler stood in the middle with Holly to his immediate right holding the board like an axe. Ollie had moved to his friend's left side.

Ollie continued to point the gun at Shawn's center mass while evident agitation was exhibited by facial twitches on the younger man. Any doubt Ollie may have had for Shawn's capacity to commit violence on them had evaporated with the attack on Tyler.

"Drop that damn gun and see if you can kill me like you did my daddy, big man," sneered Shawn. "I'll send everyone of you to hell."

Flashbacks flooded Ollie's brain. His life had come full circle.

"I don't want to shoot you, Shawn. Drop the knife," replied Ollie in a voice that sounded very distant to his ears.

"Don't throw away your life," pleaded Holly.

"It's your fault, bitch," screamed Shawn as he lunged toward the woman.

The gunshots were deafening in the basement room as Ollie fired three rapid shots into Shawn's chest. The dying man performed an almost graceful pirouette as he fell face up near Holly's feet.

His mouth opened as he tried to speak, but no words made it out. There was only blood.

EPILOGUE

Six months later

Sunset highlighted colors of the day blending into the nighttime sky. Early springtime in the country was one of Tyler's favorite times, and this evening was more special than he could have ever imagined. The change of seasons meant new life, and that's what he was experiencing. There were a few lingering effects from the traumatic events of last year, but he and the others were working their way through them.

He sat in one of the chairs on his back deck and took in nature's beauty. The harshness of winter was gone, but there was still coolness in the air requiring him and his guests to wear sweaters and light jackets.

There was a Chiminea fireplace providing additional heat for those in need, but the warmth he felt by being with Ollie and

Holly was all he desired. The smiles they shared from their nearby seats reinforced the feeling.

The barbeque grill where he had cooked juicy rib eye steaks, potatoes, and corn was still open as the coals turned to ash. All evidence of the deliciousness of the meal was hidden in their bellies.

"That was a helluva meal, Ty. I won't tell my cardiologist about it, though," said Ollie.

"Yeah, Uncle Ty, I won't be able to get in these jeans much longer if I keep eating like that," added Holly.

It tickled Tyler to hear her call him uncle. She had started doing that right after his prostate surgery in January, and it still made him smile every time she did, almost as much as now being cancer free.

"I just wanted to do something special for y'all after helping me the last few months," replied Tyler.

"You look in tip top shape to me, old buddy. I bet you could even climb that big ass tree in your front yard," said Ollie with a grin.

Tyler laughed and shook his head. He then relayed the story to Holly about his first meeting with Ollie and Libby. She listened and her face showed rapt attention.

"Enough about the dangers of tree climbing. I've got a little gift for each of you," Tyler said as he stood up and retrieved a bag behind his chair.

He first handed a nicely wrapped box to Holly and cleared this throat as if he was going to make a speech.

"For going beyond the call of duty while working on my case; for helping me during my recovery after surgery, especially getting me to my treatments when I couldn't drive; and for making me feel a part of your life as any real uncle would be proud; I now present you something worthy of a lawyer to be."

She beamed and tore into the package. As Holly pulled out a leather briefcase, she oohed and ahhed while stroking the buttery texture.

"Thank you, Uncle Ty. I'll always treasure this," she cooed.

"You're more than welcome, sweetie. Thanks again for everything," Tyler replied.

He then reached into the bag and pulled out a small box. Walking over to Ollie, he approached with his hand outstretched. After giving it to his friend, Tyler patted him on his shoulder.

"Ollie, you're the best friend anybody could ever ask for. You'll never know how much you mean to me. I've been keeping this for so long, but I've always known you should get it back in the end. I found it after Libby died. For some reason, I couldn't find the right occasion to give it back to you. Many times, it gave me comfort. Now I know, it's where it belongs."

Ollie stared at his friend as the small box remained in his hands. He appeared almost scared to open it.

***

The lawyer opened the box and couldn't believe what he saw. Libby's necklace. He touched it with reverence.

Ollie looked at his lifelong friend without speaking. After sharing the moment, he turned to see the fire glowing and then rotated his head upward to the clear evening sky. Tears swam in his eyes. He could almost swear Libby winked as the sun dipped below the horizon in a blaze of glorious colors.

The End